FINDING HOME WITH MY COWBOY

COWBOY

O'SULLIVAN SISTERS #7

SOPHIA QUINN

ISBN: 978-1-99-103432-8 (Paperback)
ISBN: 978-1-99-103431-1 (Kindle)

Forever Love Publishing Ltd
www.foreverlovepublishing.com
2022 - USA

CHAPTER 1

Chaos reigned at the breakfast table in the Donahue household, and Boone did his best not to get drawn into it.

"Pass me the sugar, pumpkin," his mother, Angela, said as he tried and failed to pass unnoticed through the bustling kitchen.

"Yes, ma'am." He reached over the heads of his little niece and nephew to grab the bowl of sugar and hand it to his mother.

"Ma, have you seen the kids' stuffies?" Boone's older sister, Kelly, stopped beside her big little brother. She might've been older than him by eight years, but she only came up to his shoulder, and he slung an arm around her, pulling her in for a side hug that also managed to keep her out of his father's way as he came through carrying luggage.

Kelly tipped her head back. "Boone, you weren't thinking of sneaking out of here without a proper good-bye, now were you?"

"'Course not." He grinned. "Just trying to stay out of the way."

"You're never in the way," his mother answered as she flipped pancakes on the griddle. "Matty and Morgan can't eat all these by themselves."

"Stay," Kelly ordered. "Keep the kids busy while we get the car loaded up."

His mother turned at the stove and, seeing him still standing there, shooed him toward the table. "Go on, sit."

"Ma, I gotta get back to the ranch to—"

"Not until you have a good breakfast," she interrupted.

Boone eyed the table where his niece and nephew squabbled over who would get the last of the orange juice. A plateful of bacon called his name, and he gave in, sliding into the seat beside his niece, Morgan. "Now what are you two fighting about?"

Their answers drowned each other out, and he laughed as he filled his plate.

"I'm gonna miss you two, you know that?" He reached over to ruffle Matty's hair.

"We'll be back for Thanksgiving," their dad, Randy, answered as he, too, walked by with a suitcase.

"Need a hand?" Boone called out.

"Nah. Your dad and I've got it."

"Your dad's a pro at helping people with their luggage," his mother added with a chuckle.

She wasn't lying. Ever since his father, Hansen, opened a boutique bed-and-breakfast outside of town some ten years back, he'd made an art out of dealing with needy tourists.

It would have driven Boone nuts, but running an upscale inn seemed oddly fitting for his outgoing mother and father. Meanwhile, he'd happily taken his uncle

Patrick up on a job as a ranch hand during high school, which had turned into a full-time job after graduation.

This past summer, he'd moved to the neighboring property, the O'Sullivan Ranch, whose cattle operation was run by his older cousin, Nash.

"Kelly, check the dryer. I washed Matty's blankie this morning," his mother called out. "And I think Randy already packed the stuffies."

Boone glanced at the clock on the microwave as he took a bite of bacon. The O'Sullivan Ranch was exactly where he was supposed to be this morning. He typically stayed at the bunkhouse but had come home to spend some time with his sister and her family before they went back to their home in Wyoming.

He'd already missed the morning chores, and he didn't want to make JJ cover for him any more than he already had.

"Come on, kids, hurry it up," Kelly called as she rushed through the kitchen. "We've got a long drive ahead of us."

"Five hours," Randy laughed as he came back in, hands on his hips as he watched his kids dally over their breakfast. "And that's assuming we don't have to make twelve pit stops like we did on the way here."

Little Matty climbed into Boone's lap, and Boone wasted no time snuggling his nephew.

"I don't wanna go," Matty whined.

Boone kissed the top of the boy's scruffy little head and reached out to boop Morgan on the nose. "You two will be back before you know it. And if you're good, I'll take you over to the park to go sledding."

Matty brightened, his cherub face nothing but adorable.

"Is Aunt Addie coming for Thanksgiving?" Morgan asked.

His mother's brows drew together as she thought that over. His eldest sister, Adeline, moved to San Diego after college, and her trips home with her boyfriend were rare. "I don't think so. She's hoping to make it for Christmas, though."

"All right, I think that's everything," Kelly announced when she reentered, their father right behind her so the small kitchen was crammed with family. "We should get going."

Boone set Matty on his feet and scraped the chair back from the table. "I've gotta head out too."

"Where are you running off to?" Kelly asked.

Boone just barely resisted the urge to roll his eyes. As the youngest by nearly a decade, he'd gotten used to being seen as a permanent kid in this family, but his pride made him point out, "I do have a job, you know."

"How's it going working for your cousin?" Randy asked.

Boone grinned. "It's great."

"Is he a better boss than Uncle Patrick?" Kelly's eyes sparkled with amusement.

Boone tipped his head from side to side as he helped herd the kids toward the door. "He's much more hands-off, you know? He trusts his ranch hands to get the job done in their own time and their own way."

"In other words, he lets you goof off," his mother teased.

Boone sighed, but he was still smiling as he returned his sister's and brother-in-law's hugs.

"I never thought of Nash as the laid-back type," Randy said. "He always seems so serious."

4

"Just quiet," Kelly corrected. She'd met Randy at college in Wyoming, and Randy hadn't spent much time with the extended family.

"And I'd bet money this new laid-back demeanor has just as much to do with that pretty wife of his, am I right?" Angela said.

Boone and his father laughed.

"Emma's definitely a good influence," Boone agreed.

"Just wait until he's a father." Hansen glanced at his grandchildren, pulling a face that made them both giggle. "Having kids has a way of changing everything."

"Don't I know it," Randy grumbled good-naturedly as he reached down to lift Matty into his arms.

Kelly already had an arm around Morgan and was tugging her away from her beloved grandma.

"I'll walk you out," Boone said.

His mother pretended to whisper behind him as she addressed Kelly. "That's Boone's way of avoiding any conversations about when he's going to settle down."

"Ma, I'm still young," Boone replied, out of habit more than anything. "Don't go getting started with talk of marriage and grandkids just yet."

"From what I hear, he can have his pick," Kelly laughed. Her singsong tone said she knew she was being a nuisance and she loved it. "Margot called him 'honeypot.' Says the bees come swarming the second he walks into the bar."

Boone rolls his eyes, ignoring his sister's wink and giggle. He could just imagine what the bartender and his sister were talking about on their girls' night out.

"He's had them swooning after him since middle school," his mother said. "Now, if he'd just pick one and settle down already…"

"'Just pick one,' she says," Boone muttered as his father laughed at the well-worn bickering. "Like it's as simple as picking out a pair of shoes."

"I'm just saying…" His mother drew the words out as they got the kids in the car and took turns giving them one last kiss and hug. "If you'd stop flirting with every woman with a pretty smile and actually found someone you can be serious with."

Boone sighed as Randy patted him on the back. "Ignore them. The right one will find you."

"That's what I've been saying!" Boone threw his hands out in an exasperated gesture that made Kelly and his mom giggle.

They loved to tease him about girls—always had. It wasn't his fault that most of the female population liked him. And he liked them right back.

And he had no qualms about settling down either. One day.

But today was not that day.

"See you later, Pops," he called to his dad as his sister's family started to pull away.

He gave his mom a kiss on the cheek before heading to his truck. "Thanks for breakfast, Ma. Love you guys."

His mother's dark hair was dappled with silver, and crow's-feet crinkled at the corners of her eyes, but her smile was bright as she waved him off, and his father's was filled was so much adoration as he looked down at his wife, it made Boone's own smile broaden.

"Just pick one," he muttered to himself with a shake of his head. As if his mom and dad had just picked each other randomly.

No, sir, if his parents had taught him anything, it was

that the real deal was worth waiting for. And if it was meant to be, it'd find him.

He drove back to Aspire, then right on through it, heading toward the ranch just outside town as the sun rose in the east, covering the meadows and hillsides in a warm orange glow.

It was no wonder the ranch he worked at was now filled with the O'Sullivan sisters. Each and every one of 'em had come to this part of the world expecting to leave within a month, but now they were settled in like one big happy family. Except for Sierra, who had whisked Cody off to South America. It had sat pretty dark with Boone for a little while, until he accepted the fact that his friend was deliriously happy living down there with the love of his life and helping out orphaned children who needed him more than the ranch did.

He bet Cody missed it occasionally, though.

And mornings like this one, it was easy to see why the sisters had stayed. How anyone could spend any time in a place as beautiful as this southwest corner of Montana and *not* want to stay was a mystery. Sure, his own sisters had gone off and started lives elsewhere, and most of his high school buddies had done the same. But Boone had never been tempted to leave.

Not even when there'd been some talk of scouts at his football games.

The long, winding dirt road of the ranch greeted him like an old friend, and he smiled at the sight of a family of deer that paid him no mind as they grazed by the road's edge.

When he pulled up to the main house, it was clear that the household was already awake and active. Nash's wife,

Emma, came dashing out the front door, beaming as she spotted him. "Hey, stranger. How was your weekend off?"

"Great. My sister and her family kept us real busy."

She laughed as she headed to her car, hitching a bag on her shoulder as she headed off to school for her teaching job. "I bet. No one knows better than I do how exhausting sisters can be."

Emma winked and slid into her car as Boone laughed and headed around the house toward the stables.

It was no secret that the O'Sullivan women had each come with their fair share of drama. Emma had been the first to arrive, but since then, five others had shown up on the doorstep, each with her own drama and her own opinions on the future of this estate.

Which made things tricky, because their estranged father made it clear in his will that in order to keep the property or sell it, all seven sisters would have to come to a unanimous agreement.

So far as Boone could tell, the five who were here in town were in favor of keeping the property. Sierra had returned to Venezuela, taking Cody in her wake, but now that she'd gotten close with the other sisters and come to understand the allure of the land, even she was rooting to keep the place.

Which meant there was just one sister left.

April O'Sullivan. Frank's youngest daughter, who was Boone's age and had gone to school with him up until she'd moved to Bozeman with Frank and her mom, when her mom got sick.

Now that both her parents had passed, she was...

Well, gone. Just gone. She'd taken off, it seemed, and Boone couldn't help but feel a nagging worry every time he thought about it.

It was driving her sisters nuts too.

Boone dove right into work, mounting his horse to ride the range and see to the chores on his never-ending list. It wasn't easy work—some days grueling, some days tedious. The morning chores had him working up a sweat.

But every time he lifted his head and filled his chest with fresh air and took in the sight of the white-topped mountains and the land that seemed to stretch into eternity…

There was no place he'd rather be.

This was his home just as surely as it was the O'Sullivans'. He might not own the land, but he was proud to work it, to take responsibility for the cattle and the livestock.

One day, maybe he'd even be able to take on some land of his own. A house, at the very least. With a happy family just like his sister had…

He gave his head a shake and stuck his baseball cap on backward to keep his hair out of his eyes. His father gave him grief for letting it get so long, and at moments like this one, he suspected maybe the older man was right.

Sure, the girls he spent time with down at the bar liked his thick dark waves, but it was getting to be a nuisance.

Thanks to the big breakfast he'd had at home, he didn't call it quits for lunch until late in the day when the sun was already starting to sink toward the peaks in the west. Rather than head straight back to his bunkhouse to grab some food, he went to the office to snag the leftovers he'd stashed in the mini fridge.

He found Dahlia in there already, head bent over the desk as she listened to someone on the other end of the line with a grim expression. Dahlia was the fourth oldest sister, and while she'd rubbed nearly everyone the wrong way when she'd first arrived—earning herself the nick-name Dragon—she'd quickly become an integral part of the family. And the business.

She took over a lot of the administrative work for Nash, allowing him to focus on the cattle operation and making a profit.

She'd also fallen in love with Boone's friend JJ while she was at it, and JJ strolled in just as Dahlia sighed, clearly disappointed by whoever was on the line.

"What's up?" JJ asked as he moved past Boone to grab a drink from the fridge.

Boone shrugged. Before he could say anything, Dahlia started talking into the phone. "April, it's Dahlia. Again. Just…please call. Please. We really need to talk to you, and—"

Boone exchanged a grimace with JJ as Dahlia made a garbled sound of frustration and slammed the phone down against her leg. "It cut me off. The dang voice mail cut me off!"

JJ hurried over to his fiancée and pulled her out of the chair and into his arms. She sank against him with a groan. "How many messages am I supposed to leave?"

Boone started to move away, not wanting to interrupt their moment, but Dahlia spotted him. "No, don't go. It's your lunch break. I'm not trying to drive anyone away." She ran a hand over her face. "I'm just frustrated, that's all."

JJ wrapped his arms around her and swayed with her from side to side until a smile tugged at her lips.

"I take it there's no recent news on April," Boone started. He didn't have to feign interest or concern. He might not have been friends with April growing up—not that they weren't friends, they just…hung out in different

10

circles—but he still had the connection with her. A shared history. And even though it had been more than five years since she'd moved away from their high school and gone to Bozeman, he could still picture her vividly.

She'd always stuck out. And not just because there wasn't a ton of diversity in their little town. Although, her dark skin and wild black curls had definitely set her apart in the looks department. But more than that, it was…well, everything.

She'd always worn colorful clothes and took art classes for fun and made her own jewelry and wasn't afraid to hang out by herself and…

Well, she was different, that was all. Artsy and cool in her own unique way.

He'd always liked that about her. Even if they hadn't been friends, they'd been classmates, and to Boone, that meant something.

So when Dahlia straightened and turned to him with a sigh, he grew uncharacteristically tense.

"We did get some news about April, actually." She looked up at JJ, who nodded with a smile.

To Boone, she continued. "You know how we all pooled our money to have a private investigator look into it?"

"Ye-ah." Boone drew out the word, his unease growing.

"Well, he found her. Finally." Dahlia added the last part under her breath. "Lord knows we paid him enough to—"

"Dahlia," Boone interrupted. He arched his eyebrows, surprised by the urgency running through him.

Dahlia winced. "Right. Well, he got us her phone number on Friday—"

"And you've been the one calling?" Boone didn't try to

hide his alarm, just like JJ didn't try to hide his snicker of amusement.

Dahlia rolled her eyes. "Don't look at me like that. I used my sweetest tone, plus Emma's tried twice, Daisy once, and we even persuaded Rose, who has to be the nicest person on the planet."

JJ grimaced. "She's obviously not ready."

Dahlia's brows pulled together in frustration. "This is ridiculous! We've spent all this time and money to find her, and now she won't play ball."

"I know, sweetheart." JJ held her shoulders and lightly kissed her, which seemed to calm her down.

Boone shifted from foot to foot, the sandwich in his hands all but forgotten as he turned this information over. "Did this investigator give you an address too?"

Dahlia nodded. "She's in Portland. We told her grand-parents, but they're in no condition to go chasing after her." She straightened, her chin setting in a resolute look. "I'm gonna have to go get her."

"No!" Boone and JJ said it at once, and the combined effect of their booming voices had Dahlia blinking in surprise.

"Well, Emma can't go, and Rose obviously can't, and Lizzy and Daisy are busy with—"

"None of you should go," Boone cut her off.

JJ nodded, his gaze filled with understanding as he turned from Boone to Dahlia. "I think he's right, hon. She obviously doesn't know you or trust you, and she's made it clear she doesn't want to see you."

"So...what?" Dahlia started to pace. "We just let her go? We just put all ranch business on hold until she decides to come on home?"

Boone was only half listening as Dahlia and JJ went back and forth on their options.

All he could think about was April.

In Portland.

Alone.

Honestly, he wasn't shocked when she'd left town in high school. Even if her mom hadn't been sick, she was the girl in their class he'd have voted as "most likely to move away." She'd been an outsider and seemed like the sort who was just waiting for a chance to run off to a big city.

And she did.

He wasn't sure why that unsettled him so much. Maybe because he hadn't spent much time in big cities so he couldn't picture where she was. Or maybe because, artsy outsider or not, she'd also always struck him as...sweet.

Maybe a little shy.

Definitely vulnerable.

And given all she'd been through these past five years, with both her parents dying and then six women she didn't know showing up and taking over her home, and—

"I'll go."

The words were out of his mouth before he actually thought it through, and he wasn't surprised to find JJ and Dahlia gaping at him when he turned to face them.

"Uh...what?" Dahlia frowned.

Boone smiled and recovered with a shrug. "Why not? After all, I've got a stake in the future of this ranch, right? And I'm the only one here who actually knows April."

"You do?" Dahlia looked confused.

"I went to school with her." He nodded.

JJ looked at Boone. "Oh yeah. She was in your class, right?"

Boone nodded again.

Dahlia's skepticism turned to hope. "So, you two were…friends?"

Boone hesitated. "Sort of."

Before either of them could ask more questions, Boone hurried on, his mind racing and his pulse pounding with an odd sort of excitement.

It was the same sort of adrenaline rush he got when he trained under Ethan as a volunteer fireman.

Finding April. Bringing her home.

It was a purpose. A goal.

He could do some real good for April and the O'Sullivans.

"I'll do it," he said again. "I'll go get April, and I'll bring her back home."

CHAPTER 2

April's studio above the coffee shop where she worked had always been tiny. But it had never felt smaller than it did right now.

"It's Dahlia. Again." The words filled the stuffy one-room apartment as April paced from one art-covered wall to another.

An artist's loft—that's what the owner had billed this place as. And the natural light and abundance of bare white walls had indeed made this spot the perfect place for April to create and display her works of art. Little white could be found any longer, now that she'd plastered the walls in oil paintings and sketches.

This loft had come unfurnished aside from a small bed. No TV, her laptop had died a year ago, and her phone's reception was nigh on useless.

"…we really need you to call us back," Dahlia finished.

Again.

April let her cheeks fill with air before blowing out a long, slow exhale.

It was one of the breathing exercises the Bozeman therapist had taught her when she and her dad—no, Frank. When she and Frank had been taking care of her mother.

It had been Frank who'd insisted she see a therapist, even though April had thought it kinda morbid to be seeing a grief counselor when her mother was still alive.

But, of course, she hadn't lived long, and April supposed those sessions had proved useful over the years.

Like right now, when she was ready to crawl out of her skin with frustration.

Her phone automatically started playing the next message. "Hi, um…this is Rose. O'Sullivan? Um, actually it's not O'Sullivan any longer. Or it won't be soon, because I'm taking my husband's name and… Oh shoot. Never mind. I'm just calling because…" Rose's defeated exhale sounded so much like April's weary sigh that she stared at the phone in surprise.

"We're worried about you, April," Rose said. "Please give one of us a call. Or…I don't know, send a smoke signal, maybe?"

April's lips curved up in a grudging smile before she stalked over to her phone where it lay on her bed and deleted the voice mail.

Silence filled the small space, and for a moment, guilt flickered up alongside frustration as she glowered at her device.

"We're worried…"

Why would they worry? They didn't even know her. And she definitely didn't know them. She suspected there was no good way to find out that one's father was actually a father to six strangers as well, but the way she'd found out…

She shook her head, pushing aside the memory. Didn't matter now. What mattered was that everything her mother and Frank had told her about her life was a lie. And all she cared about now was finding out the truth.

She had no urge to meet her father's estranged daughters, and absolutely no desire to go back to the ranch where she'd grown up.

Way too many memories still lived there…along with the six strangers her father hadn't thought to tell her about. No, actually, he'd probably thought of it a hundred times and rejected the idea, because…why?

He didn't think she could handle it?

Or maybe he was just a coward.

With a muttered oath, she turned on her heel and headed to the open suitcase that sadly served as her makeshift dresser.

One day, she'd have enough to get some furniture in here.

Or, better yet, she'd end this month-to-month lease and get a better place. Maybe one that was already furnished.

The thought buoyed her spirits as she changed out of the flowy, paint-splattered dress she wore around the house and into jeans and a button-down shirt that made up the coffee shop's uniform.

As she changed, her gaze kept flickering back to her phone, that guilt growing as Rose's voice seemed to linger in the air.

"That's probably why they had Rose call," she muttered. "She sounds so sweet, only an ogre would refuse to call her back."

All six of her newfound sisters had called so many times and left so many messages, she was starting to feel like she knew them. Their personalities were clear enough, at least. Dahlia was the bossy one, Emma was the maternal one, Lizzy's voice was always brisk and energetic, and more than once April had heard her muffle the phone to talk to little ones, so…clearly a mom.

Sierra's voice usually cut in and out because she was calling from somewhere with bad reception, and Daisy's messages were always filled with laughter.

So yeah. Whether she liked it or not, April was getting to know Frank's other daughters.

A part of her itched to hit Return Call and ask Rose how they'd gotten her number. She'd gotten a new phone and a new number when she'd left home.

Her fingers stilled on the button of her shirt, and for a second, she met her own gaze in the full-length mirror that hung on the bathroom door.

She didn't even look the same as when she'd left. Her chaotic dark curls were now wrangled into tight braids that fell against her copper skin when she didn't pull them back for work. Her black button-down shirt was a far cry from the bold colors she'd always been drawn to.

She didn't look like April O'Sullivan, and she definitely didn't feel like the same innocent, ignorant little girl who'd grown up in the blink-and-you'd-miss-it town of Aspire, Montana.

And yet somehow, her sisters had still tracked her down.

They'd accomplished what she'd failed to do, and that earlier frustration was back in spades as she picked up the notebook she carried and crossed out the name at the top of the right-hand page before tucking it into the back pocket of her snug jeans.

Then she picked up the only black apron she had left in her rapidly diminishing supply of clean clothes, snagged her phone, and headed out the door for the stairs leading down to her workplace.

Despite what her grandparents believed, she hadn't left Montana just to run away from her problems.

Or...not just that.

She'd left because she was desperate to find out the truth. After her mom died, she'd thought Frank and her grandparents were her whole world. Only to find that they'd all been lying to her. Keeping secrets.

And then when Frank passed, and her grandparents had burrowed further into their grief, she'd been lost. And the answers she'd sought hadn't been in Bozeman or Aspire...

Or Montana, for that matter.

She needed answers, and very few people could give them to her. Her mother had a life before Frank. A life her grandparents didn't want to talk about. A life here in Portland.

Was it too much to ask that one of her leads pan out?

Apparently so.

She pushed open the door that led to the kitchen and was greeted with shouts and good-natured teasing.

"You're late," one of the baristas sang as he snagged a breakfast sandwich from the counter. "Must've been a tough commute all the way down those stairs."

"Nah." Monica, one of the bakers, nudged her hip as she passed. "She just stayed out too late with me and the girls last night, isn't that right?"

April laughed, snagging one of the freshly made croissants near Monica's station. "Hey, you stayed out later than me."

Monica groaned. "And I'm paying for it, trust me."

April took a bite and sighed happily. "Mon, you make the best croissants."

"And I'm teaching you all my secrets," Monica

muttered. "Hope you're happy."

"I am," April said. And she meant it. She grinned as she wove her way through the bustling kitchen, pausing long enough to finish her pastry and tie the apron around her waist.

She'd been lucky to find this job. Not only was she surrounded by friendly, welcoming people her own age, but the owner and managers actually fostered her love of baking.

For the first time ever, she'd found a place where her unique love of art and food could flourish. She'd learned so much while working here, and considering she was as far from "home" as she'd ever been, this place was the next best thing.

Better, actually, considering Portland and this café bore no reminders of her mom, Frank, or any of the secrets they'd kept from her.

The earlier guilt and frustration melted away as she found herself caught up in the busy flow of the café. There was a line forming as the coffee shop reached its peak busy time of the morning, and April didn't hesitate to jump in. "What can I get for you?"

One after another, she filled their orders, lighting up at the ones that called for some decorative touches and beaming with pride when anyone complimented the macaroons she'd labored over the night before.

When it finally came time for her break, April was pleasantly exhausted in a way that only seemed to come about after a long, hard day at work.

She went out front for some fresh air, snagging a coffee and one of Monica's mini baguette sandwiches on her way. Her manager, Sheila, was already outside, no doubt basking in the relative calm before the lunch rush.

"April, just who I was hoping to see." Sheila beckoned her over to the small table where she sat.

April laid out her lunch as the other woman watched her.

"You've been doing great work here, hon." The older woman smiled.

"Thanks. I really love all I've been learning in the kitchen."

The woman nodded. "If you keep it up, we'll be moving you off barista duty soon enough."

April's brows arched. "Really?"

"Uh-huh. You have a real knack with pastries and confections," her manager said. "It's clear that you'd do well with a little more training."

April leaned back in her seat with a warm flush of pride. "Thanks, Sheila. I do love working in the bakery. I don't mind dealing with customers, obviously, but I definitely feel like working in the bakery is a good use of my skills."

"You're an artist," Sheila said simply. "And it shows in your work."

April felt that warm flush spreading as she reveled in the compliment and nibbled on her lunch. The sandwich was good, but she was already looking forward to the chocolate éclair that would follow, if there were any left.

Sheila sighed and took her time getting to her feet. "I should get back inside. No rest for the weary, you know."

April chuckled. "Thanks for the kind words, Sheila. I appreciate it."

"It's all true." She patted April's shoulder. "If you want to stick around, you could find a home here at Café du Monde. We'd love to have you."

April's hands stilled, the sandwich hovering in midair as Sheila disappeared inside the café.

The word *home* seemed to ring in her ears, but rather than warm her the way Sheila's compliments had, the words made her insides tighten and her chest grow cold.

The word *home* said aloud conjured so many images at once that April felt herself blinking back tears before she knew what was happening.

The word *home* made her think of sprawling meadows and her mom's bright smile. It made her think of Frank's laughter and her grandparents' cozy living room, and a purple bedroom in a house that was now filled with strangers.

She set the sandwich down, her throat too tight with emotions for her to take another bite.

Home.

Was that what she'd found here at Café du Monde?

She wished she could say yes, but the ache in her chest called that a lie. She fell back in her seat, that earlier frustration back in spades. She'd set out for Portland to get answers, and that was exactly what she needed.

She'd never be able to call any place home so long as there were still so many unanswered questions in her mind about where she came from, and who her parents really were.

Frank had six other daughters. *Six.*

And her mom had a life before him, about which no one seemed to know.

She pushed the sandwich away and jerked out of her seat. She'd be better off going back inside and throwing herself into work.

This place might not be home...but right now it was the closest thing she had to one.

CHAPTER 3

Boone got the unnerving impression that he was being watched as he turned his large pickup onto the narrow streets of April's neighborhood.

He squinted as he took in the narrow buildings that lined the packed street. A few homeless people gathered at one corner while a musician played loudly on the other.

All the while, his truck crept down the street like he was inching through molasses. "Are you sure that private detective got you the right address?"

His phone was hooked up to Bluetooth, so when JJ spoke, his low, rumbly voice filled the entire cab of the truck. "I'm sure. Looking at it right now."

"Why?" Emma's voice piped in. "Doesn't it seem like the sort of neighborhood where April would stay?"

They had him on speakerphone. He could just picture it now, all the happy couples piled into the kitchen at the ranch to check on Boone's progress.

He shrugged and then remembered that no one could see him. "I dunno. I guess I'm not very familiar with this city."

"Or any city, I'd imagine," Lizzy teased.

Daisy's laughter was a light, tinkling distraction. "Boone, don't tell me you're driving around in that big pickup wearing a cowboy hat."

Lizzy's laughter joined in, and Boone rolled his eyes even as he grinned. "No, ma'am," he shot back. "I left my cowboy hat behind." He made eye contact with a wide-eyed man who was either on drugs or visiting from another planet. "Still feel out of place, though."

"We shouldn't have let him go alone." Emma murmured—no doubt a side comment not meant for him to hear. It was so very expected he couldn't even get annoyed.

"He'll be fine, Emma. Don't you fret," Lizzy's husband, Kit, reassured her.

Well, at least someone believed he was up to the challenge.

"Hey, Boone, did you make those stops like I asked?" Nash's voice was as husky as JJ's sometimes, and it took him a second to figure out who was talking.

"Yes, sir." Boone glanced over his shoulder at the loaded-up truck. The cost of airfare from Bozeman to Portland was outrageous, and between Nash, Ethan, Dr. Dex, and his own family, he'd been inundated with requests to pick up supplies while passing through Spokane.

It was a good thing the horse trailer hadn't been free or Kit might've had him buy horses at auction while he was at it.

"This truck is full to the brim with supplies for the ranch, and Dr. Dex's office, not to mention the firehouse and—"

"See?" Emma cut in. "We've asked too much of him."

Boone laughed. "I didn't say that, Miss Emma."

Miss Emma was what her kindergarten students called her, and it never failed to make her smile when he used the name.

"Is there anything we can do to help?" Rose asked. Her voice was unmistakable. So sweet and gentle that everyone naturally went silent when she opened her mouth.

"No, ma'am, I've got this." He hoped he sounded more confident than he felt.

Not that he wasn't sure he could handle this. He'd never had a problem getting his way—especially with pretty ladies.

But the closer he got to the pinpoint on the dashboard map, the more he was feeling like a giant sore thumb. So far out of his element he didn't know which way was up. "Lizzy, darlin', this must've been how you felt rollin' into Aspire that first day," he muttered.

Lizzy's laugh was loud and made him grin. "Oh, cowboy, you don't know the half of it."

"So long as you're not wearing a ten-gallon hat and throwing the word *ma'am* around left and right, you'll do just fine." Daisy laughed too.

"We appreciate you doing this, Boone," her fiancé, Levi, added.

"Don't mention it." Boone gazed out the window, wondering how he could still be in the same country when it felt like a different planet.

This was no Montana.

"We owe you, man." Nash spoke with such quiet sincerity, Boone actually shifted in his seat with embarrassment.

And maybe just a little pride. He couldn't deny he was looking forward to being the hero when he showed up back at the ranch with the one sister who'd been MIA for more than a year now.

In the end, there'd been no question that he needed to be the one to go. Everyone else had family or work commitments that made a trek to Portland out of the question. Plus, there was the fact that he was the only one who actually knew her.

Once again, his mind's eye was full of the artsy loner he remembered. Cute, brave, and weird as heck, but in a way that everyone found endearing.

"I hope she remembers you," Emma fretted.

"Of course she'll remember him." Lizzy was no doubt throwing her arm around Emma's shoulders and giving her a little squeeze.

"She hasn't seen him since they were sophomores in high school," Dahlia pointed out.

Boone listened as the sisters bickered in a good-natured sort of way.

"Yeah, but this is Boone we're talking about," Daisy chirped.

"Exactly," Lizzy agreed.

Boone's smile grew as he spotted Café du Monde at the end of the block.

"I don't see how that makes a difference," Kit cut in.

Lizzy's tone was bland. "Don't you?"

Rose giggled, and JJ chuckled as he added, "I think what your wife is trying to say is that Boone's, well…"

"He's a legend," Daisy finished with a laugh.

Rose giggled again, and her husband was the one to respond. "A legend, huh?" A baby gurgled, and Dr. Dex started talking baby talk to the infant he shared with Rose.

"Look, I've only just moved here, and even *I* know

April's knight in shining armor is *the* Boone Donahue," Daisy teased.

"Oh please," Dahlia sighed. "You're gonna give the kid a big head."

"He's not much younger than me," Rose cut in. "He's hardly a kid."

"Thank you, Rose," Boone called out as he winced his way through parallel parking a giant truck in a cramped space.

"You're welcome, Boone," she said sweetly. "But please don't let it go to your head. We like you just as you are."

He laughed, his earlier wariness fading in the light of all these friends and their banter. "I promise I won't."

Nash scoffed. "You're kidding, right? My cousin was the youngest varsity quarterback to make the Aspire team…and he led them to states two years in a row. If his head was ever gonna get swollen, it's a done deal already."

Boone chuckled quietly, turning the key in the ignition as he waited for a pause to wrap this up.

"Mmm, and he's just as popular now as ever, from what I gather," Lizzy said.

"How is it that you still have all the gossip?" Emma teased.

"It's a gift!" Lizzy shot back.

"Y'all, I hate to interrupt," Boone drawled, "but I've just parked, and I've got a young lady waiting."

Dahlia hissed. "Oh, I hope this works."

"It will, darlin'," JJ said. Boone could picture the gruff mountain man gently squeezing the back of his wife's neck and kissing the side of her head. "If anyone can convince April to come home, it's Boone."

"Yeah, she probably had a crush on him like every other girl her age in this town," Kit added.

Boone supposed it wouldn't be humble to agree, but… he agreed.

There weren't many girls who didn't return his lopsided grin with a flirty look or a shy little smile.

"I got this," he assured them all. "Now, if you'll excuse me, I've got a girl to meet."

He shut off the phone and unplugged it, sticking it in his back pocket as he climbed out of the truck and right into crazy traffic.

The whole city seemed to be wilting under the gray skies and heavy clouds, but when he stepped into the café, he might as well have been stepping into yet another world. Bright colors adorned every wall, and knickknacks, plants, and artwork were arranged around the small seating space in a way that felt haphazard but was most likely well thought out because, all combined, the place seemed to beckon him forward, and soon he was joining a long line that nearly reached the door.

At first, he was content just to take it all in—the patrons seated at tiny tables and the ones who flew past him on their way out with to-go cups in hand. The artwork that he didn't actually get but he supposed was pretty, even if he wasn't sure what it was supposed to represent. As he got closer, he grew fascinated by the crazy pastries behind the counter, with artwork on top just as elaborate as the art that graced the walls.

And through it all, he looked for her. For April.

A little part of him was sinking fast with disappointment. The private eye knew where she worked…but not when.

Maybe she wasn't scheduled today. It might have been

years, but Boone was sure he'd recognize those untamed curls anywhere. But as he kept an eye on the employees flying around behind the counter, he didn't see any telltale curls.

He'd just wait until he got to the front of the line and ask what time April worked, that was all.

A little anticlimactic after two solid days of driving, but whatever. He could wait a little longer.

It wasn't until he was one person away from the counter that he finally spotted her. She came out from a door leading to the back—to the kitchen, he supposed. And her arms were full of a large tray laden with goodies.

But he barely noticed what she held. He was too busy taking her in.

Like a punch to the gut, he felt winded at the sight of her. Probably just all that anticipation, that was all. Not to mention the sudden surreal blast from the past, seeing an old high school pal here in the middle of a crowded café in the middle of a way-too-crowded city.

Yeah, that was it.

He drew in a shaky breath as he watched her waltz behind the display case, a smile curving her lips and forming a dimple that he definitely did not remember. Her curls were tamed now, caught in thin braids that made her look more mature…

Or maybe it was the fact that he hadn't seen her in almost a decade that made her seem more mature.

She *was* more mature. She'd grown up, just like he had.

He gaped as she turned, flashing that smile in his direction—though she didn't see him.

But he saw her.

All of her.

She hadn't grown much in height, but her features

were sharper and her eyes just as bright as he remembered. Her smile was mesmerizing, and the way her hair swung and her curvy body moved behind the busy counter with the grace of a ballerina…

He could have watched her all day. It wasn't just him. He sensed everyone tuning in to her. Just like how he'd walked into this café and felt his mood brighten, her very presence was like a visit from the sun.

The other employees returned her smile one by one, and her husky, soft laughter made the smooth jazz playing in the background feel harsh.

She was brilliant. And his heart started to pound with excitement as the employee behind the cash register stepped away and April slid into her place.

"Will that be all?" She smiled brightly at the man in front of him.

She made the change and dismissed him with a parting farewell, and then—finally—she turned her attention to Boone.

"Can I help you?" she asked, her eyes bright and that same smile on her lips.

Boone's heart tripped. His smile grew. He waited for a second for recognition to light her eyes, but instead, he saw the corners of her mouth slide, her smile faltering as her expression turned weary or exasperated or…

Or like she was waiting politely for a stranger to speak.

"Hey, April." He moved a little closer to the counter.

Surely she recognized him. His confidence waivered under her even stare.

"I hope she remembers you…"

Emma's words from earlier ran through his mind. He'd dismissed the thought as quickly as everyone else had.

"Of course she'll remember him," Lizzy had said.

And he found himself thinking it now as her wide-set, warm brown eyes met his, her almond skin glowing under the bright, cheerful lights.

Of course she'll remember…

He arched a brow, waiting. Finally, she blinked, and the last of her smile disappeared into a look that could only be described as…

No, not revulsion. Surely not.

But…she definitely didn't look pleased as she narrowed her eyes at him. "*Boone?*"

CHAPTER 4

April's heart was beating way too fast. And the café seemed to be shrinking around her as she stared at the man on the other side of the counter.

"Hey, April," Boone said again.

She gave her head a little shake, trying to get her mind working. "What...what are you doing here?"

His smile grew. Before he could answer, her manager walked past. "Is everything all right here, April?"

The concern in Sheila's tone made her aware of the fact that she'd been standing there staring for far too long. Her welcoming smile was nowhere to be seen, and—

She blinked, releasing some of the tension in her face.

Had she been glaring?

Yes. Yes she had.

Boone rocked back on his heels, his smile tilting up on one side in a way that was at once so familiar and so forgotten. She found herself blinking in confusion all over again. Boone was so tied to her memories of Aspire that for a moment, it felt like she was facing the ghost of Christmas past.

Or…the ghost of hometown past?

Whatever. The question was…

"What are you doing here, Boone?"

His gaze flickered to Sheila, who was still hovering nearby, and then he gave April a wink. A wink! Only Boone Donahue could get away with winking like that. "Just here for some coffee." His gaze lifted, and he made a show of studying the board behind her. "Let's see, how about one of those mochaccinos? They any good?"

April made a noise somewhere between a squeak and a choking sound.

Is he serious right now? Is Boone Donahue seriously in my café, ordering a mochaccino?

For Sheila's sake—and the ever-increasing line of customers forming behind Boone—she forced a smile. "Coming right up."

He handed her some cash, and it was sheer force of habit that had her going through the motions, making change and sending through the order.

Sheila's hands fell on her shoulders as they both watched Boone saunter toward an empty table by the window. "Why don't I take over the cash register?" Sheila murmured in her ear. "You can make his drink and… maybe take a break, huh?"

April glanced over her shoulder and felt a swell of gratitude at the understanding in the older woman's gaze.

Sheila arched a brow. "Let me guess. He's your ex?"

There was that squeaking, choking sound again, escaping from her throat like she was a dying pigeon or something. She shook her head. "Not an ex. Just…" The right words wouldn't come, but finally she settled on "A blast from the past is all."

Sheila smiled. "Well then, I think Roger and I can cover

for you for a while if you want to take a break and say hello."

I don't want to. April's smile was tight as she nodded. *Please don't make me.*

She didn't say that, though. Because she was no coward. And Boone Donahue was many things, but he was no one to be scared of.

April headed to the espresso maker, casting glances at Boone all the while. He looked the same as she remembered, only…better.

If that was even possible.

He still had the same dark wavy hair that fell into his eyes and made every girl nearby want to brush it aside. Still the same dark eyes that sparkled with mischief and laughter, like the whole world was a joke just for his amusement. Still tall, same broad shoulders, although…

He was more muscular than she remembered. His biceps bulged against the fabric of his T-shirt, and his back muscles stretched it taut when he'd walked away.

She turned back to the machine with a roll of her eyes. *Get a grip, April.* But her hands shook as she reached for a mug.

Boone Donahue was here. In her café. In Portland.

And yes, she'd recognized him instantly, but like an idiot she'd played dumb. *"Can I help you?"* she'd said.

Can. I. Help. You.

She resisted the urge to smack a palm to her forehead.

Boone Donahue resurfaces in her life and that's all she can say. Chirping out the familiar words like a parrot rather than acknowledging the fact that the most popular guy in all of Aspire High was standing there in her coffee shop.

She'd been shocked stupid, that was all. And for

some reason, she hadn't wanted him to know she'd recognized him. His ego was too big by far. Always had been. He didn't need her acting like some infatuated, silly girl just because he'd happened to come into her workplace.

But seriously…

As if April wouldn't recognize that charming lopsided grin anywhere.

As if his "aw shucks" smile and that crinkle at the edges of his eyes weren't forever ingrained in her memory.

Not that she'd had a crush on Boone. Of course not. She'd never been that stupid. But one simply did not get through grade school, junior high, and most of high school with a guy like Boone and not know exactly who he was.

The school had orbited around him like he was the freakin' sun. It had always been annoying, but even more so because he just…took it for granted.

It would have been better somehow if he'd been a jerk. Like, if he'd been a cruel, self-centered jock, it would have been easier to just hate the dude.

But no. Boone had been known for his kindness. Help-fulness, even.

And sure enough, every time she glanced over her shoulder, she watched him tip his baseball cap at a passing stranger or hurry to his feet to open the door for a woman with a stroller.

Gah! He was ridiculous. Who did he think he was, Prince Charming?

She took her time with the mochaccino.

Okay, fine. She took way too much time, making a design on top that was extravagant even for her. Anything to buy a few more minutes, right? Because seriously… what was he doing here?

Her brows drew together as she focused on making a picture in the foam.

Was he here…for her?

No. That didn't make any sense. She shoved the thought away as quickly as it came up. What would Boone Donahue be doing seeking her out? And in Portland, no less.

But then again…what were the odds that he'd just happened to come to Portland? That he just stumbled into this coffee shop in the middle of a city that was over-flowing with cafés?

It made no sense. But after another minute passed and there were no more flourishes she could possibly add to his drink, she couldn't procrastinate any longer.

With a deep breath for courage, she took the mug and slid out from behind the counter…and walked over to Boone's table.

"Here you go." She set it down in front of him, the saucer clinking quietly and the spoon rattling at her jerky movements.

Boone stared down at the drink. "Wow. Just…wow." He glanced up with wide eyes. "Did you make this?"

She shrugged, annoyed beyond belief by the warmth of pride that swelled in her chest. She hadn't spent so much time on that stupid saddle and horseshoe design to impress him, dang it. She'd just been procrastinating.

"So cool," he breathed.

"Yeah, well…" She trailed off when she realized she had no idea how to finish. "Boone, what are you doing here?"

His warm brown eyes found hers, and they seemed to soften with an empathy that made her want to run away.

She forced herself to stand still, her spine rigid as he

shifted in his seat, his muscular body comically large in the small chair.

He leaned forward, resting his elbows on the table. "I need to talk to you."

Air rushed out of her lungs in a whoosh. If there'd been any doubt left in her mind that his being here wasn't a coincidence, he'd just confirmed it. "You? Talk to me?"

Her laugh sounded as awkward as it felt.

His lips curved up and… Gah! If she hadn't known him for as long as she had, she might've fallen hook, line, and sinker for that ingratiating grin. "Why is that so weird? We've known each other since kindergarten."

When she didn't respond, he added, "We were in the same class all the way through sophomore year, you know. Is it so odd that I might want to chat?"

His tone was teasing, cajoling…and her head was spinning. The way he was talking, one might think they'd actually been friends. "So we went to the same school for a while. I'm surprised you even remember that."

His chin jerked back, and his brows drew down. He honestly looked hurt. "Come on. I remember you."

"Really."

"Sure I do. Little April O'Sullivan. The quiet, mousy artist who liked to wear colorful scarves in the winter and those leg warmer things. You had a rainbow pair that you knitted yourself, right?"

She swallowed hard. Memories were not her friend these days, and just the mention of those rainbow leg warmers made her heart hurt.

She had made them, but not by herself. Her mom had spent countless hours helping her decipher the pattern and learn new crochet techniques.

Boone arched his brows, prompting. He looked so

pleased with himself that it took everything in her not to roll her eyes in disgust.

Instead, she sighed. "How do you know that?"

"Because we went to school together, and I remember you." He winked and leaned forward even farther, all eager puppy vibes as that infamous smile spread across his face. "Now, can you take a break? Because we really need to talk."

CHAPTER 5

Boone tried his best to be patient, his smile never faltering as she stood there looking down at him like he was some bug under a microscope and she couldn't make out the species.

Okay, he could admit it.

This…was not going as planned.

Granted, his plan hadn't gone much further than showing up at her workplace and saying hello. But still.

When the silence grew so loaded that it felt ready to pop, he broke it. "C'mon, sunshine. Just hear me out."

One of her elegantly arched brows lifted.

Man, she looked like a queen when she did that. Her cheekbones were so high, and her features so delicate and fine…

She'd always been cute, but now she was exquisite.

His gaze was caught by the swing of her large turquoise earrings as she tossed her braids back over her shoulder. A matching necklace peeked out from behind the collar of her shirt.

"Is the black shirt a uniform or something?" he guessed.

Her lips twitched, a silent confirmation.

"I like what you've done with your hair."

She reached a hand up and touched one of those long braids, a flicker of amusement in her eyes. "Don't tell me you came all this way to check out my new hairstyle, Boone Donahue."

He chuckled. "I wouldn't dream of it, *April O'Sullivan*." His heart gave a little kick when his teasing made her lips twitch again. "But until you take a break and join me, I guess I'll just sit here and talk about whatever's on my mind."

"Like the weather?"

The amusement in her gaze was definitely grudging, but he felt a surge of optimism. She was talking to him. Maybe not about anything real, but at least she hadn't sent him packing.

An outcome that hadn't even occurred to him before he'd come face-to-face with her.

"Nah, I thought maybe we'd talk about all the small-town gossip you've missed these past few years."

"I haven't missed anything." There was a warning in her tone despite the teasing.

"Not true." He saw her stiffen before he hurried on. "Now take old Chicken Joe…"

She blinked and then let out a little laugh as a smile and a dimple transformed her from a queen to an angel.

Man, she was a pretty one.

"From the coffee crew? Is that still a thing?"

"Yes, ma'am." He nodded. "And rumor has it, Chicken Joe is in over his head with a new shipment of roosters. Dr. Bob had to go out there and take some off his hands, and now the whole town is trying to rehome a bunch of livestock."

"You're ridiculous."

"I'm serious. And then there's the hubbub at Mama's Kitchen. Don't get me started on all the hassle over their fancy new outdoor seating area."

She snickered before glancing away, like she was embarrassed that she found it funny. "Okay, now I know you didn't come to Portland just to fill me in on local gossip," she finally muttered.

He leaned back, his heart doing a weird little tap dance when her gaze met his. There was a wariness there that he didn't like. Not one bit.

He glanced over to the register, which was manned now by her manager, and other employees were busily filling orders behind her. "Can you talk now, or should I come back?"

He watched her debate her answer. Boone could all but see the battle between curiosity and the desire to send him away.

His hands clenched around the mug as he awaited her verdict.

With a loud sigh, she turned away. "I'll be right back."

He watched her head behind the counter and say something to the manager. A little while later, she was walking his way again, her earrings swaying and her mouth set in a resolute line as she set her own steaming mug of black coffee down on the table and sank into the seat across from him.

"All right, Boone, what do you want?"

He widened his eyes at her no-nonsense tone. He should've expected it, he supposed, but he found himself pondering ways he could get that smile back.

It really was too pretty for words.

April tilted her head to the side. "I'm guessing you didn't come all the way from Aspire just to reminisce. You still live in Aspire, right?"

He tipped his chin. "I do."

"Cowboy?"

He winked. "Yes, ma'am."

"Should've known," she murmured.

From anyone else, he might've taken that as an insult of sorts, but it didn't sound that way coming from her. "Yeah?"

"That's what you always wanted." Her dimple popped into place before quickly disappearing again.

Surprise made him still, his chest oddly tight as she continued.

"Youngest quarterback in the school's history." Her dark brown eyes studied him. "Everyone thought you'd be chasing down some football dream, but that wasn't who you were."

He smiled, oddly grateful that he didn't have to explain himself. For years now he'd had to go over his decision to family and strangers alike. When word spread that scouts were watching him, he'd had to face outright confusion when he spelled out that he had no desire for fame and fortune.

All he'd ever wanted was in Aspire.

"You're a country boy." She shrugged, then stirred some sugar into her coffee.

He grinned. "You remember me, too, I see."

Her cheeks flushed. "I just remember your speech from freshman year, trying to sell everyone on the fact that cowboy life is the way God intended us *all* to live."

His head fell back with a laugh. "I forgot about that."

He was still laughing when he met her gaze with a wince. "I don't know if I got the best grade for that one."

She smiled. "I wasn't there for the last couple years, but I...I knew you'd stay."

"It's home. I love it."

Her answering silence made him wish he hadn't spoken. It wasn't just his home. It was hers too.

But she obviously didn't feel that way.

He cleared his throat and lifted his cup, struck again by the awesome picture she'd made. It almost seemed a shame to drink it. "How about you, April?"

"What about me?" She sounded so defensive.

"This coffee's pretty fancy. I almost can't take a sip. Is this your dream? Making artistic drinks for people?"

She snickered. "Not exactly."

He waited her out, taking his time sipping his drink as she toyed with her spoon. Finally, she added, "I like it, though." She glanced around. "I like what I've been doing here, combining my passion for art with food and..."

Her lips clamped together like she'd said too much. Yet she'd barely given anything away.

He studied her, trying to figure out what she was thinking, what she was feeling.

"You like it here," he repeated slowly.

She nodded. "That's right."

He leaned over the table, setting down the drink so he could give her his full attention. "Is that why you haven't come back to the ranch your father left you?"

CHAPTER 6

April froze in her seat.

She should've seen it coming. Maybe some part of her had, but she'd gotten so caught up in the fact that Boone was here, and that he'd sought her out, that she hadn't had a chance to really think about why he'd come here.

But even now as she stared into his eyes, all soft with sympathy she didn't want to see, her brain couldn't quite make the connection. Her memories hitched and faltered trying to figure out how Boone was involved in the mess her father had left behind.

As if he could read the questions in her expression, he continued talking. "You guessed right that I'm a cowboy, but you never asked which ranch I'm working on."

She blinked a few times, her breath coming too sharp and shallow. "I figured you'd be working for your uncle. Doesn't he have that big property outside of town?"

She was stalling. They both knew she was avoiding the topic at hand, but Boone was nice enough to let her.

He nodded, an easy smile playing on his lips as he

shifted the mug in his hands, rotating it left, then right, as he studied her with seemingly never-ending patience. "I was working for my uncle Patrick during high school and for a few years after—"

"So no college for you?" The words seemed to jump out of her mouth. She threw in a tight, probably unconvincing smile that barely lasted half a beat.

He shook his head. His expression shifted, just slightly but it was enough. He was watching for some sort of reaction.

"What?"

"Nothing, just...most people have an opinion when it comes to that particular topic."

She gave a little huff of laughter, oddly relieved by the fact that they were veering away from talk of her father and the ranch. Even if she knew it was only a matter of time before he brought it up again.

"You think I'm gonna judge you for not going to college?" A wry smile tugged at her lips. "That would definitely be the pot calling the kettle black."

His brows arched in surprise. "You didn't go to college either?"

"Not really. Not full-time. My mom died my senior year—"

"I heard," he interrupted. "And I'm sorry."

She meant to hurry on, to babble on about something else—*anything else*—before the tsunami of emotions could grab a hold of her and drag her under, but Boone didn't give her the chance. He leaned over the table and shocked her speechless by taking one of her hands in his.

Her heart kicked, her belly fluttering as her gaze dropped to see his large, calloused fingers covering hers.

They seemed to swallow hers up, and that ache in her chest, the tightness in her throat…

It was unbearably painful, like his touch brought every emotion surging to the surface at once.

But there was also something nice about it. Something gentle and soothing and…

She blinked away tears as she stared at his long fingers, his thumb rubbing a gentle line across the back of her hand.

How long had it been since someone had touched her like this? She'd been surrounded by relative strangers for months, and having someone who knew her—or who knew about her family, at least—the casual gesture felt far too intimate.

She tugged her hand out from under his.

He let her go, and the moment he did, she felt cold. Alone…again.

Like she had been for more than a year now. Ever since she'd learned the truth about her father and his family.

She clasped her hands around her coffee mug, as if that might warm this bone-deep chill, her gaze fixed on the black coffee like it held the answers to every riddle in the universe.

"I am truly sorry, April. We all are."

Her gaze shot up. "We?"

He wet his lips, and she hated the pity in his eyes. "Anyone who ever met your mother knows that this world lost someone special."

Dang it, she hated that his words made her eyes sting even more.

"I remember when your mom would chaperone our field trips," he continued. "She'd always make the day so much more fun. She'd bring the best treats and never lost her temper…"

She swallowed hard and looked away.

"I can't imagine how hard it was for you to lose her. And then to lose your father too. I…I am so sorry for your loss."

She bit her lip, grief making words impossible. It was clear what Boone was doing. He was filling the silence so she could get it together.

His kindness was too much.

It was annoying, especially because…this was not why he was here. And they both knew it.

She drew in a deep breath and forced her gaze back to his. "What do you want, Boone?"

He met her gaze evenly, but he didn't respond to her curt tone, and that only made a flicker of guilt stir in her belly.

"I *was* working for my uncle," he said, his voice even and his tone as easygoing as ever. "But a while ago, your father left my cousin Nash in charge of your ranch—"

"Not my ranch," she snapped.

He didn't even blink. "He left Nash in charge of the O'Sullivan Ranch."

She pressed her lips together, not trusting herself to speak. The coffee shop's customers were dwindling, and she knew without looking that Sheila and her other coworkers were watching them.

The last thing she wanted was to cause a scene and stir up questions at this place that had become a respite from her family and her past.

"You shouldn't have come here," she muttered.

He ignored that. "At the start of last summer, Nash was shorthanded, and my uncle offered me up. I like working for Nash, and I guess he's been happy with me, too, because he and Uncle Patrick worked it out that the transfer could be permanent. So I'm living and working on your family's property now…"

He paused expectantly, and annoyance surged again. "Good for you," she bit out.

Really, what was she supposed to say? *Cool, so glad to hear you're living it up at my childhood home.*

She gripped the mug so hard it hurt as memory after memory threatened to devour her. Before she could stop it, she had visions of her old bedroom, the view of the land from the second-story floor-to-ceiling window, the way her mom would bake fresh bread and how the scent would fill every room in the house.

But just as quickly, the bad memories surfaced right alongside the good. She smelled the stale stench of her mother's bedroom when she hadn't been able to leave her bed for days. Those awful months leading up to their move to Bozeman, when she'd been in the hospital more often than not.

Those long nights sitting by her mother's side while she was sick and her body grew thinner with every passing day.

April stood up abruptly, and the sound of her chair scraping the floor drew more than one pair of eyes. "Just get to the point, Boone. What are you doing here?"

"Look, I know this is awkward, but I'm here to ask you to come back with me."

Her fingers started to tremble, and she clenched them into fists.

"Even if it's just a visit," he continued, his hands coming up like he was surrendering. "Your sisters have been looking for you, and since I'm the only one who knows you, I volunteered to come and bring you home."

There were so many things wrong with that sentence. Like the words *sisters* and *know you* and *home*.

She shook her head, that trembling in her fingers spreading to her arms and legs. Did he have any idea what he was asking?

Could he possibly understand how mistaken he was in coming here? She stared down into his warm, kind eyes and…she had no idea how to even begin.

This guy barely knew her when she was young, and he certainly didn't know her now.

She didn't owe him anything, just like she owed nothing to Frank's other daughters.

"Go home, Boone," she rasped. "Go back to Aspire."

"But—"

"I don't have any sisters." It came out louder and harsher than intended, and she hated the flash of guilt that followed in the wake of his kicked-puppy expression. But she ignored the feeling. All that mattered now was pushing him away, getting him to leave before he brought up any more painful memories.

"April, just hear me out," he started. "I just want—"

"You *don't* know me, Boone," she interrupted. "And Aspire isn't my home. It hasn't been for a long time."

Her words hit their mark. She could see it as his brows came down, a mix of hurt and confusion in his eyes. "It *is* still your home. There are people there who care about you."

She shook her head, pushing the words away as well as the painful emotions they conjured. "You shouldn't have come here. I didn't return any of those calls for a reason. I don't want any part of that ranch or those sisters who I didn't even know existed until—" Her voice cut off, emotions clogging her airways. Dang it.

"April." Boone came to his feet, and he reached for her.

She pulled away, stumbling back until her bottom hit the back of another chair. "Go, Boone. Go back where you belong."

"I'm not going home without you." His voice was soft, but his firm gaze told her he was serious.

She pressed the back of her hand against her mouth while her stomach trembled violently.

Home, he'd called it.

Home.

Once upon a time, it had been.

Aspire. The ranch.

It had been the sweetest, safest, most beloved home a girl could ask for.

But that was the past. And it had all been make-believe.

She didn't live in that fairy tale anymore, and she had no idea how to make Boone or any of her so-called sisters see that.

She stumbled away another step, this time heading back toward the cash register. "You should go." She raised her chin toward the door. "I have to get back to work."

Then she bolted toward the entrance to the employee station, ignoring Boone's voice as he called after her.

CHAPTER 7

Welp, that had been…not great.

Boone watched April walk away, her name echoing in the café as other customers turned to stare at him.

Okay, maybe it had been…bad.

Nope. Awful.

Boone scrubbed a hand over his face and fell back into his seat with a sigh. Okay, yeah, that had been outright awful.

He wasn't sure how long he sat there, watching April work. Ignoring the narrowed, suspicious glares from her overprotective coworkers. Sipping his cold coffee until he lifted it to his lips only to find that it was empty.

All the while, he kept watching and waiting. But April hadn't just gone back to work. She'd gone into hiding.

It was disconcerting, really, watching this vibrant young woman shut down in front of his eyes. Her dimpled smile was still there when she greeted customer after customer, and she still floated behind the counter with that effortless grace. But the light that was so uniquely April just…dimmed.

And he hated that.

He hated even more that he was responsible. His gut twisted as he watched her, trying to rid himself of the memory of the hurt in her eyes—the pain, the grief, the anger.

His heart thudded painfully as he held his empty cup, willing her to look his way.

But she never did.

Eventually he left. He'd already disrupted her workday enough as it was, and even if she were to give him some more time…what was there to say?

He didn't want to hurt her any more than he already had. He'd do just about anything to take away the pain in her eyes, but…how?

As he headed back to his truck, his steps were slow and halting. He nearly ran into another pedestrian as he crossed the street because his mind was still back at the coffee shop.

Shoulders slumped, he climbed back into his truck and caught a glimpse of his reflection. He nearly laughed at his brooding expression and defeated posture.

Man. What a change from the confident swagger he'd had when he'd first pulled up. He'd been so certain that all it would take was a smile, maybe a little flirty banter, and he'd have April in his passenger seat and back at the ranch in no time.

He exhaled loudly, running a hand through his hair before pulling out and heading to the motel where he'd reserved a room for the night.

The place was no frills, and he didn't need a local to tell him that he was in a dodgy neighborhood. The sounds of shouts, cars backfiring, and drunken laughter filled his musty old room.

His phone kept lighting up with texts, but he wasn't quite up for calling the ranch to fill everyone in on his failure.

He fell back on the bed with a groan.

He'd gone about it all wrong. He could see that now. He'd been sure she'd be happy to see him, and why. He rubbed at his eyes, as if that could erase the awful way they'd parted.

Or no…they hadn't parted. She'd run. From him.

Because he'd pushed too hard. That had to be it.

He scowled up at a watermark on the ceiling as guests in the neighboring room shouted at one another.

"I'm not going home without you," he'd said. And that… that had been a mistake. He'd seen her flinch when he'd said the word *home*. He'd heard the pain in her voice when she'd said she didn't have sisters and that Aspire wasn't her home.

"You don't know me, Boone."

He sighed as those words hit him between the ribs just like they had the first time she'd said them.

She was right. Of course she was right. He'd been an egotistical jerk to think he knew anything about what she'd been going through these past few years. He might have known her when she was young, but they hadn't been friends.

Not way back when, not a few years ago when her mom passed…and certainly not now.

His phone dinged where it was charging on the nightstand, but he made no move to pick it up.

Soon. He'd call them soon.

First, he ventured out of the motel to find some food,

all the while looking around and wondering about April's new life.

Was she happy here? Was this her home now?

The hurt was so glaringly clear when she spoke of Aspire and her sisters…maybe she'd never want to return.

Carrying his food back to the motel, he found himself debating how to go forward.

Was it right to try and bring her back if it caused her so much pain?

After he ate, he was no closer to feeling any sort of closure on the matter, but he couldn't ignore the texts and calls he'd gotten. He tried the ranch's house number first and got Emma straight away.

"Nash is here, and Lizzy's here with the kids," she said. "But the others have gone back home."

"Put him on speaker!" Lizzy shouted in the background.

Boone sat on the edge of the bed, leaning forward so he was resting his knees on his elbows. He found himself rubbing tired eyes as he spoke.

"So?" Lizzy's voice was high with excitement. "Did you see her?"

"Yeah." His own voice sounded dull in comparison. "I saw her."

There was a slight pause, and he guessed they'd picked up on his far-from-enthusiastic tone.

"Did you talk to her?" Emma asked.

"Yes, ma'am."

A silence fell, and it was Nash who finally broke it. "Probably best just to spit it out, cuz. These two are beside themselves with anticipation, and everyone knew you wouldn't have an easy time of it."

He winced. Everyone had known that...except for him. Man, maybe he really did have a big head.

Clearing his throat, he started from the beginning. When he finished, the silence felt like it weighed a million pounds.

"Well," Emma said slowly, "at least you got her to talk to you. That's something."

"Yeah," Lizzy added. "That's further than us sisters would have gotten."

He let out a humorless laugh. "Yeah, it was a real win."

"Don't beat yourself up, Boone." Emma sighed. "April's made it clear she has no interest in meeting us."

"Yeah, but I thought..." He shook his head, staring at the bland watercolor hanging on the wall.

What had he thought? That he'd be so irresistible she couldn't refuse?

That the thought of visiting Aspire would just magically erase all the heartache she'd been through?

He took a deep breath and tried again. "I guess I didn't realize how much she's been through...how much she's hurting..."

Emma let out a sad little sigh while Lizzy murmured, "That poor girl."

They all sat in silence for a while, each lost in thought.

Lizzy finally spoke. "You've got to try again, Boone."

Boone straightened. He wasn't sure what he'd expected, but her words caught him off guard. "I don't know, Lizzy. You didn't see her. She looked so...heartbroken. So lost."

He opened his mouth to keep going but...he was lost for words. None of them did justice to what he'd seen in her eyes.

"That's all the more reason that you need to try again," Emma said.

He pulled the phone away, put it on speaker, and set it down so he could stand and pace. "I don't know." The words came out sludgy and slow. Even he could hear the indecision in his voice.

"Do you think she'd talk to you again?" Nash asked.

"Maybe, but…" He stopped and faced the phone. "I don't want to do anything that'll cause her more pain, you know? She's been through enough."

Everyone was quiet at that. Boone supposed they were surprised. Heck, he'd surprised himself. He was normally the most easygoing person in any given room.

He didn't do confrontations or serious conversations. But this was important. He might not have been friends with April, but despite what she'd said, he did know her. He knew her well enough, at least.

Just the thought of her made his chest swell with a protectiveness he wasn't used to. "I know y'all need her to make a decision on the ranch, but maybe she doesn't have to be there in person, you know? Maybe I can just explain the situation and see where she stands."

Another long silence fell.

Nash's voice was low and serious, as usual. "Boone, you're worried about her, aren't you?"

"I am." He shifted from one foot to the other, wishing like heck this dumpy old motel had a gym so he could work off some of this tension. He settled for rubbing his neck muscles as he considered his options.

The thought of leaving without another word didn't feel right. But also… "I'm not gonna push her."

"No one's asking you to force her into coming home," Emma said quickly.

"We all want what's best for April," Lizzy chimed in. "It's not just about selling or keeping the property. We want to get to know her, to let her know that she…she has family."

"I don't have sisters."

He couldn't bring himself to repeat her words back to them.

"Please try one more time, Boone," Emma said. "Maybe it would help if she knew this was what her father wanted."

Boone had been there when Sierra and Cody had returned from April's grandparents' with Frank's journal. He knew what she meant.

"Tell her…" Emma hesitated. "Tell her what Frank wrote. Tell her that it was his wish for all of his daughters to come together. Her returning wouldn't just be for us, or even for her… It would be to honor her father's last wishes."

Emma's voice trailed off, but her words seemed to linger.

"If she's miserable when she gets here, no one's going to stop her from leaving again," Lizzy added.

"But O'Sullivan girls have a tendency to stick around once they get a taste of the ranch life." Nash was smiling— Boone could hear it in his tone.

That lightened the mood some, and he fell back onto the bed with a sigh. "That's the thing, though. This isn't the same for April. She grew up there."

"I remember," Nash said. "She was my little next-door neighbor."

Boone huffed. Of course. He'd nearly forgotten that. But they'd been far enough apart in ages that Nash and April likely hadn't interacted much.

"I remember her living out here," Nash continued slowly. "She's about ten or so years younger than me, so I didn't pay too much attention to her. But I used to see her as a little girl, skipping through the fields and riding her horse, always laughing and smiling. She seemed to love it here."

Boone opened his mouth to remind him of how much had changed for her since she'd left the ranch, but he closed it just as quickly.

"It might be just what she needs," Nash added. "Coming home, making peace with the past…"

"Maybe," Boone mumbled. Once again, the uncertainty was clear in his voice.

And man, he wished he knew for certain.

Everyone sounded a little tired and dejected as they started to say their goodbyes.

"Check in tomorrow?" Lizzy asked.

"Yes, ma'am."

"Don't you 'ma'am' me," she teased.

It'd become something of a joke between them, and Boone smiled. "Yes, ma'am."

Lizzy laughed, and he could hear the smile in Emma's voice when she chimed in. "Thanks for all you're doing, Boone. We'll understand if you can't persuade her, but please…don't give up on her yet."

His chest felt tight as he nodded and murmured a promise that he wouldn't.

When she put it like that, his protective instincts rose up all over again.

April might not think she needed him or any of them, but she needed help. That much was clear.

He couldn't walk away from her. Not while she was in pain and looking so lost and lonely.

But was bringing her back to Aspire the right thing to do?

He still didn't know for certain, but what he did know was that he needed to see her again. To talk to her again.

And maybe this time he wouldn't walk away feeling like he'd left his heart behind.

With a weary sigh, he sat back on the bed and flipped on the TV, only to turn it off again a little while later.

Tired from the drive but his mind still racing, Boone turned off the lights and lay down to sleep.

But instead, he found himself praying. "Lord, please help me. Help me to know if bringing her back is what's best for April...what's best for everyone, and..." He sighed, staring up at the ceiling with a shake of his head. "If it is what's best, then let me know... How am I supposed to convince this woman to come with me?"

CHAPTER 8

The next morning, April's head was pounding, and her mood perfectly matched the gray, overcast day.

Her eyes were gritty from lack of sleep, and the coffee she'd downed in her studio hadn't done a thing to make her feel any more awake. Even so, she was glad to be heading into work—and not just because the café provided an endless supply of caffeine. She was glad for the distraction, and even managed her usual smile as she greeted the others already working the counter.

"Can I help you?" she asked a frazzled young woman with a toddler perched on her hip.

The woman rattled off an order, and April was up and running.

She might've been exhausted, but staying busy was surely better than dwelling in her own thoughts upstairs. And that was what she'd been doing ever since her shift had ended the day before.

She should've taken Monica up on a girls' night out. She should have gone dancing or gone to a gallery…

But all she'd been capable of when her shift had ended was the short trek up the flight of stairs leading to her studio. She'd fallen onto her bed and barely moved the rest of the night.

She should have felt rested for all the lying around she'd done, but it had been a long, cruel night battling memories—good and bad.

Sometimes she wasn't sure which was worse. The good memories were so bittersweet these days. They only made her miss her parents more, and it was impossible not to recall those happy times with the knowledge she had now.

It was impossible not to relive those moments and see the lies that lay beneath it all.

Her perfect family had never been perfect.

It hadn't even really been *hers*.

She blamed Boone for the bad night and bristled with irritation when one of her well-meaning coworkers teasingly asked what had happened to the hottie from the day before.

"Did you meet up with him after work?" the barista asked.

Monica overheard and joined in. "She must have. That's why she didn't go out with us."

They were both grinning, and April had to duck her head to hide a scowl.

"Go on, admit it. The hot country boy is your ex, right?" The barista nudged her playfully.

"I just know there's juicy drama there," Monica added.

April's face hurt from her forced smile. "No drama. He's just an old friend, that's all."

Friend.

Ha! Hardly.

She punched numbers into the cash register with way too much oomph, hurting her finger in the process.

But really, what right did Boone have to show up here? They hadn't been friends. He barely even recognized her existence back then. He'd said it himself—back then she'd been mousy, artsy April O'Sullivan, and he'd been...

Well, he'd been Boone. The center of attention. His family's pride and joy. The guy every boy wanted to be and every girl wanted to date.

The fact that he'd remembered her at all was a minor miracle, so how on earth did he think it was his place to walk into her life and stir up old memories?

She handed over a brown paper bag to a waiting customer and forced a cheery "Have a nice day!" before letting her smile fade as her anger spiked.

The nerve of that guy.

Part of her wished she'd told him off for having the self-righteous cockiness to ask her to come home...on *their* behalf.

Obviously, he'd only come because they'd sent him. Frank's other daughters.

She gripped the edge of the counter as she waited for the next customer to stop hemming and hawing over the menu and place their order already.

She drew in a deep breath. Okay, fine. Maybe work was good for her sanity in her current state...but she wasn't exactly fit for work.

The smile was getting harder and harder to summon as a fresh wave of anger toward Boone swept over her.

Truthfully, the anger was kind of nice. So much better than the guilt and the betrayal and the grief she'd been dealing with all of last night.

Anger was good.

Anger made her feel more in control.

Her eyes narrowed when the bell above the door rang and Boone walked in.

Anger…had a focus.

"What do you think you're doing here?" she hissed when he reached the front of the line.

Boone's smile made her heart race and her nostrils flare as she tried her best to keep her voice down. "I thought I told you to go home."

He leaned over the counter, dropping his voice so low she could have sworn she felt the rumble. "And I told you I'm not going anywhere without talking to you first."

"We talked."

"We didn't." His crooked smile was still in place, but his gaze was serious. Insistent. Maybe even a little pleading. "There's still more we need to discuss."

She looked away first. "I heard all I needed to hear."

"Well, I still have more to say," he shot back.

She'd looked to the side, and now she found herself facing curious stares from her coworkers. She tried to force a smile, but her cheeks weren't having it. Her lips quivered as her grip on her emotions started to unravel.

"How dare you do this to me here," she finally blurted.

She'd tried for another sharp hiss of anger, but to her horror, it came out breathless and pathetic.

She glanced up, and the change in Boone was almost comical. The cocky swagger was nowhere to be found as he stared down at her with wide eyes.

"April, I didn't…I didn't mean to…"

"Everything all right?" Monica sidled up beside her. Nearly a foot taller than April, and with a glare that scared the toughest of men, Monica turned that withering scowl on Boone right now.

But Boone never looked away from April. And the way he looked at her...the way his eyes softened with sympathy and understanding, the way he was all but pleading with her to give him a chance to explain...

She swallowed hard as another memory surfaced that was beyond inconvenient. It was of Boone, back in middle school. Seemingly overnight, the girls had formed little clique groups, and the boys were either drooling over girls or mocking them to get their attention.

There was one boy who hadn't fit in at all. Trent Wagner. He'd been gangly and awkward, with a stutter and no athletic abilities whatsoever. And it was Boone who'd crossed the gymnasium during phys ed and talked to Trent when every other boy in class had ignored him.

It'd been Boone who'd picked him first for his team, and Boone who'd made it clear that it wasn't cool to bully Trent.

And for whatever reason, that was the memory that chose to rear its ugly head right here and now as she faced off with Boone across the cash register.

It had her letting out a long exhale as some of her anger faded.

Boone might've been cocky, and popular, and yeah, apparently now he was working on her dad's land...

But this was Boone, and he'd always been kind. Whatever he was up to right now, she had no doubt that he had good intentions.

"It's fine, Monica," she said, her tone just as grudging as she felt. "I was just telling my old pal Boone that I'd meet up with him when my shift is over so we can...talk."

Boone's eyes lit with a happiness that was irritatingly adorable. "Thanks, April." He grinned, already stepping aside so the next customer could move forward. "Here's my number." He grabbed a business card and scribbled down the digits. "Just tell me where and when, and I'll meet you."

His grin was so infectious, his look so eager...

She found herself giving him a little smile despite herself, just before he turned away.

Man. Between his inherent charm and his genuine kindness, the guy was impossible to hate.

"Can I help you?" she said to the next customer.

Her newfound sisters had either gotten lucky in choosing to send Boone...or they were diabolical. As she watched him walk away with a grin and his typical swagger, she cursed those women who'd sent him back into her life.

But with each passing hour of her shift, the business card with Boone's number burned a hole in her pocket.

She wouldn't back out of it. She'd said she'd meet him, so she would.

But what would she say?

What would *he* say?

He'd push her to return again, that much was obvious. But why? It wasn't like he had anything at stake, right?

When the front of house emptied out, she made herself busy in the back, finding comfort in the soothing, methodical steps Monica had taught her in prepping dough.

"Want to talk about it?" Monica's tone was no-nonsense, and April appreciated that.

She'd never been fond of people using syrupy sweetness when a simple question would do. People either wanted to talk or they didn't. And April...

"No," she said simply.

Monica nodded. "Fair enough. But in my experience,

you can only deal with life on your own for so long, you know?"

April didn't answer. She just kept kneading the dough.

"Comes a point where you have to learn how to trust someone if you're ever going to settle down and find a home."

Home.

There was that word again.

April blinked rapidly as the dough in her hands blurred. Was it that obvious that she had no roots and no place to call home?

Maybe.

"Look, you know Sheila and all the managers love you. We all love having you here," Monica said. "But if this isn't where you need to be right now…"

"It is."

But maybe she'd said that too quickly, because her new friend gave her some serious side-eye. "Uh-huh."

They worked in silence for a minute.

"What?" April finally snapped. "What do you mean by 'uh-huh'?"

Monica shrugged and nudged her hip with her own. "Just that Mr. Hunky Cowboy seems to think you have unfinished business back…wherever it is you're from."

April had to work to swallow. Monica was probably the closest friend she had in this city, and she didn't even know where April was from.

Which was April's fault. She'd shut the door to her past so firmly, she couldn't bring herself to mention it casually like any normal person would.

She shifted from foot to foot.

"So?" Monica finally said.

"So what?" April shot back.

Monica dipped her head with a laugh. "Girl, if that's the way you wanna play it, that's fine by me. You don't have to be all honest with me…"

April glanced over when it was clear Monica was waiting for her to pay attention.

Monica's brows arched meaningfully. "Just so long as you're being honest with yourself."

April opened her mouth to retort, but Monica dusted off her hands as she turned away.

With a sigh, April did the same, pulling out Boone's card before she could overthink it any further. Biting her lip, she considered the time and place for a second before choosing a cheap outdoor taco stand a couple blocks away when her shift ended at three.

She shot off the details and then tucked her phone back in her pocket, not pulling it out when she heard the almost instantaneous response come through.

She refused to think about what she'd say for the rest of her shift. Maybe she wouldn't have to say anything at all. She'd let him say his piece once and for all and then tell him in no uncertain terms that she had no business left in Aspire—unfinished or otherwise.

When three rolled around, she paused just long enough to take off her apron before heading to the taco stand, placing her order, and then joining Boone, who looked like he'd been camped out at the patio table for hours judging by all the empty pop cans in front of him.

"Waiting long?" she asked, her tone dry as she dropped down into the seat across from him.

"You're worth the wait." His lips quirked up on one side, and…man. By the way his gaze warmed, you'd think he was genuinely over the moon to see her.

Like he'd missed her or something.

She huffed under her breath as she dipped her head and dug into her taco salad, ignoring the stupid fluttering in her chest and the warmth in her cheeks.

"Okay, Boone," she said after swallowing her first bite. "You wanted to talk. So talk."

CHAPTER 9

Boone shifted, choosing his words carefully. "I know you have no interest in going back to Aspire—"

"Oh, you picked up on that, did you?"

There was no heat in April's voice, only wry humor, and he couldn't help but laugh in response.

She was always pretty, but she was outright adorable when she got all feisty.

"I might not have been a straight-A student like you," he teased, "but even this dumb jock could figure that out."

Her lips pursed, and he felt a surge of joy when he realized she was trying not to smile. Finally, she shrugged. "I never called you a dumb jock. Those were your words, not mine."

He grinned. This was good. This was nice. Definitely better than he'd expected after the way she'd greeted him earlier at the café.

She tilted her head to the side. "How do you know I got straight A's?"

He arched a brow, not hiding his smirk. "Really? You

still think I never noticed you? I was paying attention, sunshine."

"Don't call me sunshine."

"Why not? You have a radiant smile…when you choose to show it."

Her lips pressed together, and…yep. He was positive she was trying not to smile again.

Score one for the dumb jock.

"Well, you're wrong about the straight A's." She nipped a cherry tomato off the end of her fork. "I got a B once. In phys ed."

He chuckled, and then his chest tightened painfully when she gave him one of those sunshine smiles in return.

It disappeared in a heartbeat. "So?" She stabbed the fork into her bowl. "Let's get this over with."

"That's the spirit," he muttered. "Okay, here's the deal. You know your sisters are desperate to get you back home, right?"

Her fork froze, and he caught her flinch. Was it the mention of her sisters or the mention of home that had made her wince like that?

"But what you may not know is that there's actually a very practical reason for you to get back to Aspire." He clasped his hands together on the table. He'd thought long and hard about how to persuade April, and without checking with Dahlia, Emma, or any of the others, he'd decided that making a case that was as emotion-free as possible would be the best tact.

When he saw wary curiosity light her eyes, he thought maybe he'd guessed right.

"I'm sure you've gotten a million messages from Dahlia and the others since they got your number," he said slowly.

Her arched brows said that was an understatement. "How did they get my number, anyway?"

He evaded the question neatly. "I can only guess what those ladies went on about in the messages."

Those ladies… He could practically hear Daisy's laughter and see Dahlia's eye roll. *Way to avoid the S-word, Boone.*

But whatever. They may be all gung ho about welcoming another sister into the fold, but he could absolutely respect her position.

They hadn't known Frank. Not well, at least, and not for long. They hadn't been raised by him, and they hadn't grown up thinking they were his only offspring and the light of his life.

But April had, and she'd need time. And patience.

And practicality.

"See, here's the thing," he continued, leaning forward as he held her searching gaze. "When Emma met with your dad's lawyer—"

"Emma…"

"She's a kindergarten teacher. Just married Nash a little ways back, and they're expecting a baby soon," he summed up, answering her unasked question.

She nodded. "Kindergarten teacher. That fits."

He let that pass. How many messages had those O'Sullivans left on her voice mail? He could only imagine.

"Anyway, when Emma met with the lawyer, he broke the news to her about all the…the daughters."

April blinked. "She…didn't know?"

He shook his head, his heart aching at the questions in her eyes. "She and Lizzy grew up together in Chicago, but until that meeting with the lawyer, they had no clue about you…or the others."

She processed that for a moment. "Huh." And then she went back to eating.

He cleared his throat. "He also told her about a stipulation. In the will."

"What kind of stipulation?"

"Your father made it clear that in order to sell the ranch or keep it, the decision would have to be unanimous."

She worked her jaw to the side, nodding as if maybe she possibly knew this, before muttering, "Unanimous."

He nodded as she leaned back in her seat.

After a long silence, she threw her hands up. "What kind of ridiculous rule is that?"

He flinched, glancing around at the customers waiting in line for their food who were now watching them after that outburst. April didn't seem to notice.

Her cheeks grew flushed, and a million emotions seemed to play out in her eyes. "He wanted everyone to be treated equally. Better not play favorites when you have seven daughters, amiright?" Bitterness tinged her laughter as she shook her head. "I thought I knew him so well, but...I really didn't." Her voice seemed to disintegrate over those last few words, and she looked away from him, blinking and clenching her jaw.

He leaned forward, reaching for her hand before he thought it through. She stilled, her gaze darting up to meet his.

"I think..." He wet his lips and tried again. "That is, your sisters think..." Nope. That was not the right word to use just now. He took a deep breath and tried one more time. "Your father left a journal."

She stared at him in surprise. "He did?"

"Yeah. He left a journal, and from whatever it was he wrote in his last entry, your...er, the *others* think he wanted to get all of you together. At the ranch. He wanted you to…"

"To what?" she snapped when the silence stretched too long. "Come together like one big happy family?"

He winced.

"Yeah, I don't think so." She went to scoot her chair back, but he held on to her hand like a lifeline.

"Please. You haven't heard it all yet."

"I think I have." Her voice was low and grim and… man, what he wouldn't give to take this hurt away.

But that's what coming home would do…

Hopefully.

Maybe.

"Look, no one expects you to come back and just…join this new family."

She tipped her head down and looked at him. "They don't?" Skepticism dripped from her tone.

He tilted his head from side to side. "Okay, fine. Maybe that's what they'd like," he amended. "But it's not what anyone expects."

"So, what do they expect, huh?"

He held her gaze for a long, tense moment before letting out a weary sigh. "April, believe it or not, I swear I am not the enemy here."

She blinked a few times, and her whole body seemed to soften with her next exhale. "I know. I'm…" She glanced away, her skin glowing golden in the setting sunlight, the sharp arch of her brows and her cheekbones reminding him once again of a queen on a throne.

So self-possessed and graceful and smart…and lonely.

His chest twisted painfully at that realization. She looked elegant and beautiful…and *alone*.

He could see the isolation even if she didn't want to

admit to it. She needed her family now more than ever. Or if family was too hard, then she needed friends.

She needed one friend, at least. And right then and there he swore he would be that for her. He would be her ally, even if it meant going against her sisters and their husbands.

"I'll be your proxy, if that's what you want," he said. "If you really don't want to go back there, I'll give them whatever answer you decide as far as the future of the ranch goes."

Her lips parted in surprise when she turned back to face him.

"And if you decide to go back to Aspire, to see the ranch, then I'll be right by your side."

"Why?" Her brows drew together. "Why would you do that?"

"Because…" He halted, temporarily at a loss for how to answer. Why did he feel so compelled to help her? To ease her loneliness and be by her side? "Because I think you need this as much as they do."

She pursed her lips. "They need my vote. They don't need me."

"You're wrong," he said simply. "I don't know how to explain the weird family those women have forged together back in Aspire, but I think you ought to at least see them, meet them…decide for yourself if they're the kind of people you might like to call fam—"

"Don't say it," she interrupted. Her voice wasn't harsh, just…desperate.

And that made his heart hurt so badly that for a second, all he could do was stare at her in silence.

"They're not my family," she finally whispered.

He let those words lie for a moment. He'd been in

Aspire when Emma showed up and had met each sister in kind. He reckoned every single one of them said the same thing before they got to Aspire and got to know one another.

"Well then," he finally said when it seemed someone needed to break the silence, "what about your grandparents?"

Her eyes welled with tears.

"Aren't they your family?"

She sniffed. "Don't talk about them. You don't know anything about my situation."

"Then tell me."

For a second, he thought she wouldn't. But eventually she sighed, her narrow shoulders slumping. "My grandparents lied. They kept secrets. I'm sure they had their reasons..." She waved a hand as if to gesture to all the vague excuses in the world. "But at the end of the day, how am I supposed to believe anything they say after they kept my whole life a secret?"

"My whole life..."

It felt like the ground was shifting beneath him, and Boone narrowed his eyes to study her further. She hadn't known she had sisters, but was that all of it? "April..."

"I'm not going back with you, Boone. I can't."

"But—"

"I don't belong on that ranch." She held a hand up to keep him from interrupting. "I don't belong with those women."

"April—"

"They're not my family, and they never will be."

She went to stand and he reached for her hand again, but this time she pulled it out from under his.

"April, just let them explain—"

"They're not my family. I don't know how else to say it." Her eyes filled with tears as she pushed the chair back farther and came to her feet. "Frank O'Sullivan is not my father." She sniffed, seemingly unaware of the audience they were courting.

Boone hardly noticed either. His insides were twisting into knots at the pain in her expression while his mind tried to make sense of her words. She seemed to see his confusion, because with a heavy sigh, she moved forward until she was standing beside him. "I'm not Frank O'Sullivan's real daughter. All the others are, but I'm not. He adopted me when I was little. I was too young to remember or even realize." Her voice grew thick and wobbly. "I thought I was his. But I'm not. So you see…" April held her arms out to the side as she backed away. "They are not my family. And that ranch is not my home."

CHAPTER 10

S aying the truth aloud for the first time nearly undid her.

April was blinded by tears as she stumbled toward the sidewalk.

"April, wait up!" Boone's voice grew closer, and soon he was all around her. Or that was how it felt, at least. He'd stepped in front of her, and his arms wrapped around her, and before she knew it, he was shuffling them both over to a bench in the neighboring park and had her snuggled up against his side.

She should fight it.

She knew that.

But after a useless struggle to keep some distance between them while his muscular arms were wrapped around her, she gave in to the inevitable and let herself melt against his side, her face half buried against his chest as a painful sob ripped through her.

It'd been so long since she'd let herself cry, and letting out that one sob felt like opening a gaping wound.

Without meaning to, she found her fingers curling into Boone's T-shirt. Her tears wet the fabric as she squeezed her eyes shut, willing all these old emotions back where they belonged.

It had been more than a year since her father passed.

More than a year to come to grips with the truth she'd learned the day she'd found his will.

So why did it feel like she'd only learned the news yesterday?

She sniffled, trying and failing to steady her ragged breathing.

"Hey," Boone said softly when she tried to pull away. "There's no rush. I'm not going anywhere."

That made her cry all over again for some stupid reason, and when he moved one hand, rubbing her back in small circles, she felt her heart constrict at the kindness.

How long had it been since anyone had touched her like this? Held her like this?

She let out a shuddering exhale, focusing on the feel of his hand, on the rhythm of his circling palm, pressing against her work shirt with firm, measured strokes. Suddenly she had an image of Boone on her father's ranch. She could picture him clearly in the stables, rubbing down a spooked horse just like this.

The thought made her next exhale come out as a huff of laughter, and she felt his hand still for a moment.

"Don't stop." She clamped her lips shut. Ugh, how needy was she?

But he didn't point that out. He just went right back to rubbing her back, pulling her a little closer and adjusting them so he was leaning back and she was resting against him.

It was more comfortable, and it was…nice.

Soothing.

She let her eyelids flutter shut, then opened them again when she realized that between the crying and the lack of sleep the night before, she was in serious danger of falling fast asleep on Boone right here in a public park.

Reluctantly, she pushed away from the cozy warmth of his arms. "I...um...thank you," she muttered when he let her go.

She sat back beside him, and she was overwhelmed with gratitude when he made no move to speak.

Surrounded as she was in the crowded café all day, she'd nearly forgotten there were people out there like Boone.

Guys who didn't feel the need to fill the air with words the second there was a quiet space.

She took a deep breath and let out a long, weary sigh. "Sorry about that," she finally murmured when she felt the silence stretch too long.

"Nothing to be sorry about."

Said so matter-of-factly that April almost believed him.

"So." She shifted to face him, acutely aware of the fact that her eyes were likely puffy and her nose red. "I guess you see now why I don't belong back at the ranch."

His brows drew together in genuine confusion. "But you do."

He reached for her hand and covered it with his.

She stared at the connection, jolted by the comfort of it. Silly to be so thrown by him holding her hand when he'd just held her in his arms, but there it was. This gesture was freely given and not because she was in distress.

It was natural and easy, almost like he was a real friend.

Boone turned to face her. "April, you said yourself that he adopted you, which makes you his daughter."

"But I'm not." She shook her head. "And do you know how I found out?"

He stared at her, his gaze filled with so much compassion, she felt it knock the wind out of her. The words came tumbling free before she could control them.

"After my mom died, I tried to help, you know?" She sniffed. "My dad...Frank." It sounded weird to her own ears calling him Frank instead of Dad, but she'd vowed to call him that from now on, and she'd do it. "Frank was lost. I mean, I was, too, but it was kinda scary to see my father turn into a shell of himself. So I tried to step up, you know? I'd graduated from high school and was living at home with him, and I started getting more and more involved, and then..."

April swallowed, and Boone squeezed her hand. She hadn't told anyone about this, and now she couldn't seem to stop.

"I found this folder," she blurted. "He'd had it out on his desk, probably dealing with life insurance stuff or whatever. But inside I found his will and started reading about all these daughters, and—" She stopped to take a deep breath, the mere memory of the shock bringing with it a surge of adrenaline. "I guess I was too stunned to read the fine print, huh? Or else I would've known about this...stipulation."

Boone didn't laugh along with her pathetic attempt at a chuckle.

He nudged her shoulder. "And then?"

She sniffed. Right. The other shoe that dropped that very same day. "There were adoption papers in the file too. And...and the name of my real father. David Tyler."

David Tyler. It sounded no less strange to her now as it had then. How could she possibly be related to a man whose name she didn't even recognize?

"What did Frank say when you told him you found out?" Boone's voice was soft and gentle, and she realized belatedly that she'd been staring off into space.

With a sharp exhale she said, "He didn't say anything because I was too busy yelling at him for being a liar and a fraud. And then I just…I just ran out of there."

Boone's jaw clenched tight, and his hand squeezed hers again.

"And obviously I never got to…to talk to my mom about it and ask her…ask her why she lied." She waited for a response, half expecting Boone to try to smooth things over. To make excuses for her mom or Frank.

She relaxed a little when he didn't.

"I think what really kills me the most is that I can't talk to my mom about it." The admission seemed to come from nowhere. Or maybe it came from so deep inside her, she hadn't even seen it herself.

But saying it aloud, she knew it was the truth. "This lie…"

Boone shifted, and it was enough. He didn't like the L-word, but she shot him a sidelong glance.

"She lied, Boone. They both did." Her laughter was bitter. "I used to ask my mom point-blank why I look the way I do." She tugged on one of her braids for good measure. "You know, there weren't a lot of people of color in our school, and I always felt like I stood out."

He made a sound of encouragement, prompting her to go on.

"My mom would always say that she had dark skin because her parents and her grandparents came from different parts of the world, and my skin was lighter and my features were different from hers because my father was white."

She stared down at their intertwined hands, staring as if she could peer into the past. "I keep trying to remember if she outright said it was because Frank was white or because *my father* was white, and…" With her free hand, April pinched the bridge of her nose.

She would not cry again, dang it. Weeping on Boone's shoulder once was bad enough.

"Does it matter?" Boone asked.

She blinked up at him. "What?"

He lifted a shoulder. "Does it matter?"

April frowned. "After Frank died, my grandparents kept saying that my parents were going to tell me. Everything. About the adoption, about Frank's other daughters. I guess part of me could understand them waiting, you know? I think I could possibly make sense of my mom holding off."

"A lie of omission?" Boone offered.

"Yeah. I guess."

"And that would be better," he finished.

Her eyes stung with tears so quickly, she only barely managed to blink them away before they fell. "It would be better than thinking my own mother outright lied to me my whole life, yeah."

But as she heard herself speak, April realized that to Boone, it must all sound like semantics. So many secrets, so many lies. Did it really matter where the line was drawn?

Maybe not.

"I guess no matter what, it doesn't change the fact that I can't ask her now. I can't ask either of them what they were planning, what they meant to tell me." Her jaw worked as she looked away from Boone's pained expression that so perfectly reflected her own hurt.

She took a deep breath. "I can't ask my mom, and I can't be mad at her either."

Boone tipped his head down like he was trying to catch her gaze, but she looked away, swallowing hard.

"So," she said, a little louder than necessary, "I guess you can see why you wasted your time coming all the way out here, huh?"

She finally glanced back and found him studying her with such intensity, it startled her. This was not the laid-back Boone she'd known her whole life. This guy was more serious, more mature, more…grown-up. And she was suddenly, starkly aware of the fact that he was not some harmless, cocky boy, but…a man.

Her belly fluttered when he reached out and swiped a thumb over her cheek, wiping away a lingering tear. "If anything, you've just made me more convinced that coming back to Aspire is exactly what you need."

She blinked in surprise. "What? But…but I just told you that I'm not Frank's daughter. Not really—"

"You are. You're an O'Sullivan, and you have just as much of a right to that ranch as any of the others do."

"I don't, Boone. I don't even want it." She tried to pull away, but he had an arm around her shoulders that held her still. "Tell them they can sell."

Boone winced, and she stilled. "What?"

"If nothing else, you deserve to know these sisters of yours. They sure as heck want to meet you. And once you meet them, you'll see why just saying 'sell' is not gonna fly."

She sniffed. "Why not?"

Boone started talking, telling her about all she'd missed back in Aspire this past year since her father had passed. All about how Emma and Nash lived at the ranch and how Emma was pregnant, and Dahlia worked there alongside JJ, and how it'd become home base for Rose, and Daisy, and Lizzy, and Sierra when she wasn't traveling the world, and...basically, how selling would break their hearts.

April stared in stunned silence for a while. She'd known theoretically that these women were all there, at the ranch where she'd grown up. But hearing about their lives, about how things were moving on without Frank or her mother...

She wasn't sure how she felt, to be honest. But she wasn't sure she could handle seeing it with her own eyes.

"This unanimous rule is stupid," she finally muttered.

Boone surprised her with a laugh. "I don't think anyone would argue that. But it's the way it is, and the others are sure that your father had a good reason for it."

April bit her lip to keep from saying something mean. How could these strangers know what Frank wanted when he'd raised her and she didn't know a dang thing?

"April..."

"Tell them they can keep it, then," she clipped. "I don't care."

Boone sighed, and she hated how much she didn't want to disappoint him. Or them, for that matter.

She didn't care about anyone in Aspire or what they thought of her.

She peeked over at Boone.

Or...she didn't want to, at least.

"Just think about it, okay?" He gave her a crooked

smile that would've made her knees go weak if she'd been standing. "They want to meet you, April."

She sniffed. "Why?"

He leaned over and nudged her shoulder with his. "Because you're their sister. Whether you like it or not."

CHAPTER 11

Boone half expected April to go off on another rant explaining how she wasn't really their sister.

When she didn't, he was relieved. He wasn't so naive as to think she suddenly understood she belonged in the O'Sullivan family, but at least she wasn't arguing the point any longer.

Boone meant what he'd said. He was more convinced than ever that she belonged there. Not just at the ranch but among her sisters.

He'd been hanging out with those ladies long enough to know that each and every one of them had issues with Frank, and some with their own mothers and their pasts. But they'd found more than just closure by visiting the ranch.

They'd found a home. A place where they belonged and a family that gave them unconditional love.

And if anyone needed that—if anyone *deserved* that—it was April.

He leaned forward, his elbows on his knees so he could

see her face when she dipped her head. "Say you'll come back with me."

She met his gaze, and to his surprise, her eyes lit with amusement. "You really are stubborn. Has anyone ever told you that?"

He nodded. "Mrs. Pearson said it just about every day in sixth grade."

"Mrs. Pearson. I remember her." Her lips twitched upward, and Boone found himself willing her to smile.

He'd give all the money he had to see that smile again right here and now.

His heart melted when she finally lost the battle and her face split with a grin so sweet it made his pulse race.

"She never said the final report could be on a graphic novel."

He held a finger up. "She didn't specify it *couldn't* be a graphic novel either." He joined her when she started to laugh, oddly elated that she remembered what, at the time, had felt like an epic battle of principles.

"I suddenly feel a whole lot of sympathy for Mrs. Pearson."

"Really?" He grimaced in mock horror, and she gave a snort of laughter.

"No, not really. Mrs. Pearson was mean."

"Amen to that."

"And she really should've been more specific with her guidelines," she finished.

He widened his eyes. "Right? This is what I'm saying!"

She giggled, and the sound had him smothering a goofy grin as his heart did gymnastics behind his rib cage.

"So stubborn." She shook her head with an impish grin that was downright adorable. "So, how long are you going to nag me about going back to Aspire?"

"Depends. How long are you going to fight the inevitable?"

She rolled her eyes, and he was reminded of what she'd been like in the sixth grade. "*Black Beauty*," he said suddenly.

April's chin came back with a start. "What?"

"That's what you did your report on in Mrs. Pearson's class." He scrubbed the back of his neck and looked away from her searching stare.

Man, why did he remember that? And why had he said it out loud?

"Um…"

"So clearly you like horses," he continued, trying and failing to get them back on track.

Her brows drew down in confusion. Rightfully so. He was giving them both whiplash with this turn in conversation.

"Just because I liked *Black Beauty*…"

"Oh don't go trying to pretend you weren't into horses," he said. "We were in 4-H together, remember?"

She looked like she might argue, but her lips twitched with mirth instead. "Who could forget?"

They shared a little smile, and he knew without asking that they were both remembering the old days. Way back before he was popular and she was the artsy loner, when everyone had been friends just because they were in the same class.

He nudged her shoulder with his again. "So I know you must miss the stables at the ranch, if nothing else."

Her huff of laughter sounded like it was meant to be sarcastic, but he caught the real amusement there as well. "You're a regular Sherlock Holmes."

He grinned. "I have my moments. Come on, April…"

"Boone, I can't." At his arched brows, she added, "I really can't. I've finally found a place to stay, and I have a job, and…" She trailed off at his look of disbelief. "What?"

"You really can't take off for one week? Tops?"

"I don't have money for airfare or—"

"I'll drive you."

She blinked at him like he'd just claimed he was an alien.

"N-No, you don't have to—"

"I want to."

She turned to face him with a huff. "Boone, you're missing the point."

Now it was his turn to try and smother a smile. It wasn't like he was trying to irritate April, but he had to admit that she was cute as a button when she got riled.

"The point is," she said slowly, "I don't want to go."

"But you have to."

"I don't have to."

"If you ever want to see the money that would be your rightful inheritance if you sell, you do," he pointed out. "Or the money that would be your rightful passive income if y'all decide to keep the ranch in the family."

He caught her little flinch at the word *family*, but he was heartened by the fact that she was clearly considering his words.

"Angry or not, you all deserve to get some closure." He picked up one of her braids, lightly running it through his fingers. "And trust me when I say that I'm not the only stubborn one in Aspire."

Her brows drew together in question.

"Your eldest sister, Sierra? She's pretty pigheaded. And that's nothing compared to Dahlia." He frowned. "Come to think of it, stubbornness seems to be a shared trait among the O'Sullivans." He narrowed his eyes at her meaningfully. "Present company included."

Her smile was small but sweet. Then she seemed to remember what she was arguing about. "It's not just the job or the airfare. I'm here in Portland because..." She blew out a sharp exhale and threw her hands up. "I'm here to find David Taylor, okay?"

"Your biological father?"

"Yes."

He stared at her for too long in silence. He had so many questions, but he didn't know where to begin. Also, he didn't want to lose what little ground he'd gained during this conversation.

He was making progress, he could feel it.

When he hesitated too long, she continued on, her tone defensive. "Look, I know it's a long shot. And I don't even know what I'm hoping to find. It's just...I don't know. He's my one link, you know? My one chance to get the real story of where I came from and how...how Frank came to be my only father and..."

"I get it." He interrupted her when she started to falter. He hated the waver in her voice, the hint of uncertainty that undermined her strength.

At her wary look, he added, "I do. I get it, April. With all you've been through, it makes sense that you'd be curious to get to know your family. All your family..."

She groaned. "It's not the same thing."

"Isn't it?"

Her lips set in a thin line, and he could practically see her starting to formulate an argument.

He held his hands up in surrender before she could. "Okay, fine. It's not exactly the same."

"Thank you." She leaned forward as well so they were

both resting their elbows on their knees, watching passersby as they talked.

"So…how's that going?" he finally asked.

She turned her head to face him. "What?"

"Have you made any progress tracking down this David Taylor guy?"

"Some." She looked away before adding quietly, "Not much."

"Hmm."

She straightened. "It's harder than you'd think, finding some stranger with so little to go on. I know my mom went to college in Portland and stayed here for a while after, and…" April trailed off with a sigh. "Do you have any idea how many men named David Taylor live in this city…or have lived here at some point over the last twenty years?"

He winced. "I can only imagine."

"Yeah, well…it's a lot." She pursed her lips. "And I may have kinda…hit a brick wall."

He straightened as well when an idea took hold, but April clearly misconstrued his new excitement.

"That's not to say I'm giving up," she said quickly, a warning in her tone. "I just…I…"

"You need a new way forward," he finished for her.

She nodded. "Yeah. Exactly. I need to know who I am." At his questioning look, she added, "I mean, how can I know who I am if I don't know where I'm from, right?"

Looking into her eyes, that…didn't quite sit right. But he hated the confusion he saw there and vowed to do whatever it took to clear it away. "Then…maybe we can strike a deal."

She turned until they were facing each other, the rest of the world forgotten—for him, at least—as it all came down to him and her, and the very few inches that separated them.

All at once he was remembering how it had felt to hold her in his arms. So soft and delicate, so sweet and so…real.

So very genuine. There was nothing at all inauthentic about this girl, and there never had been as long as he'd known her.

"April…" He waited until she met his gaze. "You might not know your biological father, but I think…I think you know who you are."

Her lips parted in surprise.

He dipped his head, feeling foolish. But he'd come this far, so he forced himself to finish. "You know *where* you came from, and that's a start. And despite what you're feeling right now, it seems to me you've always known who you are."

"Boone…" Her voice quivered.

"I've always admired that about you, you know." He flashed her a smile. "You've always been true to yourself, and that takes courage."

Her gaze flickered back and forth as she read his features and his gaze. "And you think I'm a coward for not wanting to go back to the ranch?"

"I didn't say that."

She frowned down at her feet and kicked her toe into the dirt. "No, you didn't say it. I did."

He rested a hand on her back, wishing he could pull her back against him. But she wasn't crying any longer, and it wasn't his right to hold her just because she felt good in his arms.

Right now, staring down at the ground, lost in thought, she looked more adrift than he could stand.

"April, if you come to the ranch with me, I'll do everything in my power to help you find your dad. We all will. They paid a private investigator to find you—"

"They did?" She sat up straight, and his hand fell away. "That's how you found me?"

He nodded.

She looked a little stunned.

"And, April, for them, it's about more than just settling up business at the ranch. They want to meet you. They want to get to know the daughter who their father stuck around for...you know?"

Her eyes grew wet with tears, and her throat worked as she swallowed.

"But if that private investigator could track you down, maybe we can do the same to find your father. Right?"

"I don't have the money to—"

"I do."

"Boone, I can't take your money."

He thought about arguing. He lived rent-free on her father's land. He had nothing to do with his money but save it and spend it on the odd night out in town.

He couldn't think of anything he'd rather spend that money on than her. But her brows drew down, and she looked ready for a fight.

"The ranch makes money, and part of that is yours," he continued. "And I know once your sisters realize how important this is to you, they'll want to help out as well."

Her expression was pure disbelief, but her brow was furrowed, and she was clearly thinking it through. "And I'll do whatever I can to help too," he added, for whatever that was worth.

"Let me...let me think for a second," she said.

"Fine." He shifted, his gaze moving down the block. "But I have a serious question."

Her gaze was wary again. "What's that?"

"Would you think better if you had an ice cream in your hand?"

Her gaze followed his to the homemade ice cream shop across the street, and she laughed. "Definitely."

He clapped his hands on his legs before moving to stand. "That's what I thought. Be right back. Don't go anywhere."

CHAPTER 12

"**D**on't go anywhere."

That was all it took for her mind to leap into action.

She could run. She could literally just stand up and bolt, and leave Boone, with all of his searching looks and his heartfelt speeches, in the dust.

But she didn't move. Instead, her gaze tracked Boone's tall, athletic form as he wove his way through the ever-crowded sidewalk to the ice cream shop.

Part of her wished she'd gone with him just so she could see his face when he read the flavors at the artisanal creamery.

The thought had her lips twitching with amusement.

Dang it. She didn't want to be amused by Boone. Or touched by his kindness.

She'd been just fine with him being a memory. The popular, self-centered jock role had fit him just fine.

But now she couldn't shove him back in that pigeon-hole, no matter how much she tried.

When he disappeared inside the shop, she sank back against the bench with a sigh. It was decision time.

She could stay here where she was comfortable. But, if she was being honest, she'd been feeling for weeks now like she was just spinning her wheels. Biding her time until…what? David Taylor just magically popped into her life?

She pursed her lips and tugged on one of her braids. She'd already followed every lead she could find and had hit nothing but dead ends. Maybe it was time to admit she needed help.

But from her sisters?

She winced. The S-word was still not sitting right. But…

She slumped even farther down in her seat. There was no use arguing with reality, and considering what Boone had just told her about the will, Dahlia and the others would never stop until she showed her face at the ranch.

The ranch.

She squeezed her eyes shut against an onslaught of emotions that ranged from painful to bittersweet.

So many radiant childhood memories that were now cast in the shadow of her parents' secrets and lies.

The wind picked up, and April wrapped her arms around herself, shivering in the cold.

Funny, she hadn't noticed the chill before when Boone was sitting beside her, but without him, there was nothing to block the breeze.

A feeling of loneliness crept up inside her, twisting in her belly and spreading into her chest.

She swallowed hard, willing it away. She wasn't lonely here in Portland. She'd made friends.

But not one of them knew her parents, or anything

about the family situation she was going through. And while she'd told herself that all the answers she needed could be found outside Montana, Boone's words had hit hard and made her wonder.

"They want to meet you. They want to get to know the daughter who their father stuck around for…"

She frowned down at her feet as she kicked at the dirt and grass. Was that how they saw her? The daughter Frank stuck around for?

Her throat ached, and her chest felt like it was being crushed in a giant's fist.

Why had he left the others? And why had he stayed for her?

And why hadn't she given him a chance to explain?

Her eyes welled with tears, and she shut them quickly. She'd cried enough for one day, and no amount of reliving that fateful last encounter with her father would help her now.

She opened her eyes, her parting words still ringing in her ears. *"Why should I stay and listen to you? You're not even my real father!"*

She'd stormed out in a rage. Ran away in shock and fear, telling herself she'd never return. But Frank wouldn't give up. He came looking for her. He…

The knot in her stomach tightened so hard and fast it physically hurt.

"April!" he'd called from the truck window.

She'd jolted to a stop in the street, and even from where she stood, she could see the anguish in his eyes, the desperation to fix the rift between them.

"Honey, please," he'd begged.

And what had she done?

She'd raised her chin and turned away. She'd run

down the street as fresh waves of anger coursed through her.

She'd been expecting him to pursue her, and her insides had been bubbling with words of rage and accusation. But he never did…and it wasn't until the next morning that she found out why. Her grandparents finally tracked her down and told her about the wasted driver who'd shot through the intersection without looking. She'd hit Frank's car at speed, and he'd died on impact. Died trying to chase after her.

It was a cruel twist of fate. A brutal, gutting reality that April had never had the courage to face.

What she wouldn't give to go back and do it all over.

You can, a little voice nagged at her. *You can go back. That's what Frank wanted. It's what your mom would have wanted too.*

Maybe she couldn't go back in time and give her father a chance to explain, but…she could see what he'd had to say in his journal.

She could meet the daughters he'd left behind and hear their memories of him and find out what they knew about his marriage to her mother…

She didn't even realize she'd made up her mind until Boone was standing before her, handing over a cup of ice cream with a look of bemusement. "I got you cardamom-flavored ice cream."

April clamped her lips shut to stifle a laugh.

"It was either that or carrot habanero, and I just…" He looked so distraught as he shook his head that April lost the battle with laughter. "I couldn't do that to you. I just couldn't do it."

She took the cup from him with a snort of laughter. "Thanks. Cardamom is my favorite."

He narrowed his eyes. "You're kidding me, right? I don't even know what cardamom is."

She stood with a sigh of feigned exasperation and reached up to pat his shoulder. "Then it looks like you and I will have a lot to discuss on the drive."

He turned to follow, his eyes widening in surprise. "Wait, so does that mean…?"

She dipped the plastic spoon into the ice cream and took a bite. "Oh my gosh, so good." Enjoying his confusion, she tossed him an expectant look. "You coming?"

Less than an hour later, they were on the road.

"Okay, next time one of my sisters tells me that no woman can pack quickly, I will use you as my proof to the contrary," Boone said as she slid into the passenger seat. He eyed her duffel bag. "Is that all you're bringing?"

"I'm not staying long, remember?"

Truthfully, she was saying it more for her benefit than his. He wasn't pushing her for any more than she was willing to give.

He'd spent the past hour bending over backward to help her prep for this impromptu road trip. There wasn't much he could do, but once she'd talked to her manager about swapping out some of her shifts, there really wasn't much left.

"And your boss is cool with this?" Boone asked as he slid the truck into traffic.

"Yeah. I think my manager was waiting for something like this to happen ever since you showed up."

He shot her a sidelong glance. "She could see from a mile away that I'd win you over, huh?"

April rolled her eyes, trying not to smile. "Don't get cocky, Donahue. I'm only going to get Frank's daughters out of my hair and because you promised to help me find my biological father. This isn't personal."

"Whatever you say, O'Sullivan," he teased.

Silence fell, and she shifted in her seat. She'd been the one pushing to leave town quickly, and right now it was clear why.

She supposed deep down she'd known that if given half a chance to really think through what was to come, she'd wuss out.

Looking out the window, she started to squirm. "You think we can listen to some music or something?"

"Sure thing." He flipped on the radio, and country music filled the air. It was a sappy, slow number about missing home.

They shared a grimace that made them both snicker.

"Maybe not this station," she said.

"Tell you what." He handed her his phone and a cable. "Plug this in, and you can listen to whatever you want."

"Yeah? You trust me to be DJ?"

He chuckled, and the low noise sounded oddly intimate in these close confines. "I trust you."

She started to plug it in, a smile tugging at her lips as she put all her focus on the songs she'd pick. How would hometown hottie Boone like some hip-hop?

"But you know the rule, right?" he continued.

She turned to face him, and his wink made her blush. "Driver gets full veto rights."

She rolled her eyes, studiously ignoring the heat that crept up her neck and into her cheeks as he watched her.

Seriously. Only Boone Donahue could make something as cheesy as a wink seem sexy.

CHAPTER 13

Boone stared down at the flat tire as a steady, insistent, never-ending rain came down on his head.

As far as omens went, this was not a good one.

April leaned out the passenger's door, using her hoodie to cover her head from the rain. "Um, maybe we should call for a tow truck."

He made a *pshhh* sound as he planted his hands on his hips. "Don't insult me, woman," he teased.

She rolled her eyes, but he heard her laughter, and that was what he'd been after. "Don't call me woman, *man*."

He grinned. "I got this. Don't worry about it."

"You, uh…do you want a…a hand, or maybe…?"

The hesitation in her voice had him glancing over, and he didn't know whether to laugh or groan when he caught her…well, there was no other word for it. The girl was ogling him.

Lips slightly parted like she was in a daze, her gaze was fixed on his wet T-shirt, which was currently clinging to his chest and abs like a second skin. "Uh, April?"

She blinked and her eyes darted up to meet his. Her

lips clamped into a thin line, and her skin flushed as embarrassment crept into her expression. "Yes?"

He used two fingers to point to his face. "My eyes are up here."

Her nose scrunched up in a wince that was so cute he couldn't help but chuckle. "Sorry. Yes. Um…" She took a deep breath. "Did you need a hand?"

"Nah, I got this." He made a show of flexing, which had her falling back against the seat with a laugh. "You stay dry. I'll be done in no time."

"No time," it turned out, was a bit of an exaggeration.

The rain wasn't making his task any easier, and the clouds and setting sun weren't helping either.

He wanted to tell April to get back in the truck and stay warm, but when she used her windbreaker as a sort of canopy to protect him from the rain and aimed the flashlight on her phone so he could actually see what he was doing, he could only say, "Thank you."

"No problem."

With her help, he managed to get the new tire on relatively quickly, but by the time they climbed back into the truck's cab, they were both soaked through, and April was shivering.

Boone turned on the heater, but what she needed was dry clothes.

He caught her stifling a yawn.

Dry clothes and a good night's sleep.

"What do you say we pull over at the next exit and check into a motel?"

She shifted beside him. "What? Why? It's not that late. If you're tired and you want me to take a shift—"

"No, it's not that." He glanced over at her, his heart giving a tug at the shadows under her eyes. "I just think we're both tired, you know? And it's not like we can get there in one day anyway, right?"

"Yeah." She looked so disappointed, and she didn't sound convinced.

"You that eager to get back, huh?" He'd hoped he could tease a smile out of her, but she seemed to be growing more withdrawn and serious by the second.

"Of course not. I just… I'd rather not stop, that's all."

He eyed the road. He could keep going, but soon he'd be tired enough that driving wouldn't be safe.

"You know what? It's fine," she said quickly, her voice clipped. "If you want to stop for the night, we'll stop." She pulled out her phone. "I'll see what our options are."

Boone kept driving, his pace snail-like as he negotiated the slick roads. His primary goal was to get April back to the ranch in one piece, and he'd take every precaution necessary to make that happen.

"Our options are slim to none." April sighed.

"Oh yeah?" He tried to sound like this didn't bother him, but the tension in his body said otherwise. They needed to get warm and dry. April's teeth were chattering as she continued hunting on her phone.

"A flat tire and now n-no rooms," she muttered. "Is it just me, or does this tr-trip already feel d-doomed?"

"Nah." He tried to sound upbeat as he cranked the heater as high as it would go. "We just need to get dry and a good night's sleep, that's all."

"Then I hope you're okay with sh-sharing a room."

She said it offhand. A throwaway, mumbled comment. But his whole body responded like he'd just been zapped by lightning.

"One room?" he echoed.

Crap, was that his voice? It sounded crazy gruff, like

he'd just woken up. With a cold. After a night of shouting his head off at a heavy metal concert.

He cleared his throat and tried again. "That's all you could find?"

She turned to cast him a glance. "I can look at the next town, if you want. But it'll be close to an hour before we get there."

He hesitated. But right then the rain that had been coming down in a steady stream started to crash down so hard that even going full blast, his wipers could barely keep up. He leaned forward, peering ahead of him but only able to see a few feet.

"Yeah, um…" April lifted her phone, the bright glow of its screen lighting up her face. Her teeth had stopped chattering, which was a relief.

She looked like an angel. Those sharp cheekbones and her delicate features…

She was too beautiful for mere mortals, that was for sure.

April glanced over and frowned when she caught him staring. "You okay?"

He quickly turned to keep his eyes trained on the road. "Yup. I'm fine. You?"

There was a slight pause, and her voice held a tinge of amusement when she said, "I'm fine."

"Good."

"Great."

He peeked over at her. "Perfect."

"Right as rain," she shot back.

He groaned. "Really? A rain pun? You're better than that, April."

Her laughter cut through the truck like a ray of

sunshine, and he found himself grinning like a fool as he got off at the exit she pointed out.

They fell silent again except for her occasional directions as she navigated them to the only motel with a room available.

Her silence drove him nuts. Especially when he glanced over to see her staring off into the distance.

She clearly had a lot on her mind, and maybe it wasn't his right to know all that she was thinking, but he was beyond curious. Considering he'd only known this girl as "that little mousy, artsy chick," this overwhelming curiosity was odd.

But it was also undeniable.

He was worried about her, truth be told. She'd been through so much this year, and now he was dragging her back home to deal with even more upheavals and family drama.

But he couldn't make her talk if she wasn't ready, right?

He pulled into the parking lot, and they both walked into the reception area. One room, like it'd said online.

One room with one bed.

He shot her a sidelong look when the front desk clerk asked if that was all right. But April didn't hesitate. "That's fine."

When the clerk turned away, she caught him looking. "What? I'm sure there's a couch or a foldout cot or something."

He nodded, stupidly at a loss for words.

How was it that she could be so cool with this and he…

Well, he was having an internal nuclear meltdown.

Every time he thought about sharing a room with this

woman, his whole body responded like someone had lit a fire inside him.

But April was cool, calm, and collected as he handed over a credit card and she filled in the paperwork.

"Is there a couch in the room?" she asked.

The clerk assured her there was and that it folded out into a bed. She nodded, never faltering in filling out the registration form.

It wasn't until he'd come back in with their bags that he caught a flicker of unease as she fidgeted with the room card in her hand.

"You ready?" He held the door open for her.

She nodded. But she was quiet all the way to their room, and after he let them in, that silence seemed to swell until it filled every inch of this dingy, one-bed room.

The silence got so thick, he wasn't sure he remembered how to breathe.

He tugged at the collar of his T-shirt as he set the bags down.

"Do you want to, um…" He glanced around. "You wanna watch TV?"

"I was actually thinking I might take a shower."

He held his breath as his runaway mind went off at the very idea of her taking a shower in the tiny bathroom with only a door to separate them.

He cleared his throat. "Right. Well, um…you hungry? I can go down the road and grab us a bite."

"That would be great," she said, so quickly he got the feeling that maybe he wasn't the only one who needed some space.

"Cool, okay then."

"Wait," she called when he went to leave.

He looked back with an arched brow.

"It's still coming down like cats and dogs out there," she pointed out. "Probably not the safest weather to be driving in."

He nodded, tucking his hands into his pockets. "You're right. It'll likely pass soon. I'll just wait it out."

She eyed the bathroom and then looked at him again. "I'll wait with you."

He pressed his lips together and nodded, all the while his brain scrambling to come up with any topic to fill this silence.

There was one question that had been nagging at him for hours, so he finally blurted it out. "Hey, April…"

Her head came up, her gaze alert. "Yes?"

"Can I ask…what made you change your mind? About coming back to Montana with me, I mean."

She shifted from foot to foot, her lips pursed. Finally, she shrugged. "I realized you're right. If I'm going to find my biological father, I'm gonna need some help."

He studied her. That wasn't the only reason she was going back, but before he could ask her anything more, she shot him a cute little smirk.

"Besides, now that I know how stubborn you can be, I've got this horrible feeling you'll be hounding me for the rest of my life if I don't give in."

"Dang straight. You'd never be rid of me."

She started to laugh, but then her gaze was caught by whatever she saw out the window. "The rain's lightening up."

He didn't hesitate. "I'd better go while the weather holds out, huh?"

"Yeah, good plan."

She made no move toward the bathroom. And when he closed the door behind him, he caught one last glimpse of

April, looking fragile and sweet...and alone...right before the door snapped shut.

But she's not alone, he reminded himself as he took a deep breath of the fresh, rain-soaked air.

She had him.

"I've got this horrible feeling you'll be hounding me for the rest of my life."

His lips curved up a bit. April had him...

Whether she liked it or not.

CHAPTER 14

April lingered for way too long in the motel's tiny bathroom.

Bare bones and smelling of bleach, the humid little room was hardly an inviting spa, but April found herself rearranging her toothbrush and toothpaste, and lining up the tiny bottles of complimentary shampoo and conditioner.

She was stalling, plain and simple. Facing her reflection, she ordered herself in no uncertain terms to pull up her big girl pants and walk out there.

She straightened the nightshirt she was wearing with some sleep shorts and put her hand on the doorknob.

But when she heard Boone in the other room, walking around and flipping channels on the TV, she froze.

Again.

One room? She cast her gaze upward, staring at the popcorn ceiling as she had a little chat with the big guy upstairs. *One room? With Boone freakin' Donahue?*

Was this some sort of test of her virtue?

A trial by fire to see if she could, in fact, die from embarrassment.

She closed her eyes, stifling a groan at the memory of how she'd basically leered at Boone while he'd been changing a tire.

But honestly, the man should come with a warning sign. It wasn't right for one human to be so dang sexy. And if one guy had to contain so much sex appeal, would it be too much to ask that he have an ugly personality?

But nooo.

She'd heard him come back in just as she'd gotten out of the shower, and the smell of burgers and fries seeped into the bathroom.

Her growling stomach wouldn't allow her to hide out in here a second longer. With a deep inhale, she reached for the knob and came out of the bathroom.

Boone held up a grease-stained paper bag in triumph. "Behold, I present you with the world's finest burgers."

She giggled when she realized that "World's Finest Burgers!" was printed on the bag. "Wow. 'World's finest,' huh? Wonder who gave them that award."

He laughed and stepped aside, gesturing to the tiny desk covered in fast food with a flourish. "Dig in. I already ate, but I'll take a shower while you're eating."

He didn't give her a chance to respond before grabbing his things and heading into the bathroom.

She sighed with relief as she sank onto the edge of the bed and popped a french fry into her mouth. Was he as weirded out as she was about spending the night alone together here, or was he just being considerate in giving her space?

She wiggled back farther onto the bed, curled her legs up beneath her, and reached for the remote.

Either way, she was grateful that Boone was making this as tension-free as possible.

The sound of the shower's spray joined the murmur of voices coming from the TV as she flipped through reruns and twenty-four-hour news channels.

She tried hard to focus on the screen and not the fact that Boone Donahue was currently naked in the adjoining room.

Nope. She was not going to think about that. Just like she was not going to think about that horrifically embarrassing moment earlier this evening when he'd caught her drooling over him in the rain.

She groaned and shoved the burger into her mouth, as if maybe she could chew away her humiliation.

What had she been thinking?

She *hadn't* been thinking. That was the problem. For a second there, she'd entirely forgotten who Boone was and what they were doing together. For the briefest of moments, he'd ceased being Boone-the-cocky-quarterback she'd known her whole life, and he definitely hadn't been Boone-the-ranch-hand-sent-by-her-sisters either.

He'd just been…hot. Crazy hot with his too-long dark hair falling into his face and his T-shirt clinging to every surface of his skin.

Seriously. Who had muscles like that?

She supposed the answer was obvious—a former quarterback turned cowboy had muscles like that.

And he knew how to use them.

She shifted on the bed, peering at the screen like maybe if she looked hard enough, she could trick her brain into paying attention.

But no. Her mind was fixated on that incident. On the way he'd taken charge and moved so naturally. This was a guy who was no stranger to manual labor, and there'd been something so alluring about that.

Not just the fact that it added to his sex appeal. He didn't need any help there.

No, it was something more primal than that. Something about his competence and his strength that, for a second there, she'd felt…safe. Like she was in good hands, and he wouldn't let anything bad happen to her.

She shook her head as she set down the burger and reached for the soda he'd bought for her.

It was silly. She was a grown woman who'd been taking care of herself just fine this past year.

But maybe…

She swallowed hard, completely ignoring the commercial that suddenly blared from the TV as her gaze landed on the food he'd brought.

Maybe it was nice to have someone else to rely on. Just for a little while.

The sound of the water shutting off had her straightening, tension returning as she finished her dinner and then waited for the inevitable.

By the time Boone came out of the bathroom, April had moved back to rest against the pillows propped up on the headboard. She glanced over but refused to let her gaze linger again, even if he did look hot as heck in a black T-shirt and sweats.

"What do you think?"

April looked up to find Boone standing next to the cheap coffeemaker in the corner. He was holding up two packets of instant cocoa.

He arched his brows. "Dessert?"

A laugh bubbled up inside her at his hopeful expression. "Ice cream and burgers and now hot chocolate? Boone, you are a bad influence."

"Nah, I'm just worried a strong breeze is gonna blow you away before I can get you back to Aspire." He winked and then turned, busying himself with making hot water.

April looked down at herself. She supposed she had lost weight since she'd left Bozeman. Definitely since he'd last seen her in Aspire.

She supposed years of watching your mother die a slow and painful death would do that to a girl. And this past year...

Well, money had been tight, and she'd had more stress than she could handle.

She tugged her T-shirt down farther, self-conscious.

"Hey, I'm just teasing," Boone said as the bed sank beside her. He handed her a steaming paper cup. "What are we watching?"

"Oh, um..." She glanced up at the TV. "I guess we're watching *The Office*."

Because that was where she'd happened to land when the bathroom door had opened. Not that he needed to know that.

"Oh, cool." He settled in beside her with his own cup of cocoa. "I love this show."

She felt a smile tug at her lips. "Me too."

The cocoa was so hot she had to blow on it, but there was something oddly comforting about the taste.

"I think this is the same brand Mama's Kitchen uses," Boone murmured, blowing gently before taking another sip.

April stilled as memory after memory flooded through her. Good ones of sitting at a booth with her mom and dad, ordering hot chocolates as the snow came down outside. Coloring on the placemats and listening to the soothing hum of her parents' voices as they talked about their days.

Those were the good times. Before her mom got sick. Before they'd moved to be closer to the hospital. Before the beginning of the end...

"You all right?" Boone asked.

"Yeah." She took a sip of the cocoa and let the drink and the memories warm her chest. "Just a blast from the past, you know?"

"Mmm." She felt him watching her, but he didn't pry. Instead, he nudged her arm with his elbow. "This is the best scene."

She brought her head up and then started to laugh as the lead character, Michael Scott, drove a car into a lake because his navigation device told him to. Boone's laughter beside her was nice. Warm, low, kinda rumbly in that manly sort of way.

She had this urge to lean over and rest her head against his chest so she could hear what his laughter sounded like up close.

She didn't. But by the time the episode ended, she realized they'd both shifted toward the center, their weight forming a sort of sinkhole in the middle of the bed.

Now they were pressed shoulder to shoulder, arm to arm, and...

And it wasn't weird.

"Want to see what else is on?" Boone picked up the remote but made no move to shift away from her.

"Sure."

And that was how they came to be not quite cuddling, but not *not* cuddling as they watched a silly buddy cop comedy, alternately laughing and chatting about nothing in particular.

April wasn't sure when the exhaustion from her day kicked in, but at some point, her mind stopped following the plot of the movie, and then her blinks got longer and longer as she struggled to keep her eyes open.

The next thing she knew, April was waking up with a start…

In Boone's arms.

CHAPTER 15

Boone woke slowly to the feel of…jostling. He squeezed his eyes shut against daylight and groaned as he took in the weight on his arm and the fact that something was digging into his side and pushing against him and—

April.

He opened his eyes, inhaling sharply in shock—which was a mistake. Because now not only was he well aware that she was squirming against his side, but she also smelled like heaven. Her hair was right beneath his nose, and his arms…

Oh heck.

He released her quickly, and she sat up with a gasp.

His arms had been clasped around her.

They stared at each other in wide-eyed silence until he cleared his throat. "Sorry, I, uh…"

Sorry I was clutching you like you were my favorite stuffie? Sorry for the snuggle but you felt like heaven in my arms?

What was he supposed to say? There was no rule for this sort of thing. At least, not that he knew of.

"I'm sorry," he said again. And he was. Because, man, he absolutely hated seeing that wary look in her eyes as she inched away from him toward her side of the bed. "I swear, I meant to go to the couch, but then you fell asleep and…"

And you looked so crazy sweet and adorable with your head on my shoulder…

"And I didn't want to wake you," he continued. "I thought I'd just give it a minute and then lay you down, but I guess I dozed off. I'm really sorry, April. I—"

"No, it's okay." She blinked a few times and the wariness was gone, replaced by embarrassment as her gaze dropped and then darted around the room. "I'm just gonna, um…brush my teeth. And then we should probably get on the road."

"Yeah. Definitely."

He waited until she disappeared into the bathroom before falling back on the bed with a groan.

Way to start the day, man.

That was supposed to be a reprimand, but he had to fight a grin. Waking up with her in his arms was an epic way to start the day, and he couldn't help wanting to do it again.

As soon as she popped out of the bathroom, he bolted off the bed and got ready to go. They wasted no time getting some miles under their belts. The silence might have been deafening if it hadn't been broken by the songs April picked out for them.

"You have good taste," he said at one point.

She shot him a funny little grin. "Surprised?"

"Nah, I should've known the weird, artsy chick would be into cool music."

She laughed. "Weird, artsy chick, huh? So that's how you see me."

He narrowed his eyes teasingly, loving the sound of her laughter after so much silence. "And how do you see me?"

She lifted a shoulder, but he didn't miss the way her cheeks flushed before she turned her head to look out the window. Okay, now he was *really* curious.

Shifting in his seat, he half turned to face her. "I mean it. How do you see me?"

She screwed up her nose in a grimace. "Do not make me play this game."

"Why not?"

"Because you know very well how people see you."

He waited her out, and she gave in with a sigh of exasperation that made him chuckle under his breath.

"Okay, fine." She pursed her lips for a second. "You're the hot, charming, popular quarterback, okay? Envied by men, wanted by women, beloved by all. Happy now?"

He burst out in a loud laugh. "Is that really how you see me?"

She tilted her head as if considering him, her gaze steady and warm. And all at once he wished he was in her head. He desperately wished he knew the real answer to this question.

Did she like what she saw? Not just his looks but... everything. All of it. He wasn't oblivious to the fact that his friends and family thought he was a good man but not the sort you take seriously.

He was the kind of guy you went to a bar with or could be counted on to flirt when a pretty lady came wandering over to your table.

He was fun. He was handsome. And yeah, all right,

maybe he'd heard himself called "charming" more than once.

But right now he wished he knew if that was all she saw.

If maybe that was all there was to see...

"I'll admit," she said with another sigh, "I used to think you were...shallow. Not to mention entitled and self-absorbed."

He winced. "Jeez, you're not pulling any punches, are you?"

"But," she added quickly, her voice warming, "I've recently had a change of heart as far as that's concerned."

It was a little alarming how his insides reacted to that pseudo-praise.

"I think, in hindsight, maybe you're the kind of guy who's easy to underestimate."

The simple statement, said so casually, made his heart kick against his ribs and his world feel like it'd been flipped upside down.

He had no doubt whatsoever that her offhand remark would stick with him for a lifetime. "I..." He stopped.

She'd gone back to looking out the window, not at all fazed by the conversation.

He forced a huff of amusement. "And here I thought you were immune to my charms."

She rolled her eyes, but her lips were still curved up in a smile. "No woman on earth is immune to your charms, Boone Donahue."

He grinned, his chest swelling with warmth at the compliment, all the more powerful for how grudgingly it was given.

"Oh, don't even look at me like that," she said with a laugh.

"Like what?"

She turned, too, so now she was facing him as he turned back to the road. "Don't pretend that you don't know the effect you have on women." After a beat, she added, "On *every*one."

To his surprise, he felt an unfamiliar warmth creeping up his neck. "Hey, you hungry for breakfast?"

She hesitated, probably thrown by the sudden topic change. "Uh, yeah, sure. Let's do it."

He glanced at the clock. It was still early. Most restaurants wouldn't be open. But at the next exit, they headed into town and found a diner that said "Open 24 Hours" in big neon letters.

"I think we found our spot," April murmured.

He parked, and over breakfast the last of the morning's tension eased as they downed waffles and bacon.

"Breakfast of champions," April said through a mouthful of food.

He moaned his agreement, making her laugh and then recall the best waffles she'd ever had.

"It was the week I arrived in Portland. A little 'out of the way' restaurant that you wouldn't even know was there unless someone told you about it." She smiled. "Sounds like the worst marketing, right? But *everyone* talked about it. Because the food was so dang good. I checked it out after I heard someone at the grocery store going on about it, and the second I walked in the door, I felt like I'd entered this secret club. Like I was earning my place in Portland somehow." She licked a blob of maple syrup off her finger. "But seriously, best waffles ever. If I got nothing else from Portland, I would still be grateful I went."

Boone paused with his next mouthful halfway to his

lips, wondering if he should ask but then deciding to just go for it and hope it didn't kill their conversation on the spot. "So, how far did you get tracking down this David Taylor?"

She grimaced. "Not far. Turns out being curious and having a gung-ho attitude does not automatically make one a crack detective."

"Ah."

"Precisely." She stabbed her waffle with her fork. "Without the funds to hire someone to help, I've been doing the best I can with what little I know of my mom's past and what I can find on the interwebs."

"I see." He leaned forward, not fooled in the slightest by her joking tone. "That's gotta be frustrating."

She pressed her lips together in silent agreement.

"And your dad…" He started and stopped, well aware he was treading on thin ice. "I mean, your adopted father—"

"Frank," she supplied, her tone blunt.

"Right. Frank's file didn't give you any information that was useful or—"

"No." Her tone wasn't just blunt, it was cold as ice. But the look in her eyes was anything but.

He felt a swift kick to his ribs at the mix of emotions he saw there before she pointedly looked away.

"I didn't get a chance to really study the documents in that folder, and he…he never had the chance to explain."

"Right." He winced. Of course he hadn't. He'd died right after she'd found out. Sympathy swelled, but before he could say another word, her low voice cut through the silence.

"Don't."

"What?"

She shook her head, her eyes wet with unshed tears as she glared at him. But again, it wasn't anger he saw there. It was grief, and it was betrayal, and it was…

"Don't pity me," she said. And under her breath, so quietly that he almost didn't hear, she added, "I don't deserve it."

He frowned.

Guilt.

That's the other emotion he'd seen swimming in her gaze.

Guilt.

But why would April feel guilty?

"I don't think I can eat another bite." She pushed the plate away, her tone returning to normal, if slightly strained.

"Yeah, I'm done too," he said. "I'll go pay the tab."

She nodded. "I'll just…wait outside."

April scooted out of the booth and headed toward the door before he could stop her. "I just… I need some air."

He stared after her.

The girl was drowning, that much was clear, but it wasn't just air that she needed.

He watched her walk out and got to his feet at a slower pace. She needed a minute. He could understand that.

He just wished he could figure out what else she needed.

All he knew for certain was that it wasn't back in Portland. She shouldn't be on her own right now, not when she was grieving and dealing with so many revelations.

He'd been right to take her away from there. That wasn't where she needed to be in order to heal. She needed family. She needed a home.

He handed over the tab and some cash to an older woman behind the counter.

But was her home in Aspire?

He didn't know. But man...he hoped so.

CHAPTER 16

April stepped out into the sunlit morning and took a deep breath. Wrapping her arms around her waist, she headed toward the truck but didn't get inside.

She tipped her head back instead, closing her eyes as she reveled in the feel of warm sunshine soaking into her skin and the wind toying with her braids.

It'd been a slow, gray fall, and it felt like it'd been way too long since she'd seen the sun.

Her insides were still coiled up in a knot behind her sternum. That's how it felt, at least. That's how it always felt when her thoughts went back to Frank…back to that day.

It was worse than ever as she sat across from Boone.

The cowboy was basically a superhero in disguise. He was Clark Kent and Barry Allen and…well, not Bruce Wayne. He wasn't nearly dark or moody enough to be Bruce Wayne. But he was all the others combined.

He had a good heart and a ridiculously hot body and the sort of do-gooder spirit that would have been laughable if it weren't so dang sweet.

It wouldn't surprise her if one day he ripped off his shirt to reveal a spandex costume underneath. To find that he was just a cocky ranch hand by day, but at night he was battling the darker elements of Aspire, Montana.

Which, to be fair, were few and far between.

Her lips twitched at the mental image of a costume-clad Boone taking on the high school bullies, who were quite possibly the worst villains Aspire had ever seen.

Her smile faded fast. Boone was so kind and lovable and good. How was she supposed to tell him that Frank was dead because of her?

That his real daughters would never get to know him... because of her?

She took a deep breath, willing her thoughts to evaporate and that knot in her chest to disappear.

It didn't work, but the sunshine did feel nice. And the mental image of Boone was enough to make her lips curve up in a smile despite her pain.

"Well, hello there, sweetheart."

A man's voice had her eyes flickering open, and she backed up with a jolt, bumping into the truck's door when she realized the man talking was standing close.

Too close.

With a shaved head and a sneer that made her stomach turn, the guy moved into her space. He was near enough that he could reach out and touch her.

So close she could smell the alcohol that was wafting off him in nauseating waves.

She pressed herself back against the truck.

To be nice or to be rude? Which would de-escalate the situation?

"Hey," she said softly, not trying to hide her wariness.

She heard laughter, and that was when she saw that the drunk, leering dude had friends.

Drunk friends.

They must've been up partying all night, and there was a glassy sheen to their eyes that made her stomach turn.

"What's a pretty little thing like you doing all alone out here, hmm?" He reached out and touched one of her braids.

She swatted his hand away. "Don't touch me."

"Ooh," his friends hooted and cackled, and her insides heated in anger.

"Miss Thing thinks she's too good for you, Leo," one of the men said.

"Is that right?" The leering drunk moved even closer until she wrinkled her nose in disgust. "You think you're too good for me?"

"I'm here with someone." She hoped her voice was strong enough. She couldn't bring herself to look away from the guy crowding her, afraid of what he'd do if she showed any vulnerability. "I'm just waiting for him."

"Well then, why don't we wait with you, hmm?" His tone was cajoling, but it was all for his friends' benefit, trying to give them a laugh at her expense.

He wanted to make her uncomfortable. Wanted to make her afraid.

She lifted her chin. "I'm fine on my own, thanks."

His friends laughed hard at that, but the drunk man's amusement faded and that sneer turned ugly and cruel. "You saying no to me, sweetheart?"

His voice was sharp and dangerous, but she'd be damned if she let him see how much it scared her.

Her chin came up higher, her insides trembling as she tried to form a response.

But then she heard it.

Boone's voice.

Close enough to level out the quaking in her stomach and help her take a breath.

"I believe my girlfriend made herself clear."

April's head whipped to the side to see him, her insides jolting as she took in his expression. Surely that was not Boone. That hard-as-steel tone and lethal gaze could not have come from her kind, easygoing friend.

Her lips parted in shock when she saw his anger grow a few shades darker. It made his chiseled jaw look like it was formed from granite and his dark eyes sparkle with a fiery rage.

"Is that right?" the drunk guy drawled.

"That's right." Boone paid no mind to the friends, who watched with a sick sort of eagerness.

They couldn't wait for a fight, but not one of 'em was man enough to start it. April glared at them with contempt, but she turned her attention to Boone when he reached her side. "It's fine, Boone. This guy was just—"

"I ain't goin' anywhere, sweetheart." The drunk guy snickered. "We were just getting acquainted, you and I."

His singsong tone was a taunt and a dare.

"Step away from my girl."

The drunk guy's grin was sudden and terrifying. Like he'd been waiting all night for this sort of encounter. He shifted away from April, moving into Boone's space instead, leaning in close, so his foul breath hit Boone square in the face. "Or what?"

Boone didn't waste a heartbeat.

One minute the drunk guy had been standing there leering, and the next he was flat on his back. April gaped down at him, her gasp as loud as the drunk guy's shouts.

Boone had knocked him out flat with one punch. One perfectly landed punch to the face, and…

Holy crap.

She turned her gaze to the still-fuming cowboy.

Boone Donahue had just punched a guy. For her.

Her jaw was hanging open, but there was nothing to be done about it. She was in shock. And she almost pitied the drunk dude's friends. Their eyes went wide with fear as Boone stalked toward them, but before he could reach them, they scattered.

April caught Boone by his arm, tugging him toward the truck. "Come on, they're not worth it. Let's get out of here."

It wasn't until they were in the truck and back on the highway that April realized she was shaking.

"Are you okay?"

She turned to see Boone watching her with such fierce protectiveness that it made the trembling a hundred times worse. She threaded her fingers together and wedged them between her knees to keep them from jiggling up and down. "I'm fine." And she was.

Because of him.

"Thank you," she said belatedly. "Thank you so much for—"

"Don't thank me." His hands moved on the steering wheel, and she caught the white of his knuckles and the way his jaw was still clenched tight. "I should've come out sooner. I shouldn't have left you alone."

"Hey." She reached out and touched his arm and… whoa. His bicep was flexed, his muscle as hard as rock. But worry won out over appreciation. "Hey. Are *you* okay?"

He looked surprised. "I'm fine. Why?"

"Why?!" She couldn't help it. A laugh bubbled up inside her chest before she could stop it.

It was everything. The guilt and anger that had come up about her dad—no, Frank. The anger and helplessness facing off with that drunk guy. That and…

"You were like a superhero!" It burst out of her along with a loud laugh. She clapped a hand over her mouth, but it was too late. Her eyes welled with tears, and for the first time in who knew how long, they were tears of laughter, not sadness.

His face split with that ridiculously handsome grin of his as he glanced over once, then twice. "You find this funny?"

"Yes. No. I mean…" She wiped at her eyes as laughter rattled through her. "I'm sorry, it's just…wham!" She punched thin air, pretending to be Boone.

He gave a snort of laughter. "Is that how I looked?"

"No, you looked amazing," she gushed. "You looked hot."

He shot her a wide-eyed glance, but she shoved aside the embarrassment, giving his rock-hard bicep a shove. "Oh come on, you have to know you looked hot. Clark Kent has nothing on you, my friend."

He started laughing in earnest. "You're nuts."

"Maybe. But you're freakin' bad to the bone." She drew the words out with a snarl that had him laughing even harder.

Soon they were both cracking up all over again.

"I'm serious," she finally said through a wheezing giggle. "I'm so sorry you had to do that, but man…" She sank back in her seat with a sigh. "It was sooo satisfying."

"Yeah?" He shot her a smug grin, his eyes glinting with

laughter and warmth and…something else that she couldn't quite name.

Something that made her belly flutter and her heart pound.

It was something that made her forget the knot in her chest…at least for now.

CHAPTER 17

*O*nly *April.*
Only April could turn that churning, consuming protective rage into…laughter.

His lips quirked up at the memory of it even hours later as they drove through endless cornfields. He opened his mouth to break the companionable silence they'd fallen into but stopped short because…there it was.

She was singing.

He pressed his lips together to contain his smile, his chest constricting so fast and fierce, it was kinda painful.

But worth it.

This was the second time he'd heard her sing. The first had been when she'd been in the shower at the motel. She probably hadn't heard him come back in, and for that he was glad.

In the shower, she'd been belting it out, but here and now, she was singing under her breath as she gazed out the window.

He wasn't even sure she knew she was doing it, and he didn't want to speak up for fear she'd stop.

Because the thing was, her voice was gorgeous. As sweet as she was, and filled with that same intangible, inexplicable lightness that made being around her so easy.

Considering the darkness she was surrounded by right now, with her family drama, it was nothing short of amazing that she'd managed to maintain the light he remembered from when she was young.

His hands gripped the steering wheel as she sang the wrong words to the chorus, his heart lurching as his mind conjured up another song—one he'd heard Daisy and the kids do a cover of.

It was that song "Riptide" by Vance Joy, where he talks about loving it when she sang that song and getting a lump in his throat because she was gonna sing the words wrong.

"What?" April's question ended her singing abruptly, and he looked over in surprise.

"*What* what?"

Her lips twitched as she wiggled a finger in his direction, suspicion in her eyes. "What's with that smile?"

"Nothing!"

He said it too quickly, though, and she narrowed her eyes. "Are you laughing at me?"

"No! Of course not. I just…" He couldn't stop another grin. "I like your singing, that's all."

She gasped and then swatted his arm, making him laugh. "You *are* laughing at me."

"I'm not!" He pretended to cower from her smacks, but really she was the lightest of lightweights. "I'm serious. I was just thinking how much I love hearing you sing."

She pouted at him, clearly dubious.

"Seriously!" He started to laugh at her suspicion. She

was stinkin' cute when she was trying to glare at him like that.

"*Now* why are you laughing?" She sounded put out, but he saw the twitch of her lips.

He gestured to her face. "Because your mean face needs some serious work."

She pouted again. "I don't like being laughed at."

"April, I'm not kidding. I love your voice. It's gorgeous. Actually…I was just thinking that it reminds me of Daisy."

"Daisy…" Her brows shot up. "My sister? Or half-adopted-sister or…" She waved a hand. "Whatever?"

"Yeah. Her. You know, I know you're not related by blood, but hearing you sing…you remind me of her a bit. She's got a killer voice too." He glanced over, concerned that maybe he was driving her away with talk of her sisters, but while she had a bit of wariness in her expression, she looked curious too. "Plus, she's a free spirit, you know? Very artistic and marches to the beat of her own drum." He shot her a sidelong glance. "Like a certain mousy artist I know."

She gave a huff of amusement. "Sounds like you like her. Daisy, I mean."

"I do. I like her a lot. She came to town with a whole boatload of baggage—"

"Seriously?"

"Oh yeah. She had big ol' secrets and even some shady bad guys who followed her to town."

"No." April couldn't hide her surprise.

"It's true. You know she ended up getting involved with the sheriff—"

"Is it still Sheriff Baker?"

"Yep."

"Wow. I used to babysit for his kids back in the day."

He grinned "You won't even recognize 'em now, I bet. Those kids have grown so much since you left."

"I bet," she murmured.

He couldn't tell where her mind had gone when she fell silent, so he gave her some space.

"They lost their mom to cancer too," she finally said.

"They did. Having Daisy in their lives has been real good for 'em," he murmured. "For all of them. I think they've been just as good for her as she was for them."

"Huh," April said softly. "That's nice."

He nodded. They were in fragile territory. One wrong step and he had a feeling she'd hop right out of this truck —moving or not—and run back to Portland if she had to.

He adjusted his hands on the wheel, waiting for a cue from her if she wanted to talk more about her family or put off the inevitable until they rode into town.

"Did you…um, I mean…" She blew out a sharp exhale. "I'm guessing you told them I was coming back with you, right?"

He nodded. "I texted JJ last night. You remember JJ?"

She shook her head.

"He must've come to the ranch after you moved to Bozeman. He's married to Dahlia. Really good guy. Quiet, tough, but one of the kindest people you'll ever meet."

She stared at him long and hard. "And that's *Dahlia's* husband?"

He burst out in a laugh. "Yeah, no one really saw that coming. But again…" He shrugged. "They're good for each other."

"What else did you tell JJ?" She shifted, tugging at the hem of her flowy shirt. "About me, I mean."

"Not much." He glanced over. "I didn't tell them that

you're adopted. Or that you're looking for your biological father. I figured that was your news to share when you see fit."

She nodded, her expression sober. "Thanks."

The silence stretched long and heavy. "I know it's not my place to say so, but I've gotten to know your sisters pretty well these last few months, and…they won't care that you're adopted. They're ready to welcome you with open arms, no matter what."

She met his gaze with one so serious and unreadable, he didn't know what to make of it.

He thought maybe she'd tell him.

Maybe she'd open up about whatever it was that was haunting her so badly. But instead she turned to face straight ahead with a sigh. "Tell me more about them," she said.

"What?"

"My sisters." She shrugged. "I started to get a sense of who's who from their voice mails, but I don't really know anything about any of them. So…" She turned toward him, yet her whole demeanor was defensive, like she didn't really want to be asking. "Tell me about them."

"Yeah?"

She glanced at the passing countryside. "I mean, it's not like we have anything better to do, right?"

He gave a snort of amusement. "True. All right then…I guess I should start with Emma. She was the first to arrive…"

His stories about her sisters kept them occupied all the way through their lunch stop, which was far less eventful than breakfast. Boone had never really considered himself much of a storyteller before, but he found himself relishing her laughter when he told her about fashion diva Lizzy's first days on the ranch, and how she and Kit took to each other like oil and water.

He loved the way she gasped and made sympathetic little "ahh" sounds when he told her about Rose showing up pregnant and lost, and how she'd found the love of her life with the town's favorite doctor.

They were both laughing when he told her about how Dahlia and JJ bonded because they were snowed in at a cabin together in the middle of nowhere.

"Poor JJ," she giggled.

"Amen to that."

She went quiet when he got to Sierra, the most recent sister to arrive at the ranch. She seemed to take it to heart when he told her all the anger Sierra had shown up with, all geared toward the father who'd abandoned her.

"I wonder why he did that," she whispered.

He didn't know how to answer, so he kept quiet.

"So she didn't stick around, then?" she asked eventually.

"Nah. Sierra had a job waiting in Venezuela, and Cody went with her."

"Cody Swanson." She smiled. "I remember him."

Cody was older than them by a few good years. He found himself casting curious looks in her direction. Something about the way she'd said she remembered him made his insides coil in irritation. "You remember him, huh?"

"Yeah. He was always nice to me."

He nodded. Of course Cody had been nice to her. She'd been a loner and a kid back then.

He tapped the steering wheel, willing himself to let it go. But then, out of nowhere, he heard himself blurting, "Did you have a crush on him?"

She blinked. "What?"

He shrugged, kicking himself. "Nothing, it's just...I know a lot of girls in our class had a crush on him."

"Uh, yeah, how could you not?" She laughed, seemingly unaware that she was stoking a fire he had no business feeling. "He was always so nice. Not a flirt like his brother, but so easy to talk to and so nice to everyone and..." She shrugged. "Who *didn't* have a crush on Cody Swanson?"

"I didn't," he muttered, making her laugh.

"But you are friends, right?"

He nodded. Petty jerk that he was, he didn't feel like owning up to his friendship with Cody at the moment because he was finding the mere thought of the guy annoying.

Of course, the fact that Cody was currently off working as a volunteer at a children's clinic in Venezuela was one reason it was hard to stay annoyed for long.

The fact that he was there with the love of his life was another.

"I'm glad to hear he found himself a nice woman." April smiled.

And the last of Boone's annoyance dried right up. "So, what else do you want to know about what you're heading back to?"

She pressed her hand to her belly with a quick shake of her head. "You know what? We still have a lot of hours to go before I have to face the inevitable. Maybe we should change the topic for a while."

He nodded. "Fair enough."

"What do you say we play some more music?"

She wanted a distraction, and he couldn't say he blamed her. "All right," he drawled. When she reached for the plug to connect his phone, he added, "But one condition."

"What's that?"

"You've got to sing along."

She started to laugh, like he was joking.

He wasn't. He really, truly wanted to hear her sing some more.

"Fair enough," she said. "But I've got to warn you, I don't know all the words to this next one."

His heart gave a sharp kick, and all he managed to whisper was "That's fine by me."

CHAPTER 18

The joyful, laughing mood in the car quickly dampened the moment they crossed the border into Montana.

It wasn't Boone's fault. He tried his best to keep her distracted and entertained with music and stories about their old classmates. But the more familiar the terrain became, the more she couldn't ignore what was to come.

"Do you, uh…do you want to go to Bozeman first?" he said. "Spend the night with your grandparents, maybe, or—"

"No." She swallowed hard. "I mean, I check in with them occasionally and…" She could've ended that any number of ways.

I should really go see them.

I should let them know exactly where I am this time instead of giving them vague answers about my life.

I should really apologize for being a distant granddaughter when we used to be so close.

But in the end, she sighed and spoke the truth. "I can't put this off any longer."

Boone nodded like he understood. Like anyone could understand. With a humorless laugh, she dropped her head into her hands.

"What is it?"

"I was just wondering…" She stole a glimpse of him, soaking in the sight of his now-familiar profile. Everything about him spoke of strength and confidence and an assuredness, and it was impossible to imagine him having any sort of family drama. But she'd never known his family well, so she found herself asking, "What's your family like?"

"Mine?" He seemed surprised.

She shrugged. "You've heard all about mine. Actually, you know mine better than I know them. It's only fair you share."

He laughed. "Not much to tell. My parents are happily married, and they own a boutique inn just outside town now."

She shifted. "Really? That's awesome."

"It is, yeah. They're living their dream together. And now that the business has grown, they've hired more staff, bought their own house in town, and actually have time off every week."

"And you have sisters, right? I don't remember them…"

"That's because they're way older than us. There's eight years between me and the second youngest."

"Wow."

"Yeah. I am what you would call—" He winked at her. "—a happy accident."

She laughed, and the sound shocked her. She'd been so anxious just a second ago. How did Boone manage to make her laugh when she was on the verge of a panic attack?

She shook her head, clueless.

"So, did your sisters pick on you or dote on you?"

He hesitated, and she started to laugh.

"Oh man, they totally doted on you."

"I wouldn't say doted. But they did love dressing me up in baby clothes and making me have tea with their dolls."

Her head fell back with a laugh. "Oh my gosh, I can totally see it."

His grin was crooked and wry, and so freakin' sexy it took her breath away. She swallowed hard and looked out the window.

"Must be nice," she said eventually. "To have a close family like that."

He was quiet for a beat. "It is. I was especially lucky because we had so much family in town. There was never a lack of aunts and cousins in our house…although I was always the youngest by far, so…"

"So treated like the baby," she finished.

"Yep." He ended the word with a popping *p* sound that made her giggle. "Sometimes I'm positive that my mother thinks I'll starve to death if she doesn't send me home with leftovers once a week."

She smiled but didn't laugh because she was the tiniest bit cynical. "They care. That's a good thing."

He shot her a wry smile. "You're right. I know. I guess I just feel like I've got something to prove."

She nodded. "Yeah, I get it. But I'm guessing they don't see it that way. They probably just want to protect you."

Her own words hit her hard, and she looked out the window.

When Boone spoke, his voice was filled with under-standing. "I guess that's what parents do, huh?"

She nodded. Her mom and Frank...they'd been trying to protect her. She got that. But it did little to make her feel better right now.

"We're almost there," Boone murmured when the silence stretched way too long.

She nodded.

"You ready?"

They exited the highway, and the landscape wasn't just recognizable, it was intimately familiar.

There was the coffee shop her dad insisted on going to even though it was in the opposite direction of town.

"They have the freshest beans," he'd say.

Her lips wobbled. Dang it, she was not allowed to start crying like a baby. They hadn't even gotten there yet.

But in what felt like no time at all, Boone pulled onto the long dirt road that led up a hillside to the ranch house.

Her breath caught, and it wasn't until Boone's hand covered hers that she realized she'd been gripping the edge of her seat like it was a lifeline.

"You okay?" he asked.

She nodded. *No.*

With every turn in the switchback road, the memories came flooding back. The last time she was here, driving away with her parents and looking back.

Even then she'd known.

She'd known that once they left this magical place, nothing would be the same.

She understood somehow that there was no going back. Not really.

And right now, she understood it in a whole new way.

As the house came into sight, her breath left her in a shuddering exhale. It was the same, but different.

It was so achingly familiar, but also so much smaller and less grand than she remembered it.

It was her beloved home…and at the same time, it felt like something foreign.

Boone squeezed her hand as he parked the truck among a handful of other vehicles, and two men emerged from the far side of the house.

"You've got this," Boone said.

She looked to him, and she couldn't hide the flare of panic that made her eyes widen as she flipped her hand to squeeze his.

He leaned in close. "I'm not going anywhere. I live in the bunkhouse, and you can't get rid of me this week if you try."

Her lips quivered, and for the life of her, she didn't know if she wanted to laugh or cry at that comment.

How did he know that was exactly what she needed to hear?

He arched his brows in a silent question: *You okay?*

She nodded, swallowing hard and letting go of his hand just as Kit Swanson reached her truck door and opened it. "Well, well. April O'Sullivan."

Kit looked exactly as she remembered. Which was to say, too handsome for his own good.

That was what her mom used to say.

It was impossible not to return his lopsided grin as he held out a hand to help her down.

"Aren't you a sight for sore eyes," he finished as he set her gently on her feet, then let her go.

She turned to find Boone hurrying around the front of his truck to reach her side, and gratitude washed over her.

She'd known he meant it when he'd said he wasn't going anywhere, but having him at her side made her stand a little taller as Nash Donahue joined Kit and gave her that small, kind smile she remembered so well.

He stuck a hand out, and she shook it automatically.

"I'm guessing you don't remember me," he said in that quiet voice of his. "But I lived next door—"

"I remember you." Heaven help her. With everything going on, she could not possibly be blushing right now.

But yup. There was that telltale heat in her cheeks, and she could swear she felt Boone's gaze searching her in response.

She avoided looking up to make eye contact because there was no way she was going to explain to Boone that she'd been massively infatuated with the cowboy next door growing up.

She hadn't lied about having a crush on Cody. But that was different. She'd thought he was cute and sweet in that older-boy-next-door sort of way. But Nash, the *actual* boy next door...

Well, he hadn't been a boy. He'd been too old for her, by far. Which was part of the appeal, she'd supposed. She'd had a crush on him like most girls her age had drooled over their favorite boy band member or the latest star on TV.

And now here he was, greeting her as if maybe she didn't remember him.

She might've laughed if at that moment Kit hadn't snagged her bag from the backseat and Nash wasn't leading the way inside.

"We'd better get in there." Kit laughed out the words as he glanced back at her. "The girls are about ready to explode with excitement. In fact..." He shifted her bag onto his shoulder and pulled out his phone. "I told Lizzy I'd text the moment you arrived…"

His brow furrowed as he dipped his head and typed a text to his wife.

Lizzy. The fashion designer. Right.

She glanced up in time to see curtains parting, and a warm glow seeped out from the living room. Voices too. Between that and all the cars they were passing on the way to the kitchen entrance…

"Is, um…is everyone here?"

"Mostly," Kit said. "Lizzy and the kids will be here in time for dinner."

"And JJ's still riding the range," Nash said.

Boone made a sound of impatience beside her as his hand came to rest on her lower back.

Heat bloomed where he touched her, spreading through her veins and into her limbs, making her feel…

Well, unsettled, in a way. But also…safe.

She took a deep breath, letting herself revel in the support.

"Everyone's here?" Boone sounded irritated. "Didn't anyone think maybe April might want to ease into the craziness that is the O'Sullivan clan?"

"Dahlia tried," Nash murmured with a wince. "It didn't take."

Kit laughed. "*You* try telling these women to stay away when their youngest sister is finally here."

"Their youngest sister."

April felt the words crash into her like a wave. That's how everyone here saw her?

The youngest sister? The rogue sister?

"The daughter Frank stayed for." Wasn't that how Boone had described her?

Her feet stumbled, and she nearly came to a stop. She might have if Boone's hand wasn't guiding her gently, a constant reminder that he was there. That he wasn't going anywhere.

Nash opened the back door and gestured for her to go first. "Welcome home, April."

CHAPTER 19

Memories flooded April the moment she walked through the door, so overwhelming and filled with so many emotions, she couldn't think her way through them.

The kitchen hadn't changed much, and its warmth was so bittersweet, her chest tightened painfully.

Nash paused behind her, Kit following right after him. But it was Boone who came to her side and threaded his fingers through hers. A reminder that he was there.

She squeezed his hand tight as her mind filled with images, one more vivid than the rest. Her mom singing along to the radio as she bent over the stove, smiling and laughing. And Frank coming in from outside, taking off his dirty boots as he oohed and aahed over how great it smelled.

April's gaze fell to the large table by the window as if she could actually see her former self sitting there, doing homework and giggling at her dad's exaggerated compliments. Then he'd come up behind her mom and make her mother giggle, too, as he nuzzled her neck and hugged her from behind.

He wouldn't quit until she shooed him away, telling him to go clean up for dinner.

It was so real. So vivid. So…good.

Her throat tightened. This past year, she'd only been able to remember the bad parts. Thoughts of the ranch only conjured images of her mom's sickbed and her father's secrets.

But here, now…

How had she forgotten this?

"My mom loved to cook," she whispered.

Boone leaned down, his breath warm against her hair. "Yeah?"

April nodded. "This was her happy place, you know?"

No. He couldn't know. He hadn't been around back then. But she had to tell someone. It seemed crucial suddenly that she not be the only person who remembered her mom in this house.

"My mom would remember her cooking," Nash said from behind her.

Gratitude swelled in her chest.

"Every once in a while, she'd come over," he continued. "And she always came home talking about how your mother should open a restaurant."

April smiled, a huff of laughter escaping. "Really?"

Nash nodded, his smile sweet and understanding. "I'm pretty sure she still cooks some of the recipes your mom shared with her. It's food you don't forget in a hurry."

April nodded, trying to blink away tears. "Yeah."

Boone squeezed her hand. "That must be where you get it."

She glanced up at him in surprise. She never really

thought of herself as a cook. Sure, she loved food, and she'd found true joy in baking, but now…

A wave of satisfaction rippled through her as she looked around the kitchen.

"Yeah, I guess you're right," she murmured. There was a hint of awe in her voice, and a smile tugged at her lips despite the sadness weighing her down.

"My mom saw cooking as an artform," she said.

"Just like you," Boone finished.

They shared a sweet little smile of understanding.

"You want this bag up in your old room, April?" Kit asked, breaking the moment.

"Oh, um…"

Her old room.

Her stomach turned even as her heart lifted.

"Yeah, I guess, if no one's using it…"

"Nah, they've been saving it for you." Kit winked and grinned.

"Is that her?!" The quiet moment with these three men was interrupted by the sound of a familiar cheerful voice, and a second later, a bubbly blonde with riotous curls swept into the room, her arms spread wide. "Oh my goodness, you're here!"

And then April was enveloped in a hug so tight that, for a second, she couldn't breathe. Boone gave her a wincing smile over the woman's shoulder as he reluctantly let her hand go.

April wasn't sure what to do, so she just sort of awkwardly patted the woman's back.

"Daisy, give the girl some room to breathe," another woman said.

April would recognize Dahlia's voice anywhere, but she didn't recognize the pretty brunette who entered with a tolerant smile and a shake of her head.

Daisy pulled back, but she didn't quite let April go. She held her by her shoulders as she took her in. "My goodness, you are so beautiful. All those pictures don't do you justice."

April stared. "All those pictures?"

Dahlia moved forward. "We'll get to that later. Daisy…" She arched her brows as she pointedly looked at Daisy's hands on April's shoulders. "Let the girl go."

Daisy sighed but did as she was told, beaming at April all the while. "We're so happy you're here. We just can't wait to get to know you and—"

"Easy, girl," Dahlia muttered, gently shoving Daisy back.

April pressed her lips together, amused at the dynamic between these two.

"Have you met Dahlia?" Daisy asked, ignoring her sister's attempts to nudge her away. "We're twins, you know."

April's eyes widened.

"Good grief, let the girl get settled in." Dahlia rolled her eyes. "There'll be plenty of time to chat later."

"But—"

"Besides, don't you have kids to pick up?"

"Why? What's the time?" Daisy turned to look at the kitchen clock and gasped. "How is it that late already?"

Dahlia fought a laugh as she shared a quick look with April. "Daisy's stepmother to three kids—"

"Levi Baker's kids." Daisy rushed around the dining table, obviously hunting down her keys. "He told me that you used to babysit for them when they were little. They're so excited to see you again."

April smiled. "I didn't think they'd remember me."

"Mikayla definitely does." Daisy snatched her keys, then glanced at the clock again and winced, but the expression was soon morphing into another one of her sunshine smiles. "I'll catch you soon, sweet things." And she flew out the door just as another blonde with big blue eyes and a brilliant smile walked in.

"Hi. I'm Emma." She beamed, coming to stand beside Dahlia. "And you must be exhausted." She turned her attention to Kit. "Why don't you put her bag in her room —you do want to stay in your room, don't you?"

Kit laughed. "We were trying to do just that before April got overrun by sisters."

"Oh." Emma cringed as she took in the scene. "Sorry about that. We're just…really excited to have you here."

"Yeah, I'm getting that." April darted a glance at Boone.

He sidled closer to her. "She knows where her room is." He grabbed the bag from Kit. "I'll take her up, and let's give her a second to settle in, huh?"

Everyone was quick to agree—if not a little surprised, it seemed to April—that Boone was the one taking charge.

She stayed close to his side as he led the way through the crowded kitchen and up the stairs.

"Thanks," she breathed when they were alone in the upstairs hallway.

"I'm guessing their excitement is a little overwhelming." He shot her an empathetic smile.

She stopped in front of the floor-to-ceiling window that overlooked the sprawling hills of their property. Her heart fluttered and then settled, like it had been waiting for this moment.

She was quiet, and Boone gave her space.

"This used to be my favorite spot." She glanced over

her shoulder to make sure he was seeing it too. With the sun sinking over the horizon, it looked more majestic than ever out there.

But he wasn't looking at the view. His gaze was locked on her.

She swallowed hard at the heat in his eyes, the fierceness and the intensity. Their gazes met and locked, and the moment felt charged. Her heart pounded like she'd just gone for a run, and her belly grew warm and tingly.

"I should, uh…" She took a deep breath and tore her gaze away toward the hallway leading to her old room. "I should get this over with."

He nodded and let her lead the way. She paused only for a heartbeat before throwing open the door and choking on a sound that was halfway between a sob and laugh.

Boone came to a stop so close behind her, she could feel his warmth on her back. "That's…a lot of purple."

She let out another choked sound before clapping a hand over her mouth. So. Much. Purple.

And just like that, she remembered the day her parents had painted it and she'd "helped." *Helped* being a subjective word. She'd been so insistent that it be this particular shade of grape. It seriously looked like a Hubba Bubba monster had exploded in here.

A laugh bubbled up as she remembered her parents covered in splotches of it, the room filled with music as they'd all worked together.

She shook her head and dropped her hand. "I can't believe no one repainted it."

"We wanted you to see it first," Emma's voice startled her from the hallway.

When April turned, Emma gave an apologetic smile

and held out a stack of towels like an offering. Boone shifted out of the way so April could take them from her.

"We figured you might want to freshen up. Maybe take a nap…" Emma shifted from one foot to the other. She was wearing a loosely fitted long-sleeved T-shirt, and April never would have guessed she was pregnant if it wasn't for the way her fluttering hand came to rest on her belly.

"We really did mean to give you space," Emma said with another apologetic smile.

"It's fine." April brushed her hand through the air. And then, because this woman was so sweet and kind and looked so worried, she found herself adding, "It's better than showing up here and finding out you're all angry with me for being MIA for so long."

Emma shook her head quickly. "We're not angry with you. Far from it. We were just worried about you, that's all."

April nodded, her throat too thick to speak. She didn't deserve their concern, or their sympathy.

Boone's hand settled on her shoulder and squeezed, and for one crazy second, April was sure he'd read her thoughts.

Emma moved forward, giving April a quick, hard, impulsive hug that left the towels squished between them. "We're just happy you're home now."

She pulled back with a smile and walked away… leaving April winded.

"Home," she whispered. That wasn't what this place was. Not without her parents here to fill the rooms with love and laughter.

It might be their home, but it wasn't hers…not anymore.

Boone seemed to be everywhere all at once. He'd set

her bag down and wrapped her in his arms. With his height and his broad shoulders, she felt enveloped.

With a sigh, she let herself be held up by his weight, turning to snuggle into his chest. Even though it wasn't her right.

He wasn't hers, not like that. But for right now, after all they'd been through, he felt like the closest thing to family. The closest thing to home.

"I'm sorry," she mumbled. "I just…"

"Never apologize," he said against her hair. And then, she wasn't quite sure if it was just his breath against her temple or his lips, but she thought maybe he'd given her a kiss that was sweet and tender and light as a feather.

A shudder racked through her at how gentle he was with her. For a guy so big and strong, he touched her like she was made of glass.

"Thank you for staying with me," she said.

She felt his smile against the top of her head. "Thank you for coming back with me."

They stayed like that for a long moment, and she was finally the one to pull away. This time she scoped out her old room with fresh eyes. It really was eerie how little it had changed. It was the same color and the same furniture, but all the little touches that had given it life and made it *hers* were gone.

There were no photos lining the windowsill, no artwork plastered on the walls, no collection of snow globes proudly displayed on the chest of drawers.

"So," she said, her voice a little louder than intended as she turned to face Boone, "that was Emma, Daisy, and Dahlia."

"Three down, two to go," he said with a grin that made her laugh.

She nodded. "Right, because Sierra's in Venezuela."

"You're catching on quick, sunshine."

"I'm guessing I'll be meeting Rose and Lizzy sooner rather than later."

Boone nodded. "They'll be here for dinner. Until then…" He looked around meaningfully. "You want some time to get settled in?"

Did she want to be left alone? Not really. But she nodded. He was already going above and beyond to be by her side and help her ease into this situation. But he had to be tired too. "You should go unpack and freshen up," she said. "I'll be fine here on my own for a little while."

He studied her, and whatever he saw in her expression, it had him nodding. "Okay, if you're sure."

She held up the towels. "I'll take a shower and get settled in."

"I'll be back in time for dinner." He said it so solemnly, like it was a sacred vow.

She couldn't help but smile in response as she nudged him toward the door. "I'm counting on it."

CHAPTER 20

April was counting on him.

The thought wouldn't stop circling in Boone's brain just like the soapy water circling down the drain. He shut off the shower, impatience warring with the knowledge that he had to give April some space.

She had to be processing a lot right now, seeing her old home for the first time and meeting sisters she'd never even known existed.

He didn't want to, though.

He'd watched April closely as they'd walked through the house. He'd seen every flicker of emotion, every squelched sob and blinked-away tear.

She was struggling. Of course she was. He hadn't thought for one second that this homecoming wouldn't be emotional for her.

What he hadn't expected was to care so much. To feel her pain like it was his own.

And when he'd set out for Portland only one week earlier, he definitely hadn't expected that he'd be the one person April let in. That he'd be the one she leaned on and trusted and—

He shut off the shower and rested his weight on a palm pressed against the tiles. He dipped his head, ignoring the water that dripped from his hair into his eyes. This tightness in his chest was new. But there was another sensation there, even more overwhelming.

He'd never been needed before. Never had anyone rely on him and trust him with their most precious memories and secrets.

April's faith in him was humbling.

And more than anything in the world, he didn't want to let her down. With that thought, he pushed away from the bunkhouse's shower wall and reached for a towel.

He'd said he'd be there for her, and he would. No matter what, he'd have her back.

Even if it meant standing against his friends and family and protecting her from them.

They meant well. He met his own gaze after swiping the steam from the mirror. He couldn't blame her sisters or Nash and the guys for being excited that she was here. But knowing the secrets she had yet to share, he couldn't help but wince with every new warm welcome and well-intentioned hug.

They were putting even more pressure on April, even if it was unintended.

He threw on some boxers and jeans, tossed the towel aside, and headed out of the bathroom. He'd only just tugged on a fresh T-shirt and was heading toward the door to go back to the main house when JJ entered, dirty and sweaty from his time out on the range.

"You're back." JJ gave him a one-armed bro hug. "How'd it go?"

"Good," Boone said automatically. And then "Well... maybe not *good*."

JJ arched his brows, the closest he ever got to prying.

Boone struggled with how much to tell his friend. If anyone could be trusted with April's secrets, it was this guy. But again, it was her story to tell, so he stuck with his own opinion. "She's been through so much, man."

JJ nodded, his expression somber. "Poor kid."

"*Kid.*" Boone shifted, crossing his arms. That didn't sit right. "She's not a kid, JJ."

The cowboy eyed him oddly but then nodded as he took off his boots. "You're right. She's not. And neither are you."

Mollified, Boone nodded again. He leaned against the kitchen counter. "I don't know that she's gonna stick around."

JJ stilled. "Not happy to be back, huh?"

"I think...I think she's got a lot of mixed emotions about it. But I should warn you, I don't think she's on board with what Dahlia and the others are thinking."

JJ nodded. "One big happy family."

Boone gave a humorless huff of amusement. "Exactly. And I'm worried that their eagerness is gonna push her away, you know?"

JJ sighed. "Yeah. Dahlia was worried about that too."

But Dahlia didn't know the half of it. That was the problem. They all thought April was grieving for her parents—and she was. But they had no idea that she was also reeling from their secrets.

She was betrayed and angry and grieving all at the same time. It was more than anyone should have to bear.

And she definitely shouldn't have to go through it alone.

"There's something else bothering you," JJ said simply.

Boone nodded. "It's not really my place to say. But yeah, there's more to it than what her sisters know."

"And it has you worried."

Boone weighed his next words. Was he worried? Yes. But not about her family and not about the future of the ranch. "She has no interest in the inheritance. She'll go along with what the others want."

JJ hmphed. "That's good news, at least."

"I suppose."

"But you're still worried."

He nodded. "I'm worried. About April."

JJ chewed that over. "You're a good friend."

Boone looked away from JJ's all-seeing stare. He shifted uncomfortably.

A good friend. Was that what he was?

He'd considered himself a good friend to a number of people, and this felt nothing like that.

"You think she'll take off again?" JJ's quiet voice cut into his thoughts.

Boone nodded, his chest tightening with something close to panic. "She might."

JJ sighed. "I'll see what I can do to get Dahlia and the others to give her some space."

"I'd appreciate that."

"She's struggling." JJ said it as a fact, not a question.

Boone tipped his chin in acknowledgment. "She's going through a lot. More than anyone realizes."

JJ studied him for a long moment, and then he surprised Boone by clapping a hand on his shoulder. "Well then, it's a good thing she's got you looking out for her."

Boone's chin jerked back in surprise, and he looked at his older, wiser, far more mature friend to see if he was kidding. But all he saw in the bearded mountain man's expression was sincerity…and maybe a little pride.

Boone dipped his head with a nod. "Thanks, man."

He wasn't even sure JJ knew what he was thanking him for, but JJ just lifted the hand on his shoulder to clap him hard on the back.

"Better go get your girl," he murmured before disappearing into the bathroom, no doubt to change and shower for dinner, leaving Boone to hurry out the door.

CHAPTER 21

The sounds coming from downstairs were just plain terrifying.

April hesitated at the top of the steps, one hand on the railing and one foot hovering.

"Just go down there already," she muttered.

Her body did not comply.

A loud peal of laughter gave her a start. Which was ridiculous, obviously. The sound of kids bickering and grown-ups laughing and chatting like one big happy family should not be making her feel like she was about to enter a haunted Halloween house.

She drew in a deep breath and let out an exasperated sigh.

This was not exactly the stuff of nightmares.

The smell of fresh-baked bread wafted up the staircase and made her stomach growl.

The sooner you get down there, the sooner you can eat.

But rather than help move her forward, the thought made her stomach twist into a knot, and her hunger disappeared.

"You're being a baby," she told herself.

And honestly, she was probably being rude too. She'd lingered way too long in the bathroom, drawing out the shower and then taking her sweet time with unpacking her meager belongings.

Procrastination is beneath you. It's cowardly, and it's pointless. You're here now. It's not like you can avoid them forever.

The pep talk helped. A little. She budged from the top of the steps, at least, and made it a full halfway down before stopping again.

This time she froze, and it wasn't because another female voice had joined the mix, or because there were now several male voices she didn't recognize.

Nope, it was because she'd caught sight of a framed photo on the wall.

How had she missed it on the way up?

She supposed she'd been too distracted by her sisters and Boone and the thought of seeing her old room. But the framed photo of her mom and dad caught her attention on the way down, and it nearly derailed her plans entirely.

She almost turned tail and ran back to her room. The thought of burrowing under the covers and not coming out until it was time to head back to Portland was a very real temptation.

She swallowed hard as she met her mother's bright smile.

She'd gotten her mom's smile. Her grandparents always used to say that with a proud look in their eyes.

For the first time, it occurred to her that not once had anyone said "you have your father's..." anything. Of course, at the time, she hadn't noticed. She was clearly a blend of genetics. Half white, half black. She'd just assumed that Caucasian aspect had come from Frank.

But now, of course, she realized why there was no real resemblance.

"Why?" she whispered to the photo of the happy couple. "Why didn't you tell me sooner? About my real father. About your other daughters…"

The picture didn't answer.

And the silence in that staircase was just another reminder that they would never answer.

She'd never know what they were thinking.

"I can't believe she's really here!" One of the female voices spoke so loudly it cut into April's moment with her parents—well, with their photo.

Shaking her head, she turned to head down…

And she froze again.

This time it wasn't out of fear, though, it was surprise.

Boone was smiling up at her, leaning against the bottom banister, his head cocked to the side as he watched her.

"How long have you been standing there?" she asked, a laugh bubbling up despite her nerves and sorrow.

It was a laugh of relief, plain and simple.

"Long enough to appreciate just how pretty you are in a dress." His wink made her blush. Or maybe it was the compliment.

He's just being nice.

Still, she felt a little better about the long, flowy dress she'd picked out from her meager stash of clothes. It had a bohemian vibe to it that her mother would've loved.

Maybe that was her way of bringing her mother's memory back into that kitchen, which was currently overrun by Frank's other daughters by the sounds of things.

When she reached the bottom of the steps, Boone held out his arm, and she choked on a laugh. "What's this?"

"Just being a proper gentleman."

She rolled her eyes, but she hooked her arm through his and let him guide her into the chaos of the kitchen.

"You got this," he murmured.

She nodded. But she wasn't so sure.

"And that's what I told him," one of the sisters was saying. "If we're not gonna have a traditional—"

The speaking stopped.

Everything stopped.

April's fingers dug into Boone's arm as she resisted the urge to flee from the silence and the stares.

Boone put his free hand over hers and squeezed back as he cut the silence with a low drawl. "The prodigal sister returns."

April didn't know whether to laugh or flinch at that description, but his remark cut the tension, and then suddenly everyone was talking at once.

"Here she is!" Daisy was back, and she crossed over to April's other side, wrapping an arm around her in a side hug. "Meet Rose and Lizzy. They've been dying, waiting for you to come down."

Two new blondes rushed her. One short and energetic —Lizzy, she quickly guessed—and the other clearly shy and with a soft voice that nearly got drowned out by the ruckus as she introduced herself as Rose.

"And this is Baby Kiara," she said, nodding toward the little one pressed to her chest.

"And I'm Kiara's daddy," a handsome young man said as he approached with a friendly smile. "Better known as Dex."

"Dr. Dex to most of town," Kit added.

April smiled and nodded, doing the best she could to keep up as she was introduced to JJ and then Kit and Lizzy's twins, who couldn't stand still long enough to say more than a quick "Ooh, a new auntie!" before they ran off again.

"A new auntie." The words clamored in her head like a gong. And for a moment, she was speechless.

But before she could fully recover from the fact that she wasn't just considered another sister but an aunt, a familiar man came forward with a kind smile and a warm hug. "April, I haven't seen you since you were Mikayla's age."

"Hi, Mr. Baker," she said softly, memories flooding her at the sight of a face from her past.

"It's Levi," he corrected as he pulled back. "And the kids are so excited to see you after all these years."

She smiled. "I was so sorry to hear about Mrs. Baker."

"Thanks." His smile grew sad and a little wistful. "And I never got the chance to say how sorry I was to hear about your parents passing. They were fine people, and I know they're missed."

She nodded, not quite trusting herself to speak. Grief was funny like that. Her mother had been gone for years, her father for more than a year, and some days she felt like she understood that fact. But then there were moments like this one where it seemed to catch her unaware.

Like she'd just lost them all over again.

She'd dropped Boone's arm when she'd returned Levi's hug, and now his hand rested against the small of her back.

She focused on the feel of it as her sisters and their partners bustled around her, bringing dishes to the table and wrangling kids.

"You're doing great," Boone murmured against the top of her head.

She didn't have a chance to answer before Levi's kids surrounded her. It was an awkward and shy start, especially since only the oldest remembered her, but soon they were competing with each other, chatting her ear off about what grade they were in and what sports they played.

"Come on, you three," Daisy called. "Last one to the table has to clean the cat litter when we get home."

The three kids nearly trampled each other to get to the table, and Daisy laughed as she winked at April. "Works every time."

April found herself smiling back. It was difficult not to smile when Daisy was around.

"April, you sit here." Emma gestured to an empty chair.

JJ had been sitting in the seat beside it, but he took one look at her and Boone, smiled kindly, then got up and moved over one so Boone could sit next to her.

April wished like heck she wasn't so dang grateful for that small kindness.

She wished she was stronger than this. That she didn't need Boone beside her to feel safe and comfortable.

But the truth of the matter was...his being by her side was a huge help. His hand on her back made her feel grounded while the newfound sisters and the memories in this house plus the easy camaraderie of this happy family...

All that combined made her feel like she was floating adrift in space.

As if he could read her mind, Boone leaned over when he took his seat. "I'm right here. And if you need a breather, just say the word."

April nodded, hoping he could see the gratitude in her eyes, because her sisters were barely giving her room to breathe, let alone speak.

"Now the only one missing is Sierra." Dahlia looked around the table as the others all found their places, like a mother hen counting her chicks. She had a satisfied, contented air about her, oblivious to the way JJ gazed at her like she was the only woman in the room as he reached for her hand, then kissed it.

April looked away with a little twinge in her heart that she couldn't quite explain.

"But she and Cody are planning on being back by Thanksgiving." Rose's tone was reassuring as she leaned across the table with a smile so shy and sweet, April found herself returning it with an encouraging grin of her own.

But alarm bells were going off in her head at the words. Thanksgiving. That was weeks away. They didn't actually think April was going to stick around that long, did they?

She glanced over at Boone. How much had he told them about their deal?

There was no time to ask because the sisters and their husbands were all talking over each other, the familiarity and connection so unfamiliar but so…wholesome. So *nice*.

It would've been like being part of some Norman Rockwell scene…

If she actually belonged here.

But she didn't. And she felt that fact more and more keenly as the last dish was set down for dinner and Nash said grace.

She tried to pray along with him, but her attention was all over the place. At one point, her mind snagged on the dishware, of all things. The china they were using, it'd been her mom's. It'd been passed down, a part of the family.

It somehow felt utterly absurd that these dishes were now a part of this family.

"…what do you think, April?" Lizzy asked from the end of the table.

April blinked in surprise and then blinked again when she realized everyone was staring at her.

"Um, sorry, I just…I was just…looking at the dishes," she finished lamely.

"These were here when we moved in." Emma looked worried. Hesitant.

Crap, now everyone was silent and staring at her expectantly.

"Is it okay that we're using them?" Emma asked.

"Oh, yeah, it's fine." April rushed out the words.

Ugh, why had she brought up the dishes, of all things? But now everyone was waiting for her to explain, and she felt Boone shift beside her, ready to swoop into action.

"They were my mom's," she said quickly, not thinking it through. "They, um…they were passed down."

Emma's brows drew together, and April caught Dahlia and Lizzy exchanging some sort of silent communication.

"If you'd rather we don't use them," Lizzy hedged, "we totally understand."

"No, no, I…" April's cheeks burned. "I didn't mean that."

Even the kids had grown quiet, as if they, too, were waiting to find out what exactly she *had* meant.

April cleared her throat. "I'm sorry. I'm being weird—"

"You're not," Boone said quickly before anyone could respond. "Coming back here would have been difficult no matter what. And given the current circumstances…"

"Anyone would be overwhelmed right now," Dahlia finished.

She said it so definitively and with such authority that April felt her tension ease a little.

She reached for her water glass and took a long gulp, gathering her thoughts. "I guess it just got me thinking, that's all. About how my mom would feel if she were here. How she'd act, what she'd say…"

Boone's hand found hers and covered it.

"I wish we could have met your mom," Rose murmured.

The sentiment was so heartfelt and sweet, it made April's throat grow thick.

"Yeah, she would've loved that too," April admitted. The truth of it hit her in the gut.

Her mom had known about the sisters—her grandparents had told her as much. And one thing April knew for certain was that her mother would have welcomed them into this home with open arms…if Frank had let her.

"She loved to entertain." April's gaze darted to Nash. "But…" She cleared her throat, nearly choking as she admitted, "Dad…Frank…was more of an introvert. He liked it just being us, and Mom understood that about him."

It was an awkward thing to say, and she could tell the people who remembered Frank knew he was kind of odd and probably didn't see the version of the man she'd seen within these walls. He liked to keep to himself, and when he left the ranch, he wore a reserved, quiet persona that April had never understood.

Maybe now she did.

The man with all the secrets. How had she never figured it out?

Nash shared a look with Levi, whose lips twitched with a knowing grin as he obviously remembered some dealing with the mysterious Frank O'Sullivan.

"So, your mom liked to cook, huh?" Kit asked, obviously trying to salvage the conversation.

A relieved smile tugged at her lips. "She loved it."

She glanced across the table at Emma, who still wore a look of wariness like she'd just been caught overstepping. "She'd be really happy to know that her things are not only still here in the home she loved, but that they're being put to good use."

Emma's answering smile was a little wobbly and then she was brushing at her eyes, muttering something about stupid pregnancy hormones.

Lizzy laughed, then changed the topic, regaling them all with a funny story about her afternoon at the store where she worked in downtown Aspire. Then Kit chimed in, prodding his twins to show their aunts and uncles the cards they'd made to send to Uncle Cody in Venezuela.

"The twins are really close with Cody," Lizzy explained to April. "They miss him, but Cody is great about video-calling whenever he can."

"And luckily they'll be visiting soon," Kit added. "Otherwise, I'm not sure I could keep my kids or my parents from booking the next flight to Venezuela just to give him a hug."

"I know they're hoping to make it for Thanksgiving." Rose smiled. "But I really hope they'll be able to stay for the wedding."

"Wedding?" April asked.

And that one word, April soon discovered, was enough to set the whole table talking.

CHAPTER 22

Boone's grip on his glass was so painful, he thought it might break in two.

No one but JJ seemed to notice Boone's tension. When he looked across the table, the burly mountain man was eyeing him with curiosity and a question in his eyes. When he arched a brow, he could practically hear his friend asking, *You all right, brother?*

Boone bobbed his head. He was fine. It was April he was worried about.

He loved every single person at this table, but right now he wished they'd all clear out.

His girl needed space. Couldn't they see that?

She's not your *anything.*

But whether she was his or not, she was clearly reeling. This, all of this...it was too much to ask of anyone. She should have time alone in this house to process the memories of her parents, to get some semblance of closure with their passing.

She should have some space to wrap her head around

all that had changed this past year and figure out where she fit into it.

But instead, she was sitting in silence beside him, seeming to shrink into herself further and further while her sisters chattered happily about wedding plans.

"I always thought I'd have a spring affair," Daisy said with a cheerful, oblivious grin. "But then we found this amazing place in Paradise Springs that's doing a special newly opened rate for us, and I let Rose talk me into a winter wedding. It's going to be amazing!"

Daisy's voice ended on a squeal as she shared a grin with Rose, who smiled back shyly. To April, Rose explained, "We're doing a double wedding, which I never thought I wanted, but it's just come together so perfectly, and I'm so excited to be getting married beside you, sis."

"Me too!"

"A double-wedding dream come true," Dahlia intoned in a dry voice that made Lizzy burst out laughing.

Dahlia's eyes sparkled with amusement, despite her cynical tone.

"A dream come true unless you're helping to plan this affair," Emma added with a laugh.

"Try being the gown designer to not one but two bridezillas." Lizzy bulged her eyes.

Rose giggled at the teasing, and Daisy wadded up a napkin and threw it at Lizzy. "Take it back. We are the easiest brides in the world."

"Of course you are." Dahlia followed this with a cough that covered the word "Bridezilla."

Lizzy laughed even harder until Kit murmured, "Takes a bridezilla to know one," which sent Emma and Nash into a fit of laughter as Lizzy pretended to glower at her husband.

"Hey, I might've been a bridezilla when we met, but we eloped, if you'll recall."

"I loved your wedding, Mama," Chloe said. "I want to evoke just like you did."

Even April smiled at the little girl's mispronunciation. But he didn't miss the way the life seemed to be draining out of her.

The others probably didn't realize how their bickering banter might make an outsider feel like…

Well, like they were on the outside looking in.

Sure enough, when the laughter faded, April pointed between Daisy and Rose, confusion clear in her expression.

"Did you guys…grow up together?"

Dahlia looked a little surprised, but she quickly leapt in. "Oh, sorry. We've done a terrible job of catching you up, haven't we?"

"No, it's okay. I mean…" She glanced over at Boone, and man, he took one look at the beauty sitting beside him and was overcome by the urge to scoop her out of that chair and into his arms so he could carry her away somewhere safe and quiet.

April smiled at him, but it didn't quite reach her eyes. "Boone filled me in some, but I guess I lost track of the family tree a bit."

Dahlia nodded. "Of course. It's confusing, for sure." She took a deep breath and then launched into a recap of how Frank had first gotten his high school sweetheart pregnant with Sierra and then left her. Then the story went on to explain how she and Daisy were twins, and they shared the same mother as Rose, and how Emma and Lizzy had been raised together in Chicago.

Throughout it all, the other sisters kept interjecting,

teasing each other and laughing about who was stuck with the most difficult sister.

It would've had Boone in stitches if he hadn't been watching April instead.

And he *was* watching, so he caught each and every flinch and wince as the sisters spoke.

He couldn't begin to guess what she was thinking, but it was clear this little "get to know the O'Sullivans" conversation wasn't making her feel any more welcome or comfortable.

"And then he met your mother," Dahlia finished. "They had you, and..." She gave April a wry little smile. "Well, I guess you know the rest better than us, huh?"

April didn't say anything.

Boone shifted, ready to intervene, but then Emma slid her chair back as well. "Since you're here now, we thought maybe you'd want to read Frank's journal. The last entry is particularly..." Her voice trailed off, and she shook her head with a watery smile.

She got up and reached for something on the counter. Boone's stomach dipped with dread, but he supposed that was nothing compared to whatever April must be feeling. Whatever was bringing that haunted look to her eyes and the pallor to her cheeks.

"I think maybe if you hear his last words, you'll see why it was so important to us that we find you and bring you back here," Emma continued gently.

April's hands gripped the edge of her seat as Emma started reading. Her face was blank, like she wasn't hearing a word, until Emma said her name. She flinched, her eyes jerking across the table to stare at the book in her sister's hands.

"My sweet April found out in the worst way possible,

186

and now I've lost her as well. I should have told her the truth from the start. I've let her down. I've let all my girls down. What I wouldn't give to tell them how sorry I am. There are no words to express the depth of my regret, and I wish there was more I could do to make amends." Emma drew in a shaky breath, blinking back obvious tears as she kept reading. "The ranch is my home. *Their* home. I'd give anything to see all seven of my daughters together. To tell them how sorry I am. To tell them how they lived in my heart even though I wasn't man enough to be there for them."

April trembled beside him, and all Boone could do was wrap an arm around her shoulders as Emma continued.

"The ranch is all I have to give, but it's not enough. I've spent too many years ignoring the call of my heart, but I have nothing left and nothing to stop me. No matter how long it takes, I will bring my family home."

"Stop," April whispered, her voice choked with tears.

Boone tightened his grip on her, casting a stern look at her sisters. "Give her time, people."

"No, it's just…" April gave him a look that was somewhere between grateful and pleading.

"I'm sorry." Emma's voice hitched, and a few tears slipped from her eyes. Nash jumped up, grabbing a couple tissues and pressing them into her hand. She mopped her face and sniffed. "I know it's a lot.

"It is," April admitted.

Boone's heart ached when he saw April lose the battle with her own tears. They slid down her cheeks unchecked as he pulled her close to his side. "Hey, it's okay. I got you."

He felt her nod against his chest.

Everyone was staring. All of the sisters had tears in

their eyes, and the kids looked scared and wary. Boone shot JJ a pleading look, and he leapt into action. "Hey, who wants to watch Uncle Kit make a fool of himself playing charades?"

Every kid at the table jumped up, eager to escape the grown-up drama, while Kit threw JJ a droll grin and stood as well.

"We'll give you ladies some space," Nash murmured, his gaze darting with concern between his wife and April before he crept out of the room.

Dex took Kiara from the baby seat. "We'll take a little walk, won't we, pumpkin?"

The baby cooed in response.

Levi squeezed Daisy's hand, then came over to pat April's head before following the others out.

Daisy gave Boone a pointed look, but it was softened by a teasing smile. "I take it you're not leaving her side."

"No, ma'am," he said.

Lizzy grinned with approval, and Rose shot him a grateful smile.

April sniffed, and the other sisters looked at each other in silent conversation.

Rose surprised everyone by being the first to break the silence. She leaned forward. "I can't imagine how hard this is for you, April. I never really met Frank. He left before…" Her voice trailed off, and she shook her head. "I always thought he must have been this heartless man. But it seemed he had regrets—"

"He wasn't heartless." April shook her head. "He was good and kind and…"

"He left us." Lizzy frowned. "He left us all."

"I know," April whispered, and Boone's heart broke for

her. Rose was right—he wasn't sure any of them could imagine what she was feeling.

And these ladies didn't even know the half of it.

"I don't know why he left," April murmured.

"We know that, sweetie." Emma gave her a watery smile.

Dahlia was watching on with clear concern. "We didn't expect you to come back here and make explanations on his behalf."

April nodded. "I know, but…but I wish I could, you know?"

Emma leaned across the table. "No matter what Frank did before you were born, we're glad he stayed with you and your mom."

Daisy nodded. "I believe everything happens for a reason. We might not know God's plan…or understand our father's heart, for that matter. But I, for one, am grateful that Frank gave me all of you." She spread her arms wide with a meaningful smile.

Emma started sniffling. "That was really sweet, Dais."

"Ah, honey," Dahlia leaned over to pat Emma's hand. "You really are pregnant, aren't you?"

This had all the sisters but April chuckling softly—a much-needed break in the emotional storm that had swept into this kitchen with talk of Frank.

April wasn't distracted, though. If anything, her features were tight with pain and frustration. "I know how he must seem to you all. And I wish I understood it. I wish he'd told me about you so I could have asked him why he'd done it. Why he'd left. And then…then why he'd stayed."

"Because he loved you," Lizzy said simply.

April sniffed with a choked sob. Her lips were quivering, and it seemed to Boone she was using all her might to keep from falling apart.

"You know, our mom used to say that Frank was a restless soul," Emma murmured. "That he was to be pitied because he'd had a rough childhood and hadn't known how to love or be loved or…or take care of others."

"But he took care of me." April tapped her chest. "He never left my mom or me. And he was there, day in and day out, even when she got sick."

"Like I said," Lizzy chimed in softly. "Because he loved you. Both of you."

April shook her head. "What made us different?"

All the others exchanged looks.

"I think that's probably what we've all been wondering," Dahlia murmured.

"My guess?" Rose said. "He didn't know what love was until he met your mother."

Emma nodded. "That's what he alludes to in his journal. He says more than once how grateful he is that he finally found a home with your mom, and you, and…" She glanced around meaningfully. "And all this."

"He did love my mom. He loved her so much." April swallowed. "He was heartbroken when she died. And I…I just…I…"

April started crying in earnest then, gut-wrenching sobs that had Boone's heart breaking as he tugged her into his arms again.

He leaned over her, trying to swallow her whole. Wishing he could swallow her pain at the same time. "I've got you," he said in her ear. "You're safe, April. I've got you."

CHAPTER 23

"*Y*ou're safe. I've got you."

Boone had said these words to her several times now, and every time it felt truer than the last.

She reveled in the feel of his arms around her now, burrowing into him like he was her safe place. Like he was...

Home.

She squeezed her eyes shut against the crazy thought. Boone was her friend, that was all. Her friend, and right now...her ally.

Straightening slowly, she tried to get a grip.

Her gaze fixed on the china pattern she knew like the back of her hand as she tried to put into words some of the confusing mix of feelings. "I miss him so much." She licked a tear off the edge of her mouth. "Every day. And my mom, of course, but my dad..." She paused, her breath catching as she looked up and forced herself to gaze at each sister in turn. "*Your* dad. His passing was so unexpected. I think...I knew for a while that my mom was dying. So by the time she passed, we'd already grieved a bit, you know?"

She looked back down. No, they couldn't know.

Boone slid his hand into her lap to catch her trembling fingers in his large grip, and she latched onto him, using it like an anchor as she sorted through feelings that threatened to carry her away.

She'd been feeling lost at sea for more than a year now, and being back at this ranch amplified the feeling a millionfold.

But Boone was here.

"I got you."

"You're still grieving for your dad," Daisy said gently. "We all understand that."

Frustration rose in her. They didn't understand. How could they? "I miss him, but I'm also so angry with him."

"Because he never told you about us?" Lizzy guessed.

April pinched her lips together before finally saying, "That's part of it."

She watched the others exchanging looks that seemed to say so much without speaking a word. And just like earlier, when they were all teasing and joking while talking about who they grew up with and how they'd found out about each other…

April felt alone.

More alone than when she'd shown up in Portland not knowing a soul. Because for the first time, she understood that these women might not have had Frank, but they'd always had each other.

And they wanted to welcome her into that connection, which was so kind. So generous, but…

"You should resent me," she said.

Though who she was even saying it to, she couldn't

say. It just needed to be said. She'd tried to put herself in their shoes ever since Boone had referred to her as "the one Frank stayed for," and it made her stomach turn to see herself like that. What made her so special?

"No one resents you, April." Emma's eyes were filled with genuine confusion, as if the idea had never even occurred to her. Was Emma really that kind? So good-hearted that she couldn't even fathom resenting a long-lost sister for having a relationship with her father?

But would she still feel that way when she learned the truth?

And she *would* learn the truth, because April had to tell them.

But under their kind, searching, worried glances, the words wouldn't come.

How was she supposed to tell them?

She couldn't do it.

I have to get out of here.

April stood abruptly, accidentally knocking aside Boone's arm from around her shoulders in the process. *Dang it, Dad. Why did you leave me in this position?*

Better question…

Why'd you have to leave me at all?

But it wasn't his fault he'd left her. It was hers.

The thought was too much on top of everything else. The urge to bolt, to run, to flee this place and never look back overwhelmed her.

It had her scraping the chair across the floor to escape, but she didn't get far. Dahlia had come around the side of the table and planted herself in front of April, enveloping her in a hug before April could so much as balk.

She stiffened at first, but Dahlia's hug was fierce, and

her voice was surprisingly warm and gentle. "It's okay, April. It's okay."

It took a minute, but April finally wound her arms around Dahlia, tears surging up all over again at the older woman's kindness.

Daisy, Rose, Lizzy, and Emma had all come to stand and were crowding in behind Dahlia, smiling gently at April over Dahlia's shoulder.

"We've all made peace with our past. With Frank," Rose said. "I think I can speak for all of us when I say we've forgiven him. And we don't resent you."

"Not one bit," Emma added eagerly.

"They're right, hon," Daisy said. Even with tears in her eyes, she had this luminescent smile, and her eyes twinkled like she was just waiting to laugh. "We're so happy that Frank found the love of his life. That he had Loretta and that he had you."

Lizzy reached out to touch her hand. "We're so sad he lost her—that you both lost her—but I'm so grateful you got to have him as a dad."

April couldn't take it anymore. Her heart felt like it was breaking in two. So much kindness, and such an inviting welcome.

And here, of all places. The one place she'd thought of as home in her life.

After more than a year of no one aside from some check-ins with grandparents who'd betrayed her just as surely as her parents. And friends who barely knew her because she hadn't wanted to let anyone in.

And now this?

Now they were just…welcoming her into their club with open arms?

It was too much.

It was wrong.

And they'd realize that just as soon as she mustered up the courage to tell them the truth.

She didn't even know she was shaking her head and pushing Dahlia away until all of the sisters' smiles began to slip, concern replacing their gracious compassion.

"April." Boone started to reach for her, but she pushed him away too.

She backed up until she was getting close to the stove where her mother had spent so much of her day.

Her laughter was still here if April listened hard enough. Frank's voice calling for his little girl to come give him a hug just before he swept her off her feet in a crushing embrace.

It was all here.

And it was all a lie.

"I can't," she sputtered, her gaze frantic as she turned it on one sister after another, finally landing on Boone with his warm smile.

"It's okay," he said. "We don't have to do this now."

She knew what he meant. He thought she wanted to escape the conversation to come. To procrastinate. To avoid the truth.

But that's what she'd been doing for the past year.

She'd been running from the truth. And all it had done was bring her more pain.

"April?" Emma's voice was tentative and soothing, like she was talking to a spooked animal. "What do you need, sweetheart?"

Her breathing was coming too quick and shallow. Distantly, she was aware of Boone's demeanor changing. He inched closer to her, his gaze growing intense. "April…"

"I can't do this, Boone. I can't be here."

Now every one of them was frowning at her. Concern, hurt, fear—she saw it all.

Her mouth went dry, and her palms started to sweat. She wanted to back away, but there was nowhere left to run.

Dahlia moved forward. "April." She said her name with calm assertion. "I swear, no one brought you here to make you feel bad that your dad—"

"He's not my dad!" The words came out in a burst, too loud by far.

Dahlia jerked back like she'd been struck. Emma gasped. April couldn't bring herself to look at the others. Instead, she tipped her head back, her gaze fixed on the molding her mom had been so fond of. "He's not my dad," she said again, this time softer.

But even though her tone was quiet, the words scraped her throat, making her feel like she'd swallowed glass.

"April, I don't understand," Lizzy started.

April shook her head. She couldn't see anything for the tears swimming there, clouding her vision. "Frank O'Sullivan is not my father. He pretended to be, but he's not. I'm not one of you. I'm not your sister." She threw her hands up. "I don't even look like any of you, because we are not related in any way."

"But—"

"April—"

"Hon, please—"

But she didn't stop to hear what any of them had to say.

She'd done it.

She'd spoken the truth.

And now all that was left was to run.

CHAPTER 24

Boone wanted nothing more than to sprint after her, but the moment he moved, a hand settled on his arm.

Rose frowned up at him, shaking her head with a quiet "Give her a minute."

He hesitated, but after seeing the way April had grown so spooked, backed into a corner, literally and metaphorically…

He sighed with resignation. "Fine. But only *one* minute."

That was all he could do.

Even that was killing him. He found himself staring at the door where she'd disappeared, worry eating at his insides, and anger right behind it.

"I don't understand," Emma said slowly. "The will and paperwork didn't say anything about her not being Frank's daughter."

"She's adopted," Boone filled in the gaps. "So, technically, she *is* his daughter."

Daisy winced. "I wonder how she found out. Her reaction just now doesn't bode well. Has she known her whole life, or was it just sprung on her?"

"How did we not know this?" Dahlia rubbed her forehead.

Boone ran a hand over his face, a sigh of impatience escaping. "Maybe she would've explained everything if you all hadn't ganged up on her like that."

He regretted the harsh words instantly, especially when he took in the stricken faces staring back at him.

Who was he to be lecturing them on how to deal with their crazy family drama?

No one. He was just the guy who'd been sent to fetch April.

"Sorry," he muttered. "I shouldn't have—"

"No," Dahlia interrupted. "You're right."

Emma nodded. "We knew coming back here would be hard for her."

"We were just so excited to meet her," Lizzy said. "But we should have given her space."

Rose nibbled on her lip. "I hope we haven't driven her away."

"She's an O'Sullivan." Daisy threw an arm around Rose's shoulders. "She doesn't scare that easy. Right?"

Boone's lips twitched with rueful mirth despite his irritation.

"She's an O'Sullivan."

He wished April had been there to hear that.

Lizzy studied Boone. "So you knew, then."

He dipped his chin. "It wasn't my place to say anything."

"No, of course not," Lizzy agreed. "I just meant…" She shrugged, a smile tugging at her lips. "You knew…"

"Which means she trusts you," Emma finished for her.

Boone's shoulder hitched because he wasn't sure how to respond to that. Also because his chest had grown so tight so quickly that he hadn't been able to speak.

She trusted him.

And there it was again. That humbling sensation that made his heart swell and his shoulders go back. April O'Sullivan trusted him. And he'd be damned if he let her down.

"Do you know when she found out?" Dahlia asked.

"At the same time she learned about you guys," he said.

All five of the sisters stared at him in horror.

"Exactly," he murmured.

"And then her dad died before he had a chance to explain?" Rose whispered, her eyes welling with tears on April's behalf.

"I think so, yeah."

"That poor girl." Daisy rested a hand on her chest, her eyes glistening with unshed tears.

Dahlia's brows had drawn down, and she was staring at the door, lost in thought.

For a second, Boone feared that she meant to go after April, but then she turned to him with a determined set to her chin. "Boone, you should go make sure she's okay."

That was all he needed. Rushing toward the door, he shoved his boots on and disappeared outside before anyone else could get a word in edgewise.

Boone didn't have to look hard to find her. The herding dogs greeted him enthusiastically, and even if they didn't start leading him toward the stables, he would've known she was there from the light that glowed beneath the door.

He found her leaning against the edge of one of the stalls, rubbing the nose of his favorite mare.

She didn't look over when he came in, but he saw her tense before letting out a long, weary exhale. She kept her gaze on the mare as he came to lean against the stable door beside her. "Coming here was a really big mistake."

Don't say that.

He kept his mouth shut, his heart aching.

Moonlight seeped in through the windows above them, soaking her in a pale glow.

She looked beautiful in spite of her haunted sadness.

"You know, this used to be my favorite place in the whole world." Her voice was soft and sweet, like she was soothing the mare in front of her.

"You were into horses?"

She smiled, and his heart gave a hard thump of relief. This girl's smile was perfection itself.

"I wasn't as into them as some girls in our class." She shot him a sidelong glance. "Remember Becky Holden?"

He let out a surprised chuckle at the memory. "She was obsessed."

"What ever happened to her?"

"She went pro." He shrugged.

"Really?" Her brows shot up. "Cool."

He nodded, giving her time. He suspected that was what she really needed. Time and space. Talking about their childhood classmates and her upbringing here on the ranch…it was a distraction, but maybe that was exactly what would help her right now.

He settled in beside her, reaching out to pat the mare's neck, earning himself a snuffling sound in response.

"So, you weren't a big rider," he said.

She lifted a shoulder. "I liked to ride okay, but I wasn't daredevil enough to get into jumping or racing, you know?"

He nodded. "Yeah, I used to go out to Uncle Patrick's just to ride. But I was the same. I just liked the freedom of speeding across the land."

"Yeah, exactly." She grinned. "Freedom is the perfect word for it. Frank…" She hesitated. "My dad…would always find me out here. He'd have to force me back home to clean up for dinner. Or to do homework."

She gave him a cute little smile.

"No wonder you always got straight A's," he said.

"Yeah, my dad was very diligent about making sure I got my homework done. My mom, too, but he was the one who had all these big college plans for me."

There was a long silence.

"He still thought I'd go back to school eventually. He understood that I needed some time after Mom died, but it didn't take long for him to start nagging me to look at college brochures even though the rest of the kids I'd graduated with were already well on their way to earning degrees."

Boone smiled. "Trust me. I understand that better than anyone."

"Yeah, I guess we're the same like that, huh?" She laughed. "The difference is you knew exactly what you wanted to do and had a job ready and waiting."

"Sounds like you're getting there," he said. "You've figured out what you love, and that's a start."

She nodded. "I'd meant to talk to my dad about culinary school, but…"

But then it was too late.

He took a deep breath, wishing like heck that the pain he felt on her behalf actually did something to alleviate her heartache. But he supposed it didn't work like that.

"So now I wonder…would he be proud of me now?"

Her voice grew so quiet, he wasn't sure she was even talking to him anymore. "And then I wonder if I even care, you know?"

She shot him a look, and he nodded.

"Yeah, I get that. I mean, it's gotta be confusing to miss someone and love someone, but also have so much anger toward them that you can't express."

She nodded, her eyes gleaming with unshed tears in the moonlight. "It's the same with my mom, just not to the same extent. I'm mad at them both, and I don't want to be. But I can't just let it go either."

"Family can be messy," he murmured. "That's what my mom used to say whenever us kids got into a fight, or my dad had issues with his siblings."

"I don't know that *messy* is a strong enough word for my family." Her tone was filled with a bitter humor, and they shared a rueful smile.

"Maybe not, but the sentiment is the same. You can love someone with all your heart and still want to strangle them. You can *be* loved by someone and still be mistreated by them."

April turned to rest her back against the stable door, laughing softly as the mare nuzzled her hair. "Do you think that's on purpose?"

"How so?"

She glanced up toward the windows. "I don't know. My mom was like Daisy. She always thought everything happened for a reason, and it was always part of God's plan."

"You don't believe that?" he asked.

She shrugged. "I want to. Maybe."

"Well…" He leaned over and nudged her shoulder with his. "That's a good start."

She smiled. "I guess."

They stayed there for a while in companionable silence.

"Thanks for coming out here," she whispered. "I wanted to be alone, but also…I didn't want to be alone." She wrinkled her nose. "Makes sense, right?"

He laughed. "Perfect sense."

She pushed away from the stall. "Want to go for a walk?"

"I thought you'd never ask."

He let her lead the way out of the stable and into the moonlight. They walked side by side for a while, and when she shivered, he wrapped an arm around her and tugged her close. "Want me to go back inside and grab your coat?"

She shook her head. "No, I…I need to face the music eventually, but not yet. And if you don't mind…I'd like your company."

"I told you, I'm not going anywhere." His voice was low and gruff, and before he could stop himself, he kissed the top of her head.

"Thanks, Boone." She tipped her head back to meet his gaze. "So…how'd it go after I left?"

He smiled. "If you're secretly hoping they're gonna send you away so you don't have to deal with them anymore, you are sorely underestimating how much these women want you in their lives."

Her eyes widened a bit, and he realized with a start that she truly had believed that.

He stopped short to face her. They'd wandered aimlessly up a hillside together, and now they stood perched on top, overlooking the ranch house and stable, only the moon and stars providing any light.

"April, I don't want to speak on their behalf," he

started slowly. "But as far as they're concerned, you're still Frank's daughter. Which means you're still their sister." When she didn't respond, her gaze distant and haunted, he leaned down to meet her stare. "Which means this place is your home."

Her face screwed up with emotion, and he caught a hint of that emotion again. Guilt and shame and...what was she not telling him? What secrets was this girl still holding on to?

"It's not my home, Boone. Not anymore."

"You sure about that?" He tried to keep his tone even. Unaffected. He tried to tell himself that it didn't matter if she chose to stay or leave.

He wasn't sure he fooled either of them.

But this isn't about you, Boone reminded himself. *It's about what's best for April.*

He tried to set aside his own desires, and this aching need to keep her close. His mind caught on the memory of how she'd looked when he'd first found her in the stables.

There'd been a serenity about her that he hadn't seen before.

"I know you probably don't want to hear this, but I think a part of you still loves this place," he said. "It owns a piece of your soul, whether you like it or not."

She turned to face him with a frown.

"Look, I know you're set on leaving, but I don't think you should rush it. Stay for a while. Hang out. Maybe being here will help you find some closure. Or...maybe not."

She arched a brow, her lips twitching at his honesty.

"I can't say for certain that being here will help you to solve every dilemma, but I do know that running away isn't the answer. I know that the sort of issues you're facing can't be outrun. And if you stay…"

Her eyes were wide with surprise, no doubt because his tone had grown urgent. Passionate. He swallowed hard trying to find his cool.

"If you stay, I'll be by your side every step of the way," he promised. "And while I know your sisters are overwhelming, they'll support whatever you decide. And you might just find…"

He paused. Was he going too far? Was he overstepping?

She reached for his hand. "What is it?"

"You might just find that they can help to ease some of your pain."

She gave him a dubious look that spoke volumes.

"I know they haven't experienced the same loss. It's not the same. At all. But they've each had to find peace with Frank and with what this ranch means to them."

She looked away, but her gaze looked thoughtful.

"All I'm saying is…I think you owe it to yourself to stay. For a little while, at least. Give yourself a chance to say goodbye, and then when you do go, you'll have no regrets."

She let out a shaky breath, and he couldn't hold out any longer. The need to touch her and hold her…it was primal and fierce.

In that moment, he was overcome by the knowledge that she was his to protect. His to care for.

For now, at least.

He stepped into her space, lightly brushing his fingers over her face, savoring the feel of her soft skin and her delicate features.

So fragile and yet so strong to have survived all that

she had. Her breath caught at his touch. But then she looked up at him, her eyes sparkling. "No regrets, huh?"

"That's right."

Her lips curved into a hint of a smile, and Boone...

Boone forgot how to breathe. He forgot how to do anything but stare in awe at the beauty before him.

She went up on her tiptoes, and before he realized what she was doing, she lightly pressed her lips to his.

His heart gave an enthusiastic kick to his ribs as surprise and desire flooded him.

Her lips were soft and warm, and she pulled away far too soon.

He stared down at her in wonder, and when he met her gaze, he saw all the surprise that he felt.

He grinned, stifling a laugh. She'd shocked herself, it seemed, and for some reason, that delighted him beyond measure. He reached out, snagging her by the waist and tugging her closer. "I'm hoping you don't regret that."

"No," she whispered, her lips curving up in a smile that stole his heart. "I don't know why I did it, but I don't regret it."

"Good." He nodded, his gaze raking over her, taking in every tearstain and every beautiful line and curve of her features. "That's real good."

And then he dipped his head, claiming her lips with his. Unlike her chaste peck, he let himself savor the taste of her, molding their lips together as she melted into his arms.

No regrets, he'd promised her. And as he tilted his head to deepen the kiss, that was a vow he meant to keep.

He'd do right by this woman. He'd help her in any way he could.

And if she still wanted to leave, then he'd watch her walk away with no regrets.

But right here, right now...all that mattered was showing this woman how perfect she was. How sweet and how beautiful and how infinitely lovable.

He tried to show her all of that in a kiss that left them both breathless.

CHAPTER 25

April found herself staring at her bedroom's bright purple walls on Monday morning, her phone clutched to her ear as her manager, Sheila, chatted away about what she'd missed these past few days.

"And you're, uh…you're sure you don't mind me extending my visit to Montana?" April asked when her friend came up for air.

"Hon, from the sounds of it, you've got a lot of family drama to sort out."

April gave a little snort of amusement. Sheila didn't know the half of it. She'd told her manager some of the story, confiding in her about her father's recent death and the inheritance.

She'd left out big chunks, but apparently what she'd told her was enough.

"Thanks, Sheila. I appreciate it."

"You take all the time you need, kiddo."

A little while later, they hung up, and April summoned up her nerve to leave her old bedroom.

She wasn't sure how long she'd be here, but she

really had to start getting used to walking around this house. It wasn't like she could hole up in this room forever…

Especially since the bright walls were giving her a headache.

The thought made her laugh, and she was still smiling when she ran into Nash in the kitchen.

"Hey, April." He held up a thermos. "I was just refilling on coffee before I head back out."

"Is, uh…" April glanced around her. "Is Emma gone?"

"Yeah, she left for school already. She didn't want to wake you to say goodbye."

"I was up," April murmured. But she appreciated the consideration.

She wasn't sure exactly what Boone had said to her sisters after she left, but she'd come back to find the house nearly empty on Saturday night, and everyone had tiptoed around her like they were walking on eggshells all day yesterday.

She'd declined their offer to join them at church but had come down for their weekly post-church lunch. She'd mostly hung out with the kids as the grown-ups were so polite around her, she wasn't sure how to relax.

They were nice, but like…too nice. When she'd said that to Boone, he'd cracked up. "Oh no, not too nice," he'd teased.

He'd spent the better part of the day glued to her side, but when she'd realized he was planning on skipping Sunday dinner with his own family just to babysit her, she insisted that he go.

"Come with me," he'd said.

She'd hesitated but, in the end, had said no. She had no idea what was going on between her and Boone, but she wasn't about to add any more complications into her life by going home to meet his family.

This morning, however, she found herself annoyingly antsy to see him.

"I just saw Boone at the stables, if you want to go say hi," Nash said.

She turned to him in surprise, heat creeping into her cheeks. Was she that obvious?

But Nash wasn't smirking or anything as he passed her on her way out. "You know, if you ever want to get reacquainted with the property or hear about the changes we're working on..." He hesitated, his grin sheepish. "Sorry. We all promised Boone we'd give you space. I didn't mean to push the issue. I just thought—"

"No, it's a kind offer." She hurried to reassure him, ignoring the flutter in her belly at finally having her suspicions confirmed. "I appreciate it. And...I think I would like that. At some point."

He dipped his head, holding his thermos out like he was cheersing her. "Just say the word. No matter what happens, this place will always be your home."

She stared after him in surprise.

His assurance seemed to come so easily. Like it was understood. Her heart swelled with gratitude.

There was still so much she had to tell her sisters, and Nash, and Boone. About the car crash, and her part in it— her insides revolted at the thought of talking about that. But she did need to tell them about her hunt for her real father.

She hadn't forgotten, and focusing on that task seemed so much easier than dealing with her sisters and her father's legacy. Granted, she still had no idea where to start looking next...

Following Nash's lead, April poured herself some coffee and headed outside. Her heart did a little leap when she spotted Boone heading her way.

His face lit with a grin that was so sexy it ought to be outlawed.

"Morning, beautiful," he drawled.

"Morning."

"How'd you do last night?" His tone was casual, but there was genuine concern in his eyes that made her 100 percent certain that if he ever had kids, Boone would be the most doting dad anyone could ever imagine.

And just like that, her mind's eye filled with an image of Boone beside her, holding a baby in his arms with that smile of his aimed at her and…

Oh my word.

She blinked rapidly. What on earth was she thinking about that for?

"Oh, um…" She glanced away.

"April?" His smiled faded. "You okay?"

"Yes. Totally. I'm good. I'm great." And she was over-selling it. Obviously.

His eyes lit with amusement as he studied her. "Okay then."

"My night was fine," she continued quickly. "Kinda chill, actually. Emma seemed tired after hosting everyone for lunch, so Nash grilled some steaks, and Dahlia put on a movie, and…it was fine." She bit her lip, remembering how she'd laughed when Dahlia had shot her a funny smirk when JJ fell asleep and started snoring in the corner as Emma battled a yawn of her own.

"It was nice," she amended. "It was far less awkward without everyone all together at the same time."

"I can imagine," he said. "Do you have any plans for today?"

"Not yet."

"Well, if you're up for revisiting some of your old haunts in town…" He hesitated, and she felt a surge of appreciation for this guy who was so incredibly concerned with her comfort.

"I think I could handle that," she teased.

He grinned. "Cool. JJ and I have to drive in to pick up some supplies, so I thought, if you wanted a ride…"

She perked up, the idea of getting a break from the ranch making her down the rest of her coffee. "Let me just grab a coat."

She left him chuckling behind her, and a minute later, she was back outside. JJ waved her over to his truck. "Hey there, littlest O'Sullivan," he said in that low, soothing voice of his.

"Hi, JJ."

Boone came along right after, and he gave her a boost into the truck, helping her get situated in the middle seat between them.

She'd never felt smaller than she did crammed in between these two big, burly men, and she squirmed to get a better view.

"We need to get you one of those booster seats," Boone teased.

She smacked his arm as JJ chuckled.

The drive into town was deliciously relaxed. Out of everyone at the ranch, Boone and JJ were by far the easiest for her to be around. Boone because…well, because he was Boone. And JJ because he seemed so laid-back, and there was never any pressure to fill the silence or answer questions.

He was good with silence...and, it turned out, listening to Boone and April laugh and bicker as they flipped between radio stations trying to find one they could agree on.

Boone helped her out after JJ parked on Main Street and they both waited for her to drink it all in.

"What do you think?" Boone asked as her gaze ran up and down the familiar row of storefronts.

Her lips twitched as a million memories surfaced, along with a slew of emotions...but a sweet nostalgia won out. "I think it looks exactly the same as I remember."

Boone smiled and shocked her by taking her hand in his. He didn't seem to care what JJ would think. And to be fair, JJ didn't even seem to notice. "I'm gonna head to the feed store." He sauntered away.

Boone pulled her to a stop. "I've got to go grab some things too. Do you want to come?"

"Actually, I was thinking I'd pop into the library. Use their Wi-Fi and do a little digging into David Taylor. Again."

She added the last word with a sarcastic tone that made Boone smile. "I told you I'd help. And once we talk to your sisters about it, I'm sure they'll be eager to help too."

She smiled back, mostly because her mind was still focused on his use of "we."

It was so nice to be a part of a "we" after so many months on her own.

"I'll pick you up when I'm done?" he asked.

She nodded. "Sounds good."

He hesitated. "JJ's got a ton of personal errands to run, too, so maybe..." He cleared his throat. "Maybe we can grab lunch?"

She smiled. "Sounds like a date."

His answering smile was so smug and sexy, the butterflies in her belly went into overdrive.

"Sure does, doesn't it?" he drawled as he backed away from her. "See you soon, sunshine."

She had to press her lips together to contain a goofy grin as she spun around and headed toward the library.

It was nearly empty, which wasn't surprising for a Monday morning.

"Welcome." A pretty redhead stood behind the front desk. She looked pleasantly surprised to have a visitor. "Can I help you find anything?"

The smiley librarian looked so eager to help, April felt a little guilty admitting that she just needed to use the Wi-Fi.

"Oh. Of course." The woman sat back down. "Do you know where the study area is, or…?"

"I do. I haven't been here in a while, but I grew up going to this library. Ms. Patterson was the librarian back then."

The woman grinned. "I took over from her. I'm Ellie."

"I'm April…O'Sullivan." April paused. How had she not anticipated how awkward this would be.

"You're the youngest O'Sullivan sister?" Ellie's expression brightened even more.

April laughed. "I don't exactly look the part, do I?"

Ellie smiled. "If you're a part of that family, then I feel like we're already friends. They've all been so good to me."

April shifted from foot to foot. "Oh, you're friends with them?"

She laughed. "I've had to play referee a time or two when they've met up here for wedding planning, so I guess that puts me in the friend zone. Plus, Emma and I hit it off as soon as she arrived in town. She's a sweetheart."

"Oh, definitely," April agreed. "Although, I'm new to the scene, so I guarantee you know them better than I do."

Ellie's smile was quiet, as if Emma had been keeping her up to play with family events. But she didn't follow it up with any gossipy questions, and April decided she straight-up loved this woman when she let it drop at that.

It might've been a while since she'd been back in Aspire, but she definitely remembered the prying. And the gossip.

So much gossip.

"I don't think I remember you from when I lived here," April said. "Are you new to town?"

"Sort of. I think I arrived after you left. I remember my husband mentioning the O'Sullivans moving to Bozeman or something?"

April nodded, sadness sweeping through her, but she managed to raise a smile...until she noticed Ellie's expression.

The librarian looked suddenly lost, a forlorn sorrow sweeping over her face.

"Ellie? You okay?"

"Oh yeah, I'm okay." But her smile seemed forced. And when April gave her a pause and a prompting look, Ellie started blinking at tears. "I'm sorry. I..." She shook her head. "He wants a divorce. He filed the papers this morning, and I'm still...processing." She let out a laugh that sounded more like a sob. "I don't even know why I'm telling you this."

April's lips parted, but nothing came out. Even if this woman wasn't practically a stranger, she had no idea how one was supposed to respond to that.

"Sorry." Ellie winced. "I'm so sorry. Please forget I said that. I haven't told anyone. Not even Emma. We've been having problems for a while, and everyone around me is happily falling in love and getting married and getting pregnant." Ellie's laugh was breathless and bordering on hysterical. "And here's me, watching my marriage fall apart and not knowing how to fix it. And now I'm blubbering in front of a perfect stranger." She swipes the tears off her cheeks, letting out another awkward laugh.

"Trust me, Ellie, I understand what it's like to need to talk."

Ellie bobbed her head, her cheeks a brilliant red. "It's just so…humiliating. Shameful, I guess. How do you tell people in this place? Everyone around me always seems so together."

April sighed. "I know that feeling well. I'm dealing with some shocks myself lately, and I'm…so out of my depth. I feel like I'm drowning sometimes, you know?"

Ellie cast her a look that was almost hopeful, because maybe it meant she wasn't alone. "Yeah?"

"Yeah." April nodded. "So believe me when I say that I am here for it if you ever want to talk. Because I…I could use a listening ear too."

She didn't realize how true that was until she said it.

She was so grateful to have Boone by her side, but he knew everyone involved, and as an employee of the ranch and a friend to everyone who lived and worked there, he had to have some opinions of his own.

The idea of talking over her own dilemmas to someone who wouldn't judge or have anything at stake was definitely appealing. "So…" April fidgeted with her purse strap. "I take it the news of divorce was a surprise?"

Ellie frowned, her gaze distant as she thought that

over. "I wouldn't say a total surprise. We had our difficulties." She winced. "Okay, we have a lot of problems. But I thought we would work on them, you know? I've been trying to get him to go to counseling or talk to the minister or...I don't know...anything, really. But it's like he doesn't even want to try."

April winced in sympathy. "That's gotta be tough."

"Maybe I should've seen it coming, but it feels like talk of divorce came out of nowhere, and I guess I'm still reeling."

"That's understandable." April kept her voice as soft and even as she could.

Ellie took a deep breath and plastered a smile on her face. "Look at me, chatting your ear off and all you want to do is work. Are you sure there's nothing I can help you with?"

April opened her mouth, wanting to ask if Ellie needed to say more but also sensing the librarian was done for now and ready to pull herself together. She was mopping her face with a tissue and swallowing, forcing a bright smile.

April was ready to say she was all set and didn't need any help. But something made her pause. This woman had just shared her most private fears, and it felt almost churlish not to share something in kind.

Aside from that...this woman was a librarian. Maybe she could help her figure out where to find information on David Taylor.

"Actually," April said slowly, "I found out recently that Frank O'Sullivan is not my biological father..."

Ellie listened wide-eyed as April recapped what she'd learned and what little she'd managed to dig up. "Is there any chance you could point me in the right direction?"

Ellie's eyes gleamed with excitement. "I can do better than that. Do you know, I became a librarian because research is my specialty. Seriously, research is my jam. I can lose myself in tracking down family trees and piecing together mysteries and—" She cut herself off. "Long story short, I'd love to help you."

April grinned, a sense of something hopeful and exciting buzzing through her. She was about to tell Ellie how grateful she was when her phone dinged with a text. Glancing at her screen, she couldn't help a small laugh.

Boone: Too hungry to do any more errands. You mind bouncing early?

And then a second later.

Boone: Also...too excited for a date.

This was followed by a winky emoji that inexplicably made her blush.

"Um, it looks like I won't have much time to delve into it today," she said to Ellie.

"Let's exchange numbers and emails." Ellie gave her a confident smile. "If you email me what you've found so far and the leads you've followed, I can pick up the trail from there."

April nodded, feeling lighter than she had in months. Ellie seemed so eager and so sure of herself. Maybe there was some hope that at least one giant question about her past would be answered before long.

She grinned as she texted Boone back that she'd meet him at the diner. She was still smiling as she waved goodbye to Ellie a little while later.

It might not have been a lot of progress, but at least she was heading in the right direction.

CHAPTER 26

O ne week.

Boone glanced over at April, who was leaning out the passenger side window, soaking in the sunshine on this brisk fall day.

She'd been here one week, and he had no idea how long she planned to stay.

He had no idea about anything, really.

Like…what were they? It felt like a girly thing to obsess about, but he couldn't help but wonder.

It was the last thing she needed to be pestered about, though. He'd promised that no one in Aspire would try to pressure her—not to open up about her past, not to stick around any longer than she wanted, and not to make a decision on what she'd do with her portion of the stake in the ranch.

He'd been included in that promise, so even though he'd been enjoying the heck out of his time with her this week, he refused to ask her now what her plans were.

And if those plans included him.

He glanced over again, and this time she caught him. Her lips curved up, and her eyes sparkled with laughter.

"What are you thinking about?" she asked, her tone teasing.

Truthfully? He was thinking about kissing her again. About what it would be like to pull this truck over, tug her into his arms, and give in to temptation for a second time.

He cleared his throat and looked straight ahead. "Just wondering how long I'm gonna be your chauffeur." He gave her a little smile to let her know he was teasing.

She rolled her eyes. "I told you I'd find another ride home."

"Or you could just come hang with me at the fire station when you're done hanging out with Rose and Ellie."

She'd been meeting up regularly this week for some one-on-one time with Daisy, Rose, and Lizzy. They took his lecture on not ganging up on her to heart and had planned it out that they'd take turns spending time with her. So far, it sounded like it was going well.

The other day, April had laughed as she'd told him about her ice cream date with Lizzy, who'd had her in stitches with stories about how she and Kit had "courted."

And then there was Ellie. April had been spending a fair amount of time with the librarian this week. Which was good. It was nice to see April making a friend.

"Maybe," she said. "I still can't believe you're a volunteer firefighter. Isn't that dangerous?"

He shrugged. "Can be. But someone's got to make sure we're protected from wildfires around here."

"And it just has to be you, huh?" she teased.

He gave her a cocky smile that had her rolling her eyes

again. But she was still grinning. And that smile of hers was still everything.

It'd been so hard to keep his physical distance ever since their kiss on her first night home.

He'd nearly given in to temptation so many times this week. Like when they'd gone for a ride together and gotten caught in a light snowfall that had clung to her hair and skin, making her appear more angelic than ever.

Or when he'd sat beside her for a slightly awkward video call with her grandparents. They were practically begging her to come visit them, and he'd nearly offered to drive her there himself, but he could sense her reluctance and instead played along with the catch-up call as though it wasn't filled with tension. She'd given him so many looks of appreciation whenever he'd stepped in to fill an uncomfortable silence or smooth over her grandparents' concerns.

Every time she looked at him like that, he felt like a dang superhero.

And he loved it.

He adored being the guy she turned to for help.

Turning off the truck, he watched her reach for the door handle, but she didn't hurry to hop out.

Here they were. Trapped in close quarters in his truck's cab, and he could cut the sexual tension with a knife.

She had to feel it too. This magnetic pull that had him clenching the steering wheel to keep from reaching for her.

Because her life was complicated. She didn't know what she wanted or where she'd go next.

He understood entirely that kissing her again, taking their flirting any further than they'd already gone…

He'd only be adding to that complication, confusing her even more.

And that was the last thing he wanted. So rather than pull her toward him so he could kiss her goodbye, he settled for returning her awkward little wave.

"Call if you need me," he said as she climbed down.

She shot him an exasperated look like she did every time he said that. Which was, admittedly, too often.

"You know I can manage to be on my own for an hour or two, right? I promise I won't fall apart."

"I know you won't," he shot back. "I just like you to know that I'm here whenever you need me."

Her gaze sparkled with laughter, but it was softened with something delicate too. A tenderness that tugged at his heart and made him want to pin her down and make her stay.

Stay for me.

Stay forever.

He tore his gaze away, clearing his throat. "Good luck with the great David hunt."

She snickered at the nickname he'd given it.

He felt a pang of guilt whenever the topic came up. He hadn't done much of anything to actually help, except be there when she'd talked to Dahlia and Emma about potentially using their private investigator if Ellie's research didn't pan out.

He wished he had a good reason, but it was selfishness, plain and simple. He wanted her to be happy, to find closure, to feel like she had a family and a home.

But every time the topic came up, it was more and more difficult not to point out that she had a home and family right here.

But it wasn't his place to say so. And it definitely wasn't his place to try and convince her to stay.

So yeah...that was just pure selfishness at work. Rather

than say anything one way or the other, he'd just ignored the topic altogether for the most part.

"I'll see you later, Boone." She smiled and gave him one more wave before turning.

He watched her walk away, grinning when Rose and Kiara came into view. April didn't even hesitate to hug her sister or pick up the baby and hold her in her arms.

Hope welled up in Boone before he could stop it, but he pushed it back down again as he started the truck and drove the short distance to the fire station.

"Hey, man!" Ethan was already there. As the only paid fireman, and the captain, it felt like he lived at the station.

Most of the volunteers took off during the off-season, but Ethan stuck around to deal with house fires and any other emergencies that came up in town.

Ethan put him to work right away, and they were cleaning the engine side by side to make sure it was in perfect working order when Levi showed up.

"Sheriff," Boone called out. "Don't tell me we're in trouble."

Levi shook his head at the lame joke as Ethan clapped him on the back. The two of them and Dr. Dex were good buddies, always hanging out, so it wasn't rare to see either man randomly pop in during a shift.

But today Levi looked frazzled. "Sorry I can't hang. I'm actually just here to ask a favor."

"Name it," Ethan shot back. Because that was the kind of guy Ethan was.

Boone nodded. "What do you need, Levi?"

"Nothing official. Just wondering if you could take Daisy and Rose to their wedding planning appointment up at Paradise Springs today." He winced. "They got some snow up there this week, so there's no way Daisy's VW can handle the trip." He sighed. "And I've had an emergency come up that I need to deal with."

At their startled looks, Levi held up a hand. "Nothing major, just a dispute between you know who." Levi sighed, and Ethan laughed.

He had to be referring to the old rancher, Mr. Cooper, and his young neighbor, Billy Buckley. Those two had it in for each other, and the smallest infraction was always called into the station...usually by ol' Mr. Cooper.

"Wish I could help you out, man, but I can't leave my post right now," Ethan frowned. "I'll see if I can find someone else."

"I can do it." Boone raised his hand. He cast Ethan a questioning look. "So long as you can spare me."

Ethan looked around the quiet station meaningfully. "I think I can handle it from here. And if an emergency comes up, the siren will blast, bringing in the rest of the volunteers."

Levi perked up. "Seriously, Boone? You don't mind?"

Boone grinned. "'Course not. No problem."

CHAPTER 27

Rose gave April an awkward half hug as Kiara fussed between them.

"I wish I could stay longer." Rose pulled back and bounced the baby in her arms with a frazzled smile. "But I don't think Kiara's going to last much longer. We're way past due for a nap. Then Dex is coming home early to take over so Daisy and I can go to the wedding venue and go over the details. Otherwise, I'd invite you over or—"

"You go," April interrupted, leaning over to kiss Kiara's head. "We wouldn't want my niece to get fussy, now would we?" she cooed to the baby. "No, we wouldn't."

Rose laughed and started to walk away, leaving April a little stunned in her wake.

She wasn't sure which was more alarming—that she'd just used baby talk for the first time in her life, or that she'd just referred to Kiara as her niece.

She was still watching them walk away when Rose turned back with a shy smile and wave. "Thanks for meeting us, April."

"My pleasure," she said.

And she meant it.

Yup, that was the most shocking part of all. She'd had fun with Rose. And when talk had turned to Frank, April had found herself sharing stories from her childhood that made them both laugh.

She gave her head a shake and turned toward the library. Ellie would be waiting for her, and they'd only just begun to make some progress in "the great David hunt," as Boone called it.

A giggle escaped as she thought of Boone.

Only Boone could make her laugh about the fact that she hadn't found her father yet. He had a way of making her laugh and smile whenever he was near.

She wasn't even sure how he did it, but he had this ability to draw her out of her own head.

Ellie perked up when April walked in, her frown dissolving into a bright smile. "Hey, you."

April sank into the seat beside Ellie behind the front desk. This library had become her favorite hangout spot when she was in town. She'd been enjoying getting to know the sisters, but when she was with them, she was never fully able to shake the memories of her childhood, or escape the questions her parents had left behind.

Being alone with Boone or here at the library with Ellie were the breathers she badly needed from all that. And judging by the air of relief in Ellie when she turned to chat with April, she had a feeling the librarian appreciated the distraction from her own family drama as well.

"How was your lunch with Rose?" Ellie asked.

"Good." April bobbed her head as she tried to explain it.

Over the course of this week, she'd opened up more and more to Ellie, so she mostly knew the history there.

"Rose seemed to really appreciate hearing about Frank. Getting to know more about him than what their mother told them."

"Good," Ellie said with a sympathetic smile. "That's good. Rose is such a sweetheart. She deserves to know there's more to her father than the bad stuff she'd heard about."

"Exactly."

"And you?" Ellie leaned over and nudged her shoulder. "How was that for you?"

"You know…" April's brows drew together as she tried to put her feelings into words. "I think it was good for me, too, to be honest." She fidgeted with the strap of her bag. "It felt good to focus on the happy memories for a while."

Ellie smiled. "I'm glad."

"How about you? Any new developments with Trent?"

She was almost sorry she'd brought it up when Ellie gave a sad shake of her head. "Not really. He moved the last of his things out, but…that's it. I guess I should be grateful he's letting me stay in his house for now. I think he's doing it out of guilt, but I'm not sure how long I can stay there. I should probably be thinking about a fresh start in a new place, but I don't know… The very idea seems like too much to handle right now."

April's heart sank on her friend's behalf. "I'm so sorry, El."

"Yeah. Me too." She shrugged as if to say *"But what are you gonna do?"* Then she turned to the computer. "Where do you want to start today? I bet if we reach out to his college's alumni group, they could give us something."

April hesitated. Part of her wanted to push, to pry.

Surely Ellie needed to talk more about this whole "fresh start" thing.

But she clamped her lips shut, because who was she to push and pry?

She should know better than anyone how hard it was to talk about the worst moments of your life.

She cleared her throat. "Yeah, let's start there."

They hadn't gotten further than calling up the website when Boone walked in. It was a little disturbing the effect his sudden entrance had on her.

She felt it before she even saw it was him.

It was like her whole body went electric with awareness, and when she caught sight of his crooked grin, her heart burst into a tap dance that would put Fred Astaire to shame.

"Hello, ladies."

His slow, low drawl must have this effect on every woman in Aspire. April was definitely not the only girl who fell victim to Boone's charms.

She was just the only one who had to pretend that she wasn't affected every day, day in and day out, seven days a week.

No sweat.

"Hey." She returned his smile with a confused one of her own. "I thought you were at the fire station all afternoon."

"I thought so, too, but an entirely different sort of emergency cropped up."

April could see he was teasing, but Ellie tensed beside her. "Oh no, is everything all right?"

"Oh yeah, everything's fine. It's just wedding prep stuff." He made a funny face, then chuckled. "Seems Daisy and

April need a ride up to Paradise Springs." He turned to April. "You can either come with—I'm sure Daisy and Rose would love that—or Levi offered to give you a ride back to the ranch when he's done dealing with a minor emergency of his own." He turned to Ellie. "Nothing serious, just bickering neighbors." Then he turned back to April. "So, what do you say?"

"Ummm…" April froze in indecision.

Some part of her really wanted to spend more time with Rose and Daisy. But being a part of their wedding planning?

That felt so very…sisterly.

Ellie nudged her gently, her tone quiet and sweet as always. "The venue is stunning. You really should see it. I know you're not planning on staying for the wedding, so think of this as your sneak peek."

"I know you're not planning on staying…"

That phrase made her simultaneously relieved and anxious, if such a thing was even possible.

But it was true. She'd made it very clear that she wasn't staying in Aspire forever.

She peeked up at Boone, studying his expression. The thought of ending whatever this new friendship was between them was…

Well, it made her heart twist and her belly tighten.

She was getting used to having him by her side, always ready to listen or make her smile….

But Ellie was right. Everyone knew she couldn't stay.

Which was why she really had to stop getting any more attached than she already was.

Boone leaned over the front desk, his smile hitching up on one side in that way that never failed to make the butterflies in her belly go wild. "So, what do you say?"

"Um…" She glanced over at Ellie, who gave her a wide-eyed eager nod of encouragement.

"Ellie's right. This might be my only chance to see this place, so…" She smiled up at Boone. "I guess I'm coming with."

"Great. I'll text Daisy the plan, and Rose to make sure Dex is there to take over baby duty." He headed out, phone already in hand.

April turned to Ellie, and her new friend seemed to read her mind.

"Go," she said with a laugh. "Don't worry about me. You should enjoy this time with your sisters."

April leaned over and gave her friend a hug. "I'll text you later, 'kay?"

Ellie nodded, and soon April was climbing into Boone's truck. Then they were collecting Daisy and Rose and heading up into the mountains.

The drive was filled with lively chatter and laughter, not to mention music thanks to Daisy, who insisted on blaring the radio and singing along when her new favorite song came on.

"I remember coming up to Paradise Springs as a kid," April said at one point, then instantly regretted it because Daisy and Rose were far too eager to hear about how Frank had taken her camping.

"Be prepared," Boone said as he navigated a switch-back turn onto a snow-packed dirt road that led them toward the lake town. "It's not the same Paradise Springs you remember."

"No?" April asked.

"I mean, there's probably still some spots where locals can camp, and that public beach on the western edge of the lakefront is still popular," he said. "But it's been developed into a real tourist trap these past five years or so."

"I hear there's some mega-mansion 'cabins' back up this way." Rose used air quotes around *cabins*, which made April laugh.

"So, not like the rustic cabins I remember…"

"More like second homes." Daisy bulged her eyes, giving away just how luxurious they must be. "But Levi says some of the families who've been up here forever still have their properties and are trying to keep the small-town feel."

"That's all the more reason I love the inn we chose," Rose said. "It's family owned and run. They're doing up the old house that's been in their family for nearly a century and making that into a rustic but classy inn, plus they've converted the old barn into an events venue. They're really trying to make a go of it."

"That's cool." April smiled. "I love the idea of using the tourism to help maintain the history."

"Exactly what we said!" Daisy beamed at her, and April couldn't help but grin back.

Daisy was like Boone in that her smiles were outright infectious.

April was starting to wonder if maybe Boone had gotten turned around in these backwoods roads, but suddenly he rounded a corner and all three women gasped in unison.

"Oh! It's even more beautiful with the snow!" Rose cried.

"I didn't think it could possibly get any prettier," Daisy said with an awed shake of her head.

Boone turned to April. "What do you think, sunshine?"

April's lips were still parted, her eyes wide with disbelief. "It's...magical."

She climbed out after the others, unable to tear her gaze away from the idyllic scene before her. The lake shimmered through a thin layer of evergreens, and those snow-dappled trees formed a large semicircle around a sprawling wood-sided main house, with a wraparound porch and stone chimneys. Just beyond it lay an old-fashioned red barn with its two large doors swung open to reveal a wonderland of strung lights, ivy, and old wooden beams.

"The main house is still under construction," Rose explained as the four of them headed toward the barn.

As if to punctuate her sentence, a hammer clanged and a chainsaw began to buzz.

The work was being done on the far side of the house, and April caught sight of workers moving about just before they entered the barn.

A tall, slender brunette greeted them with a smile. "Ah, just in time!"

"Hey, Bailey." Daisy rushed over to greet the woman with an enthusiastic hug, as if they were old friends and not clients.

Boone gave April a smile and a wink as if he knew what she was thinking. Bailey had an air of competence about her that only made April approve even more of this venue. But really the inside of the barn was even more magical up close. It somehow managed to be open and spacious while still maintaining a warm, cozy, intimate appeal.

"It's perfect," April breathed as Daisy and Bailey chatted.

Bailey greeted Rose next with a smile as she hitched the

234

clipboard in her hands to rest on her lap. "No baby today?"

"Dex is on duty," Rose said.

"Too bad. Kiara's such a sweetheart." Bailey turned to Boone and April, and Daisy made the introductions.

"Ah, one of the famous O'Sullivan sisters." Bailey grinned as she reached a hand out to shake April's. "I'm Bailey King. Welcome to my family's pride and joy." She looked around the perfectly decorated barn with pride. "Welcome to The King's Inn."

CHAPTER 28

Bailey was in the midst of laying out options for how the tables could be set up for the reception when a shorter brunette entered with darker hair that was tossed up in a messy bun and jeans that looked far more comfortable than Bailey's starched, professional dress pants.

She had an energy about her that April instantly took to. She buzzed with it as she greeted the O'Sullivans with a welcoming smile. "Sorry to interrupt." She turned to Bailey. "Tom says he needs you. ASAP."

The two women shared a grim expression in silence, sorta how April's sisters conversed without saying a word. So it really didn't come as a surprise when Bailey turned to them, her business smile back in place, to say, "My sister, Willow, will be happy to tell you more about the menu we have planned. If you'll excuse me, I've got to deal with this."

Willow gave an exaggerated wave. "Hey there! I'm Willow."

They went through the introductions again, but this time it was Boone who got the special recognition.

Willow's gaze lit with a gleam that April recognized well from high school.

Yup, that was the look of a girl instantly smitten with Boone Donahue.

"Willow King," she needlessly repeated her name, just for the chance to shake Boone's hand.

April's belly pinched, a toxic green substance spilling into her veins. She took a deep breath and ordered herself to ignore it.

She had no claim on Boone. He was not hers. Not in any way, shape, or form.

And he never would be because he was an Aspire boy and she could never stay.

And yet, despite her inner lectures, she still gritted her teeth as Willow took a keen interest in him, asking what he did for a living, then connecting over their shared love of horse riding.

April nearly piped up that she loved horses, too, but managed to curb the urge and not come across like some needy attention seeker.

They're just talking. Get over yourself.

She tried to smile as she listened, but she suspected her smile wasn't very convincing when she glanced over to see both of her sisters watching her with a hint of concern and curiosity.

When they caught her looking back, Daisy finally intervened. "I hate to interrupt," she said, stepping between the happy, flirty couple with an innocent smile, "but I'd love to hear more about the options for live music."

"Oh! Sure thing!"

April breathed out a sigh of relief but looked away quickly when she caught Rose giving her a sympathetic smile.

Crap. She wasn't sure what they'd seen in her expression, but they'd gotten the wrong idea.

Mostly.

Okay, yes, fine, she was a little jealous. But she didn't have any right to be. And she knew that. So…she was fine.

Just fine.

"But I know Bailey has some great ideas for that," Willow said. "And if you're okay with a little topic change, I'd love to go over the cake with you today." Her beaming smile was pure sunshine.

And suddenly April was paying attention again.

"We're still looking for a permanent pastry chef, but we've had some local bakers put together some options for you for our tasting today."

Willow led them to the cake station, where a tall, dark-haired man with broad shoulders was setting up.

"Is this your chef?" Daisy asked.

The man turned around, and April blinked in surprise. Goodness, he was handsome, but in an entirely different way than Boone.

Not that she was comparing him to Boone.

Ugh. Stop it.

He reached a hand out, and April couldn't help but admire his good looks. He had sharp features with a dimple in his chin and crinkles around his eyes. He looked like that guy who played Superman or something.

"Brandon," he said when he shook her hand.

"April."

Boone stepped in front of her, and she found herself blinking at his back.

"Everyone, meet my big brother, Brandon." Willow paused. "Try saying that ten times fast."

Rose giggled.

Brandon raised his hands, palms out. "I'm just the guy who picked up the cakes and brought them here. I had nothing to do with the baking, so if you have any criticisms, feel free to let rip. You will not be hurting our feelings."

Everyone dug in, and April was…unimpressed.

She had no intention of saying so, but when she caught Daisy and Rose's eyes and saw their expressions, she felt compelled to help out.

"I normally love red velvet," Rose murmured. "But this one is not what I was imagining."

Willow pursed her lips, eyeing the cake like maybe she could *see* what was wrong.

Boone nudged April's arm, and she cleared her throat. "Um, I think maybe they used too much baking soda." Everyone looked to her in surprise. "It's the leavening agent? But, uh, if you add too much, it has a bitter taste, so…"

Brandon stared at her wide-eyed like she was speaking a different language before glancing at Willow for confirmation. Willow's eyebrows dipped together as she stepped forward and grabbed a fork. After one small bite, she was nodding. "Oh gosh, that… Something is definitely not right there." Her face bunched as she swallowed down the mouthful, then dropped the fork beside the red cake. "I'm so sorry. Ugh. Why did I give this job to someone else? I should have just gotten up early and baked something myself."

Daisy beamed at April, giving her a swift wink while Rose gave a look of relief. But it was Boone who spoke up. "April here is kind of a genius with baking."

"What? Uh, no, I wouldn't say that." She shook her head.

But Boone started to go on and on about the café where he'd found her and the decorating she'd done. Willow's face lit up. "Amazing! You want to check out the kitchen? I could use your take on the pastry chef's station."

April barely had a chance to respond before Willow linked arms with her and started leading her toward the main house. Brandon smiled at her as she was being led away. "I wouldn't try to fight it. My sister might be short, but she defines the words *stubborn determination*."

"Kinda like April," Boone said, making Daisy and Rose laugh.

April and Willow sighed in unison.

"It sucks being the smallest member of a family," Willow muttered.

"Amen," April enthused.

"Well, us two shorties can slip past the construction zone, so take that, normal-sized people."

April laughed. "I think I'm gonna like you, Willow King."

Willow bumped her hip teasingly. "Right back atcha, April O'Sullivan."

They quickly became two tiny peas in a pod, as April reveled in the joy of being in what had to be the coolest, most state-of-the-art kitchen she'd ever seen.

"And then we could do a three-tier cake in the center!" Willow was wide-eyed and buzzing with excitement.

Or buzzing with caffeine, since they'd both just polished off two cappuccinos that April had whipped up in their fancy espresso maker.

"Exactly."

"You think your sisters will go for it?" Willow asked.

"Your sisters."

A hiccup of reality hit April as she fought the urge to

explain that they weren't *really* her sisters. But no, this was not the time to delve into that situation.

First of all, she liked this woman, but they'd only just met. Second, after spending time with Daisy and Rose, it felt a bit like betrayal to deny that they were sisters.

And third…she was still vibrating with so much excitement over all their plans and ideas, she couldn't be bothered to come back down to earth.

She and Willow had spent the better part of this past hour caught up in a whirlwind of ideas over all the possibilities for decorating and catering—not just this wedding but a bunch of hypothetical events as well.

April had pitched a full-fledged Christmas festival plan that Willow had vowed to make a reality.

"If they don't like it, I say we hit them with the black-and-white idea. It's so classic and elegant."

Willow nodded. "Agreed. But your sisters don't seem like they'd want the elegance so much as…"

"The fun and festive?" April supplied. Her mind caught on Daisy's flowy, artsy clothes and Rose's hatred of being in the spotlight. She gave a decisive nod. "You're right. I think they'd prefer the more casual but unique approach."

Willow arched a brow. "You think you can describe it to them as well as you did to me?"

April grinned. "I have a better idea. Do you have a pen and paper?"

After a little sketching later and a whole lot more enthusiastic chatter, they rejoined the others back in the barn, and April laid out drawings of the cakes that she and Willow had discussed. "So you see, you'd each have one. Daisy's would be covered in snowflakes and gold, and

Rose's will be covered in holly and ivy. So they'd be two different takes on the winter theme and—"

"You can do that?" Rose interrupted, her eyes wide as she ogled the picture of her cake. "I mean, I'm impressed you can even draw it this well, but you can actually make this?"

April nodded as Boone gave her a proud smile and a wink from where he was leaning against the wall behind the others.

"She can do that and more," he promised.

April couldn't believe she was blushing right now. It was that stupid wink, dang it. He really had to cut it out with the winks.

Daisy whistled. "Wow, girl. Color me impressed."

April dipped her head to hide a proud smile.

"Seriously," Brandon said. "Where did they find you?"

"In Portland, actually," Boone piped up, surprising her by sidling up next to her and wrapping an arm around her shoulders.

"Well…" Brandon smiled, exchanging one of those sibling looks with Willow. "We are very glad you're back in Montana."

"Actually," Willow said, "we'd love it if you stayed. Here, I mean."

April looked at Willow in confusion. "Uh…what?"

Another shared look, and Brandon gave a subtle nod.

What is happening here?

Willow's smile was expectant and hopeful. "I'll need to run this by Bailey first, but I'm positive she'll say yes."

"Yes to what?" April's eyebrows puckered.

"To asking you if you'd like to be our new pastry chef. I mean, you said you weren't currently employed, and you weren't sure when you were leaving, so…"

April stared, completely speechless.

"Um…" That was it. That was all she could say. She didn't know when she was leaving. And she didn't currently have a job, since she'd extended her stay so long that she felt it was only fair to officially leave Café du Monde in Portland.

But this…

Staying…

"I'll be honest," Brandon said. "There's an upscale resort opening on the other side of the lake. They're catering to the people with second homes, the one-percenters who come here to golf and ski and take their sailboats out on the lake."

"We're hoping to be the place for a more local crowd," Willow added. "People more…like us."

April nodded, not sure where this was going.

Brandon rocked back on his heels. "See, the new place…they're making it impossible for us to get workers. They're stealing our construction crews right out from under us and snapping up culinary and front-of-house talent the moment we show an interest in someone."

"That's crappy," Daisy said.

"That's the Spencers for you," Willow muttered.

Brandon moved closer. "The point is, we're desperately in need of a pastry chef for our opening. Willow seems to think you know what you're doing, and she's got great instincts."

"Well?" Boone's voice was low, for her ears alone. "What do you say, sunshine? Are you gonna stay?"

CHAPTER 29

Boone's veins were filled with something fizzy and sweet as he took in April's shock.

It was a good shock. The best sort of shock.

And it means she's staying.

"I...I think I need a minute," April hedged.

Boone set aside his own elation because he knew that expression. She was overwhelmed. Of course she was. This was not how anyone saw today's visit ending.

Taking her by the hand, he turned to the others. "Do you mind if we have a sec?"

"Take all the time you need." Brandon smiled as he waved them off, and Boone made a mental note to ask around about the guy.

He seemed nice enough, but there was a big-city feel about him that seemed at odds with their whole small-town vibe.

He led April outside and she tipped her head back, inhaling deeply as she took in the treetops overhead.

"It really is special here, isn't it?" she murmured.

"Beautiful," he agreed. But he'd never taken his eyes off April.

She met his gaze. "What do you think?"

"I think..." He turned to face her head-on, trying his best to push his own selfish wants aside. "I think I saw the way you were lit up with excitement talking about those wedding cakes. I can't tell you what you should do, obviously, but it's not every day that opportunities fall into your lap like this, you know?"

"Yeah." She let out a shaky breath. "I'm still shocked. That's like...my dream job right there."

He smiled, watching her turn it all over in her mind. "But..."

"But I don't know how long I'll be staying," she said slowly. "Boone, I know my sisters and grandparents all want me to settle down in Montana. I think...I think *you* want that too."

A new tension filled the air between them, and her expression grew wary. Haunted.

All that earlier happiness faded as he saw her pulling away from him. Maybe not physically but emotionally.

She was putting a wall up around her heart, just like he'd seen her do with her family, and there was nothing he could do to stop it.

But she was waiting for an answer, and he knew deep in his bones that this was it. Time for the truth. To not speak now, or to gloss over how he felt...

It would be a lie.

A lie of omission, maybe, but a lie nonetheless.

"I want you to stay," he admitted.

His voice was gruff with emotion, all the more so because he knew in his gut that she didn't want to hear that.

And sure enough, her expression grew pained, her features tight.

"Boone," she started.

"It's all right, April. I'm not…" He cleared his throat and glanced away, shoving his hands into his pockets. "I'm not putting pressure on you. No matter what, I'm your friend, right? I've got your back. You know that."

She nodded, her eyes shimmering with unshed tears. "I know that."

His jaw worked, and he was keenly aware of the light laughter and happy voices coming from inside as Rose and Daisy planned their double wedding.

Just a minute ago, he'd thought maybe he'd have a shot at that sort of happiness too. But one look in those haunted eyes, and he knew she wasn't there. Not yet…

Maybe never.

"Boone?" She sounded so wary, so hesitant.

It took everything in him to force a smile. "It's okay, April. But I think I should be honest, don't you?"

"Honest about what?"

"About how I feel," he said slowly. He reached out and touched her cheek, pulling his hand back when she winced. "About you."

"You can't… You don't…" She let out a shaky breath. "I shouldn't have kissed you that night by the barn."

His teeth ground together as her words hit him like a punch.

Her gaze was pleading. "I like you. You know that. And of course I'm attracted to you—"

"Don't, April."

She visibly swallowed. "It's just…I can't stay. Not for long. And if we were more…if we got too close…I wouldn't…I couldn't…."

"I get it, April. I do. But for me…"

For me, it's too late.

He wet his lips and took a deep, steadying breath. His chest hurt. His heart felt like it was breaking. Which was stupid. They weren't even a couple to begin with. This wasn't a breakup, just…

Just a letdown. But he supposed it wasn't until that moment that he realized just how much he'd been hoping.

That hope crashed to his feet when she hurried on, a forced lightness to her tone. "On the bright side, you're Aspire's most in-demand cowboy these days. I mean, even Willow couldn't take her eyes off you. Every girl in Montana would love to be your lady."

He knew she meant well, but her words dug in like a knife. "Too bad for me that I went and fell for the one girl who has no interest."

"I didn't say—"

"It's fine, April." He stopped. "No, actually, it's not fine. One kiss and you ruined me for all others. That…." He cleared his throat and tried to match her teasing tone. "That sucks for me, huh?"

"Boone…"

"But it doesn't change the fact that I care about you. I promised I'd always be there for you, and I will." When she bit her lip, he added, "As your friend."

She nodded, tears welling in her eyes. "Thank you, Boone."

He ignored that, his gaze focusing on the snow at their feet as he pushed aside his hurt and disappointment. "And solely as your friend, I can say that I think you should take this job."

She was quiet.

"Even if it's not forever, it's a good step for you and

your career. It'll be a good experience. And it's only forty minutes to Aspire, so you can have a life of your own until you get this ranch business sorted."

He looked up to find her nodding. "Yeah, I think you're right. I'll go work out the details with the Kings, although I'll need to make it clear that it's a short-term thing. I can just be a filler until they find someone else." She started to back away. "Thank you, Boone. For…everything."

He nodded his acknowledgment so she could turn away and rejoin the others, but in his head, he rejected her thanks.

He didn't want her thanks or her gratitude.

He wasn't some saint, just a man…

Just a man who'd gone and fallen in love.

CHAPTER 30

April nibbled on her lip as she eyed Boone's profile in the driver's seat.

Was it possible to feel alone when sitting so close to someone?

Yes. Yes it was.

"Thanks again for the ride," she said, breaking the silence.

Boone shot her a quick smile. "No problem."

The winding road down the mountain from Paradise Springs never failed to delight her. It was truly magical up here in the mountains, even this close to the dead of winter.

Two weeks had passed since she'd gotten the job at The King's Inn, and really, April should be ecstatic.

In some ways, she was. For the first time in a long time, her life felt like it was falling into place. The job was everything she'd wanted it to be and more. Willow was becoming a friend as well as a coworker, and Bailey and Brandon were eager to hear her ideas on how they could make the amazing inn even better.

"You heading to the ranch or downtown?" Boone asked as they pulled onto the highway.

"Oh, um...do you mind stopping downtown? Lizzy and Emma were hoping to meet up after work, and—"

"No problem." There was that easygoing smile again.

April returned the smile even though her stomach sank.

He was trying so hard to be a good friend, and she appreciated it. But there was something missing between them now, ever since she'd done what she'd had to do.

And she'd had to let him down, right?

She frowned as she looked out the window at the trees whizzing past.

It would be mean and selfish to let this thing between them get any more complicated. Not when she still didn't know if she'd stick around or for how long.

She shifted in her seat, resisting the urge to steal another glance at Boone.

He had no desire to leave Aspire, and he deserved to be with a woman who wanted that too.

Right?

She drew in a deep breath, startled when he spoke again.

"You guys meeting at Mama's Kitchen or—"

"The coffee shop," she said.

He nodded.

That was another area of her life that was going so well that she ought to be ecstatic. These past few weeks, she'd really started to form a connection with her sisters. It helped to spend one-on-one time with each of them, or to meet up in small groups. She was starting to feel a real bond with the five sisters in Montana and was growing more and more comfortable at the ranch…and that was incredible.

So really, life was going great.

She glanced over at Boone, fidgeting with the edge of her shirt. "You sure it's not an inconvenience?"

"No, ma'am," he said in that cute, teasing lilt of his. "I've got a shift at the firehouse later today anyway."

"No, ma'am." It was the same way he teased Daisy and Rose and the others. No more "sunshine" for April. No more stolen touches and horse rides in the snow.

He was still there for her.

Like today, picking her up from work. She'd been coming to dinners at his parents' house and had gone to a family gathering at Nash's folks' at the neighboring ranch. He'd taken her to the town's Halloween parade where they'd met up with Lizzy, Kit, and the kids.

They'd been having fun. So much fun.

But they were now very firmly fixed in the friend zone. Where she'd stuck them.

She took another deep breath, as if that could wash away this bitter sensation in her gut.

It was for the best.

Even if she did have to fight the urge to reach for his hand.

Even if she did lie awake at night remembering the feel of his lips pressed to hers, or the way he'd held her in his arms and let her cry…and the sadness in his eyes when she'd told him they couldn't be more than friends.

Her stomach turned like it did every time she thought of that moment.

She hated that she'd put that look in his eyes.

Hated even more that he'd taken her at her word. No… she didn't hate that. This was what she'd wanted.

She just…hadn't expected it to be so painful, that was all. She'd wanted to be his friend, but she hadn't fully realized how much more complicated and intense their bond had become until he'd pulled back and put up a barrier between them.

He was still there for her. He still made her laugh and listened to her talk—heck, he'd even helped her end her lease in Portland and had almost single-handedly taken care of hiring movers to pack her things up and ship them here.

So yeah, he was still the very best friend. And she should be grateful for having that much with him.

She blew out a harsh exhale.

"You okay?"

She nodded. "Yeah. Fine. Great."

"How was work?"

Her smile was genuine as she shifted in her seat to tell him all about the dessert menu she'd helped to create and the supplies she'd ordered for the wedding.

"That's awesome." The smile he gave her was warm and kind. "They're lucky to have you."

Heat crept into her cheeks. "Thanks. I'm pretty sure I'm the lucky one, though."

"Are we gonna fight about this?" He shot her a teasingly suspicious look. "I mean…is this gonna be our first fight?"

She giggled and looked back out the window.

"Any progress on the great David hunt?"

She shook her head, a little embarrassed to admit that she'd gotten distracted from her primary goal. Ellie was working on it, though, and in her defense, starting a new job and bonding with five new sisters was kinda time-consuming.

"Did Kelly figure out their Thanksgiving plans?" Whether or not a snowstorm would keep his older sister and her family away for the holiday had been a major point of concern for his mom when she'd had dinner at their house the other night, and now she was invested.

He shook his head. "They're not sure yet. I had a video call with my niece and nephew this morning, though, and if they have any say in the matter, they'll be here for sure."

April laughed, and for a little while, they fell into a conversation that was so easy, so familiar, it made her a little sad to see they'd parked in front of the coffee shop already and it was time to say goodbye. "Okay, well…"

She hesitated, hand on the door handle. Her heart felt like it was lodged in her throat when she turned back and saw the way he was watching her.

His gaze was warm and tender, and filled with something that was…

Well, it wasn't a part of the friend zone.

And she had to clutch the handle harder to keep from crawling across the seat and throwing herself into his arms.

"Okay, well," she said again.

"You need a ride back to the ranch later?" he asked.

That heat, the non-friend-zone intensity—it vanished right in front of her eyes.

She shook her head, her throat tight with disappointment that she had no right to feel. "I'm sure Emma can give me a ride back."

"Okay then. See ya, April."

"Yeah. See ya."

An hour later, April tried her best to be an active part of the conversation. And in some ways, she was grateful for the distraction.

It was difficult to stew over Boone when Lizzy and Emma were pestering her with question after question about the latest additions to the wedding plans.

"It's so wonderful that The King's Inn people are so invested in this double wedding," Emma said at one point when April had mentioned the lengths they'd gone to in order to ensure that Rose and Daisy got the sort of music they wanted.

"Well, they have a lot riding on this," April said. "I told you how there's a rival resort—"

"Ugh." Lizzy made a face. "Kit and I were reading about that. It's just going to draw more out-of-staters and price out the rest of us."

"Not only that," April continued, "but they're not exactly loving the competition."

"How is The King's Inn considered competition?" Emma's brow furrowed. "They're small-scale and family run. Hardly some big golf and ski resort like that other place is supposed to be."

"Yeah, but…" April shrugged. "I don't know the full story, but apparently there's some rivalry there."

One of the old guys who seemed to be permanently camped out at the coffee shop perked up at that. "You gals talking about the Kings and the Spencers up in Paradise Springs?"

"Hey, Norman." Lizzy shared a quick grin with April, who tried to hide her smile. This coffee crew and their gossip. "So, you know about the rivalry?"

He and the local veterinarian, Dr. Bob, exchanged a meaningful look before Norman whistled. "That rivalry goes back ages."

"Generations," Chicken Joe added.

"Must date all the way back to the turn of the century," Dr. Bob chimed in.

"Wow." April pursed her lips. "I'd heard there was a rivalry, but I didn't realize it was so deep-seated."

"So that's why they're trying to drive 'em out of business?" Lizzy arched a brow. "Sounds kinda petty."

April nodded. "Yeah, but whatever the reason is, the King family is dead set on making a go of this renovation and the new business. Making a splash with a big double wedding for the"—she held up her hands for air quotes—"'famous O'Sullivan sisters'…that's a big part of the plan."

"Makes sense, I guess," Emma said. "And I'm glad we can support them since they're going above and beyond for us."

"I can't wait to go back there to check it out again. The wedding dresses are almost done. Now I just have to start measuring y'all for the bridesmaids dresses." Lizzy wagged a finger between Emma and April.

April straightened with a start. A bridesmaid? Her? She hadn't even planned on being here that long, and now…

Now…what? How long are you planning to stay, April?

Her head spun as the future loomed in front of her, but neither Emma nor Lizzy seemed to notice.

Emma rolled her eyes. "Please don't measure my waist. I'm already feeling huge, and this belly is only gonna get bigger."

Lizzy laughed. "It's fine. Yours will have an empire line." She turned to April. "And yours—"

April was actually relieved when a loud siren cut Lizzy off midsentence.

She didn't even know if she wanted to be a part of this wedding, let alone have a dress handmade for her.

But then Emma and Lizzy and everyone else in the coffee shop was turning to look out the windows with concern.

That was when April realized that the siren wasn't fading like a passing ambulance or patrol car might. It was steady and insistent and—

"What is that?"

Her stomach was already sinking, her heart beginning to ache. Like some part of her already knew even before Emma spoke. "That's the fire station. That sound means there's a fire, and all volunteers need to drop what they're doing and head to the station."

Fear caught her in its grip so hard and fierce she could barely breathe.

Lizzy touched her arm. "April?"

"Boone," she breathed. "Boone's already there."

Emma leaned forward, her gaze filled with sympathy. "I'm sure he'll be all right. This is what they train for."

April nodded, and Emma came to stand. "Come on, let's get home. There's nothing we can do for Boone or Ethan or any of the other volunteers from here, but I'm sure Boone will let his family know right away when it's over."

Right. His family. Which meant Nash and his parents and…

Not her.

She closed her eyes. She was being stupid. But fear was never reasonable, was it? Before she could stop it, memories of her father's death hit her with a force that nearly crippled her.

"Come on, hon." Lizzy helped April to her feet. "Let's get you home."

CHAPTER 31

Boone had seen his share of forest fires—as a volunteer, he'd been called on plenty of times to support from the backline. But in the years he'd been volunteering for Ethan, he'd never once been called to a house fire.

"The call went out," Ethan told him as he pulled the fire engine in front of the blazing house. "The rest of the guys will be here soon."

Boone nodded, already hurrying out of the cab, grateful as heck for his few years of training, because if the actions didn't come quickly and naturally as his muscle memory kicked in, he might have been paralyzed by emotions.

It was horrible to watch forests burn, but seeing a teary-eyed family on the lawn, gaping in horror as their home burned before them…

This was something else entirely.

But he forced all that aside as he joined Ethan in affixing the hose and ensuring that everyone was out of the house.

"We're all accounted for." The father nodded, glancing down and recounting his family as if he may have forgotten one of them.

His face was pale as he clenched his jaw, his frown deepening.

"Sir?" Boone prompted him, but the man gave him a stiff headshake and clamped his lips together.

"Boone! Get that hose on the left side of the house!" Ethan shouted over the roar of the flames, and Boone flew into action.

The other volunteers showed up in waves, but Boone lost track of who was doing what. It took all his concentration just to stay on top of Ethan's orders for him.

There was one thing he knew from experience, and that was that focus was everything in high-adrenaline moments like this. One slip, one emotion let loose…

That was how men got hurt.

Well, that and just bad luck. Even firefighters with loads of experience and incredible focus could fall victim to unforeseen changes on the scene.

A shift of wind. An unexpected weakness in the building's structure…

No amount of training could make you 100 percent safe, but it helped, and Boone did his best to stay homed in on each task like it was the only thing that existed.

The task at hand and his fellow firemen's safety.

His lungs ached and his eyes stung, despite the oxygen mask strapped to his face.

"Secure the defensible space on the south side," Ethan shouted to him. "The wind's heading that way."

Ethan was calmer than ever in these sorts of situations, but the shouts, the sirens of approaching ambulances, and the roar of the fire had him raising his voice just to be heard.

"Yes, sir!" Boone took off to the south of the sprawling ranch home.

He did as he was told, ensuring that there was no way the fire could spread to any of the surrounding buildings or into the brush around the house. And that was when he heard it.

A girl screaming. "Buddy!" She sobbed and screamed again. "Buddy!"

The sound cut through all the other chaos, and he turned to see a little girl tearing around the house with her father in hot pursuit.

"Millie, no!"

"But he's still in there!" she argued when her father snatched her arm. "He's going to die," she wailed. "No! Buddy! Buddy, come!"

"It's too late, honey." His expression buckled with remorse while his daughter let out another heart-wrenching sob and crumpled for her knees, crying and coughing as the smoke blew over her.

"Ricky!" Boone shouted, beckoning a newly arrived firefighter to his side. "Take this." He handed off his hose duties and raced over to the little girl, whipping off his mask and crouching down beside her. "Who's Buddy?"

"My puppy." She sobbed out the words, pointing toward the back door of the house. "He's in his crate in the kitchen, and now he can't get out."

"I'm sorry, honey." Her father scooped her into his arms, cradling her head against his shoulder. She cried and coughed, clinging to his sweater.

"Take her around to the ambulance," Boone instructed. "They can give her some oxygen. Go. Go!"

The man ran back to the front of the house while Boone stared at that kitchen door, pulling his mask back on and making a decision that he knew he'd get in trouble for.

But it wasn't even a choice.

Running for the house, he dove through the smoke and made a beeline for the kitchen.

"Boone!"

He heard his name shouted but didn't pause. A fearful bark and pitiful whine pulled him farther into the house, and he soon found Buddy pawing at his cage.

"It's okay. It's okay," he tried to soothe the terrified animal. Thankfully, he was a little thing that could easily be scooped into his arms. As soon as the cage door was open, Buddy tried to bolt, but Boone snatched him up.

He wriggled and squirmed at first, but Boone clamped his arms firmly around the pup. "All right, Buddy, it's you and me." He could barely hear his own voice through the mask, but he turned back the way he'd come and started toward the door.

Flames licked the edges of the room, the roar and heat growing with intensity. But he could see a clear path to the outside and ran for it.

Glass smashed as a window popped. He ducked, covering the dog and turning away from the dangerous shards.

The dog wriggled and whimpered as a gust of wind cut through the kitchen, smoke swirling around them. The sound of crackling flames from behind turned the fire into a living beast, racing toward him as if it wanted to swallow him whole.

Boone ducked and dodged the flames, heading for that door only to be thrown by another loud crack from above.

He looked up in horror as a burning beam fell from the ceiling, crashing to the floor and blocking his path to freedom.

CHAPTER 32

April paced the kitchen like an animal in its cage.

"I promise, April." Nash watched her pace from where he stood leaning against the kitchen counter. "If anyone can handle himself in a fire, it's Boone."

She nodded. He'd said something to that effect before —a couple times, in fact.

And April was starting to wonder if he was trying to convince her or himself. Because despite his steady tone and his placating words, she saw the worry in Nash's eyes as they waited for word on his cousin.

Fear had turned April's blood into a toxic acid on the ride home, and now her stomach was swirling with nausea.

Memories of her father's crash kept filling her mind every time she stopped actively pushing them away, and with every breath, she found herself chanting Boone's name like she could somehow summon him to her side.

She kept thinking about his smile when she'd gotten out of his truck. The sadness that tinged his gaze whenever he looked at her.

Dang it, why had she done anything to make him sad? After all he'd done for her, she'd gone and hurt him.

Better to hurt him now than ruin him in the end.

Her heart twisted with a sharp ache.

You don't belong here, and you know it. He deserves better. That's why you turned your back on him. That's why you kept him at arm's length.

"Because he deserves better," she whispered, and got a curious look from Emma, who was watching her from the table.

"What's that, sweetie?"

April shook her head, wrapping her arms around herself. "Nothing."

He did deserve better, but right now she couldn't stand the thought that he was in danger and she was…here. Safe. Comfortable. Unable to do anything to help.

What if he needed her?

What if he wanted her?

What if he went into that fire not knowing that she was thinking of him every second of every day?

Regret swamped her. Shame filled her.

It might be selfish to want him for herself when she had no idea where she belonged or where she'd end up, but with his life in danger, all her reasoning paled in the face of the fact that she needed him to know how she truly felt.

She was desperate for him to understand that his feelings weren't one-sided. Because if anything happened to him…

Her mind called up that sickening moment when she'd found out her father had died. With her shouts of anger still lingering between them. The way she'd turned her back on him when he'd called out to her. The desperate look on his face, the pleading in his eyes...and she'd bolted.

He'd chased after her, determined to make things right, but...

She shuddered, her muscles clenching as she willed the memories away.

She'd never had a chance to tell him one last time that she loved him.

She'd never told Boone how she felt...

She squeezed her eyes shut tight. This was not the same.

This couldn't be the same.

The back door opened, and April's eyes flew open.

"Hey, Dahlia," Emma said. "You all right?"

Dahlia's features were pinched as she nodded. "JJ just left for the fire."

Everyone went silent.

"Is he...is he a volunteer too?" April asked.

Dahlia shook her head. "No, but he has some experience working for the forest service, so they called him in." She drew in a deep breath, her shoulders squaring. "It's all hands on deck, because the ranch house backs onto a forest area, and they're desperate to keep the flames from jumping to the trees."

April frowned. "It must be bad, right?"

Dahlia's gaze was serious, but her voice was reassuringly calm. "It just means it's the off-season and they're understaffed."

April drew in a sharp breath, but Dahlia came over and placed a hand on her shoulder.

"Which means they're calling in everyone who has any experience. But that's a good thing. They're gonna have more hands than they know what to do with."

Nash nodded. "They'll have this under control in no time."

"Let me make you some tea to help you relax," Emma murmured. She didn't wait for a reply, and honestly, April wasn't sure who she'd said it to.

Maybe all of them.

They all needed to relax, but April was certain that tea wasn't gonna cut it.

"Any minute now, we'll be getting a call." Nash kept his gaze on her.

April pressed her lips together as she nodded. She wished she could feel even a hint of their calm.

Although she could sense she wasn't alone.

They were trying to make her feel better, but not one of them was nearly as at ease as they sounded.

Emma was frowning over the kettle, deep in thought as she went about the process of making tea. Dahlia sank into a seat at the table before leaping back up again. She took her cell out of her pocket and then stuck it back in, then drew it back out like she'd forgotten she'd just checked two seconds ago.

All the while, Nash stared at his phone on the counter like he was willing it to ring with good news.

The seconds and minutes ticked by, each more tense than the last, until April couldn't take it any longer.

"I'm gonna go upstairs," she suddenly blurted.

Everyone's heads whipped around to face her, their eyes blinking as if she'd pulled them out of a dream.

Or rather…a nightmare.

Dahlia nodded. "We'll let you know as soon as we hear anything."

April tried to smile in return. She had a feeling it came across as a grimace.

Her legs felt heavy as she headed up the steps to her room. The moment she entered the garishly purple space, she knew it was a mistake.

Being alone meant there was nothing to stop her from caving into the emotions. And the walls of this room were enough to remind her of her father…and how he'd died.

Because of me.

Without knowing I loved him.

The tears welled fast and fierce, part grief for Frank and part worry for Boone. The two seemed inexplicably tied.

She couldn't lose another person she cared for.

And she couldn't stand the thought of Boone in danger. Even worse was the thought of him in danger and not knowing…

She sank onto the bed with a sob, her whisper barely coherent, but she knew God could hear her. "Please don't let this happen again. Please don't take another person I love."

She fell onto her knees beside the bed and clasped her hands together, her posture harkening back to her childhood days when her mother would be beside her as she said her nightly prayers.

"Look after Boone, God. Keep him safe. Let him know he's loved and needed, and that he has to come back to his family and…and to me."

She cried and sniffled, her head buried against the comforter. For a second, she thought she felt her mother's soothing presence, and she almost heard Frank's low, reassuring voice.

It was memories.

Only memories.

This room was filled with them. But right now, for the

first time since she'd arrived, those memories were a comfort rather than a curse. She let herself dwell in the feel of Frank's embrace and her mother's soothing shushes until the sound of a phone ringing had her darting to her feet, racing toward the steps so quickly she nearly tripped.

She heard Nash's voice as she reached the bottom of the staircase.

"Okay. Thank you. Yeah. Keep me posted."

He was frowning, and Dahlia and Emma came to either side of her. Dahlia wrapped an arm around her as Emma clasped her hand. And all three of them watched a grim Nash impatiently until he hung up.

"What?" April asked as soon as he moved the phone from his ear.

"JJ's fine," he said to Dahlia, who shuddered with relief beside her. Then Nash's gaze moved to April, his mouth curving down in a concerned frown.

"What about Boone?" Dahlia said.

"Nash, is he…?" Emma started.

"Boone ran into the fire to rescue a dog, and…" Nash talked slowly. Way too slowly for April.

"Is he alive?" She tore herself away from Emma and Dahlia. "Tell me he's okay!"

"He's alive."

April clapped a hand over her mouth as a sob of relief escaped. *Thank you, God. Thank you!*

"But they're rushing him to the clinic," Nash finished.

Emma wrapped an arm around her waist, and Dahlia's hand settled on her shoulder.

April realized then that she was shaking. "Can I…? I need to…"

Nash grabbed his keys. "Of course. I'll take you to see him."

Nash kissed Emma goodbye, promising her and Dahlia that he'd call to give them an update as soon as they got there.

April barely heard because she was already on her way out the door, her heart pounding with the need to see Boone.

CHAPTER 33

D r. Dex readjusted the oxygen mask as Boone tried to get comfortable on the narrow hospital bed in the clinic's back room.

"How you feeling?" Dex asked.

Boone lifted the mask. "Like I inhaled a chimney."

Dex chuckled. "You look like it too."

Boone tried to laugh and ended up in another coughing fit. His chest heaved as his lungs fought for clean air. The fit ended, and he winced because all that hacking jostled his injured leg.

Dex noticed his discomfort. "The pain meds should be kicking in soon. And a week or two of R&R will see you good as new."

"Thanks, Doc."

The door to the exam room flew open, and Boone winced again when he instinctively sat up. He went to stand when he saw April panting in the doorway, her eyes wet with tears and wide with panic.

His heart gave a sharp tug.

Crap. He'd done that. He'd put that fear there.

"April," he started.

But Dex came over and held him down. "Easy, tiger."

"Is he gonna be okay?" she asked.

Dex gave her a kind smile and let go of his grip on Boone. "He's gonna be just fine."

"And the dog?" Nash asked from the doorway.

Boone hadn't seen him enter, but his cousin gave him a nod and a smile. "Good to see you doing all right, cuz. Bet your mom is ready to whoop your hide, though."

Boone winced, which made Nash and Dex crack up. But April was still staring at him with that panicky look, her lower lip trembling. He reached a hand out toward her, and when she slid her fingers into his palm, he tugged her close so he could speak just to her. "Hey," he whispered, squeezing her arm. "I'm fine."

Her gaze flickered over him. He hadn't looked in a mirror, but he had no doubt he was a sight to behold.

"You're not fine." Her voice quaked.

"But I will be." He squeezed her hand again, and her gaze finally landed on his. "I promise."

She swallowed hard, biting her lip as she nodded.

"And to address Nash's concerns, the dog's gonna be just fine too. Dr. Bob had a look at him, and he's already back with his family."

"He's doing better than you." Nash grinned when Boone pretended to be put out.

Dex and Nash looked to April, who was still silent and clearly battling emotions. The two men exchanged a look, and then Nash nodded toward the waiting room, Dex following him.

"April, you take all the time you need," Nash called back. "I'll just wait out here."

April stared at Boone with tear-filled eyes, and Boone's

274

heart nearly beat its way out of his chest.

What did that look mean? Was this the concern of a friend, or…

Nah, he couldn't let himself go there. He'd mistaken what they'd had once already. He wouldn't do it again. He gently let her hand go, resting back against the pillows.

"I should warn you, my mom will be back any minute, and trust me when I say you do not want to hear her lectures on how stupid it is to risk your life for a dog."

He'd meant to make her smile, but she sniffed, her whole body shaking. "Why'd you do it?"

He coughed and took another inhale of oxygen with a shrug. "I couldn't let a puppy die."

April sniffed and moved toward him. "How badly were you hurt?"

"My leg got a little beat up when I was trying to get around a beam that had fallen from the ceiling, but Ethan and Tony came in to haul me out." He snickered and shook his head. "Ethan chewed me out for being reckless, and then I got here and my mom was waiting to chew me out as well. I was more worried for my life at *that* point than I was when I was inside that burning house."

She let out a watery laugh, and a tightness in his chest eased slightly at the sound.

She moved closer, and it took everything in him not to reach for her, to hold her close and bury his face in her hair.

Truth be told, he had feared for his life for a moment there too. It'd probably only been thirty seconds, but it had felt like hours.

Enough time for him to regret taking a risk. To worry about how his family would fare if he didn't make it.

Enough time to think of April and get frustrated as

heck at the life they wouldn't get to share.

He looked away from her wide eyes and that fierce gaze that wouldn't stop drinking him in, like she still wasn't sure he was here safe and sound.

If she kept looking at him like that, he'd definitely get his hopes up. Again.

"You shouldn't have done it," she murmured, playing with the neckline of his T-shirt. "If they hadn't gotten to you in time, or if...if..."

"Hey." He shook his head, a reassuring smile on his lips. "Don't go there, okay?"

"I'm just saying, you shouldn't have done it."

"Trust me. My mom made that point very clear."

She ran a hand down his arm like she had to make sure he was there.

The soft caress made his insides tighten with need and hope and...

"Anyway, my family will all be coming soon, and you won't wanna be here for that..."

He couldn't look at her. The concern in her eyes, the way she was touching him...it made a guy think maybe she wasn't just a friend.

"Where's your mom now?" she asked.

"She's gone to get me some fresh clothes. But she'll be back soon, fussing and bossing me around. Lecturing me for trying to be a hero."

"She's right, you know." April's voice quivered. "You need to take care of yourself."

"I'm okay," he assured her. But his words didn't seem to get through.

If anything, she looked more pained. Her features pinched as she fought against tears. Her hand trembled as she lightly touched his cheek, and then her gaze met his and she was lurching forward, pressing her lips to his in a kiss that made his heart soar and his body ignite.

His mind quit thinking altogether, and he buried his hands in her hair, holding her close as he met her touch with a kiss of his own.

He was a drowning man coming up for air, drinking her in as light and joy and heat suffused his body like it'd just been waiting for this moment.

She broke the kiss to drag in air, but she didn't move away. She kept her forehead pressed to his as she perched on the edge of the bed, their hands clasped between them.

Then she was cupping his face between her palms, dropping sweet, light little kisses on the edge of his lips. "I was so worried about you," she murmured between kisses. "The thought that I'd never see you again nearly killed me." She kissed him some more until he thought he might float away. His heart was so happy.

"April..." He forced himself to clasp her hands between his, to give them both space to breathe.

"Yes?"

"Sunshine, I know you were worried. But if you still feel the same...if you still don't want anything more than—"

She kissed him so hard and hungrily, he couldn't help a moan.

When she pulled back, her eyes flashed with fire. "I don't want to just be friends anymore."

A grin split his face, and his heart soared like it'd finally been set free. "Whatever you say, ma'am."

She let out a watery laugh, and this time when she leaned in to kiss him, he pulled her close so she was pressed against his chest, in his arms.

Exactly where she was meant to be.

CHAPTER 34

April grinned down at her phone as her sisters battled it out.

"I can take her," Lizzy said.

"Don't you have to be at the store?" Dahlia shot back. "I'll drive April."

"This is silly. I wanted to go up there anyway to take a look at the space one more time," Rose said.

April was only half paying attention. It'd been two weeks since the fire, and she was starting to grow accustomed to the sisterly banter and bickering that was forever going on around her.

Like now. Over who had the privilege of driving April to work at The King's Inn. She ought to intervene, but she was too busy giggling at the texts flooding her phone screen.

Mostly GIFs. The first was a kangaroo in a boxing match. The second was a disco dancer from the seventies, and the third was an old lady doing the salsa.

. . .

Boone: Any guesses?

April giggled. He was trying to make her guess where he was taking her out for dinner tonight, after her shift.

April: My guess is that you're an idiot.

Boone texted a GIF of an old cowboy being shot in the heart with an arrow.

She laughed aloud. Maybe too loudly, because the ranch's kitchen suddenly grew quiet.

"Uh-oh, somebody's in love," Lizzy teased. She wiggled a finger in April's face. "I know that smitten smile."

"Yeah, because you've seen it reflecting back at you in the mirror ever since you met Kit." Dahlia smirked.

April and Rose laughed at that.

Rose caught April by the arm. "Come on, I'm giving you a ride to work."

"Are you sure? Because—"

"Dex has Kiara, and I'd love to see the space again," Rose interjected.

"I just feel bad. I really need to get a car." But getting a car meant investing what little money she had in savings, and she was holding on to it because…

Well, what if she had to travel to see her birth father? Or what if she decided to go back to Portland?

Getting a car of her own here felt like she was making a decision that she wasn't 100 percent ready for.

Not that things weren't going well in Aspire. They were. They were going great.

She dipped her head as another text came through, making her heart flutter and her belly dip.

Boone: See you tonight, sunshine.

He ended it with a heart emoji, and she knew it was ridiculous to swoon over an emoji. She really did.

And yet she still swooned.

Rose giggled. "They're right, you know."

April looked up. They'd left the house and the others behind and were climbing into Rose's car. "About what?"

Rose pointed to her face. "You are a smitten kitten, my friend."

Heat filled her cheeks as April laughed and shook her head. But she couldn't deny it. Now that she'd given in to this wild chemistry she felt with Boone, she'd been on cloud nine.

It was funny because in some ways, nothing had changed. They still did the same things they'd been doing. But now there was no wall between them. Nothing to keep her from linking her fingers through his when he was driving them into town. Nothing to keep him from holding her in his arms as they joined her sisters and his family for the town's fall music festival at the fairgrounds. They swayed in time to the music together, and she felt like she was starring in her own personal Hallmark movie.

There'd been nothing to keep them from ending their outings with kisses that never failed to leave her breathless.

So yeah…

Her happy sigh sounded sappy even to her own ears.

She could absolutely understand why her sisters were teasing her.

"Thanks for giving me a ride, Rose," she said as they got onto the interstate.

"My pleasure! I feel like I barely got to see you this week."

April smiled. She'd seen Rose plenty. She'd seen all of her sisters plenty. But they had a way of always making her feel wanted and in demand. Part of her wondered how much of it was because they liked hearing stories about Frank and feeling like they were getting to know him.

And another part of her wondered if their persistence was because they suspected that she wouldn't be around for long.

April pushed the thought away, just like she did every time the future nagged at her.

She'd made no promises to anyone, not even her new work.

Boone understood her feelings on the matter and said he was okay with it. Her sisters too.

But at some point, she'd need to figure out where home was.

"Do you want me to stick around?" Rose asked.

April blinked. "Sorry, what?"

Rose smiled. "I was just seeing if you wanted me to stick around in Paradise Springs so I can give you a ride back when you're done."

"Oh, that's really sweet, but you don't have to do that. Boone's picking me up."

"Date night?" Rose guessed.

April nodded.

"Where are you going?"

"I don't know. He's teasing me by making me guess. He knows full well I hate surprises."

"You do?"

"Yeah, and I blame Frank."

Rose laughed. "Really?"

April smiled at the memory. "When I was turning eight, he got it into his head that I'd like a circus-themed birthday party. What he didn't seem to realize—what no one seemed to get—was that I had a massive fear of clowns."

"Oh no." Rose's laughter made her smile grow.

"Oh yes. It was like my worst nightmare come to life when I got home from school and found the backyard filled with clowns."

Rose giggled. "That's so funny. And so sweet."

"Yeah, he…he had his moments."

An awkward silence fell, and Rose gave her a sympathetic smile. "Thanks for sharing your memories with us, April. I'm sure it's not easy for you, but…we really appreciate it."

"No, it's nice, for the most part. It's good for me to remember the good. I was so angry for so long."

"I bet." Rose's sigh was sweet. "I still wish I could've met him. Just once."

Guilt flared so bitter and so unexpected, it knocked the wind out of April. Rose would've met Frank if only he hadn't died chasing after her.

She caught her lip between her teeth to stifle tears. The guilt was always there to some degree. She was starting to understand that it would always be there, haunting even the happiest of her memories and tainting the new life she was attempting to create here with Boone and her sisters.

But she'd never be able to be content here.

She shut her eyes against the thought. Because if this wasn't her home, that meant what she had with Boone couldn't last, and what she was forging with her sisters was only temporary and—

"I'm sorry, sweetie." Rose covered her hand with her own. "I didn't mean to make you feel bad. It's not your fault."

Those well-intentioned words only made her feel worse, but April nodded, like she knew she was supposed to.

"And besides," Rose continued, "I'm guessing you understand exactly how I feel. You feel the same way about your birth father, right?"

April nodded. This was true. She might not love being their sole source of a connection, but she could relate to the sisters wanting to know their father—even if he hadn't been involved.

Wasn't that the reason she and Ellie kept digging into David Taylor?

"I just want you to know, we—all of us sisters—have been talking about it. And we want to help you like you've helped us. So, if you end up hitting a dead end with Ellie, I hope you know we'll all support you in hiring an investigator."

April's throat was tight with gratitude. "Thanks, Rose."

A little while later, they pulled up to the inn, which April was rapidly starting to think of as her happy place. She waved to Brandon, who was on the phone pacing the tree line. He gave her a distracted wave in return.

Bailey's voice carried from where she was doling out instructions to the construction crew.

But it was Willow who flew out the front door. "Yay, you're here!"

April turned to Rose, already vibrating with excitement over the baking and experimenting to come. "Do you mind…?"

Rose laughed and waved her off. "Go, go. Have fun. I'll see you back at the ranch later."

"Thanks, Rose." She kissed her sister's cheek before bounding up the steps, beyond excited to get started.

Willow waved to Rose and then led the way into the kitchen.

"If she's not sticking around, does this mean I get to see lover boy when he comes to pick you up?" Willow waggled her brows in a silly way that made April laugh.

"You're ridiculous."

"And you are adorable." She booped April on the nose. "Has anyone ever told you that you grin like a fool when you're in love?"

In love…

Was that what this was?

Her belly fluttered and her heart went wild, but April ducked her head, smothering a grin. "Yeah, I've been told."

CHAPTER 35

B oone normally loved his work, but today he couldn't get out of there fast enough.

"Go on, Boone," Nash laughed when he took one look at Boone hurrying around the stables. "We can handle it from here."

"I'll finish up for you, man," Kit added. "You'd better get on the road before the snow starts up."

"You don't want her stuck up on that mountain again," JJ said.

As if Boone needed the reminder. It'd only happened twice in the past couple weeks, and April seemed to have enjoyed getting to stay in one of the inn's newly remodeled rooms. But tonight Boone had plans for them, and he didn't want to take the chance.

"Besides, you need to go shower and change first if you're gonna take your girl out somewhere special," Nash added, nodding toward Boone's dirt-covered jeans.

"Thanks, guys." He grabbed his truck keys and headed for the door.

A short while later, he was freshly showered and

changed and on the road for Paradise Springs. He had one stop to make to pick up her surprise, but even if some snow started up, he'd likely still get there before the end of April's shift.

But that was just fine by him. He loved to watch her work. The pride she took in every task was awesome to see. And the way she got on with Willow, and how much she seemed to respect Bailey and Brandon...

She'd found a workplace where she really belonged. She could thrive and grow there. That was something, wasn't it?

He stopped at the roadside steakhouse, and the order was ready and waiting. "Thank you, kindly," he called out as he headed back to his truck, paper bag in hand.

He couldn't stop a grin from spreading as he turned onto the road for Paradise Springs.

Yes, sir, it was something, all right. April had barely mentioned leaving these past couple weeks. And the way she kissed him...

He pounded the steering wheel in time with the music that blared from his speakers.

She was falling for him the same way he was falling for her. He was sure of it.

Did it get any better than this?

His tires skidded a bit on the slick winding road, a reminder to slow down despite his eagerness to reach April.

He grudgingly slowed his speed. But it was fine. They had all the time in the world, right?

Just the other day, he'd watched her laughing and chatting with Frank's other daughters like it was the most natural thing in the world. Sure, there were still some moments when he saw that haunted look return...

288

But that was to be expected.

He shifted in his seat, annoyed at those few and fleeting memories that threatened to rain on his parade.

Of course she was still dealing with some issues—he didn't expect her to just magically find closure because they were finally together the way they were meant to be.

And sure, she was still looking into David Taylor, but these days it seemed to be an afterthought.

He settled back in his seat, slowing when he spotted a few deer grazing by the side of the road, just waiting to dart out into his path.

He had to pay attention. He kept that focus all the way until he reached the inn, and the moment he parked, the main doors flew open and April came bursting out.

His sunshine.

That's exactly what she was when he spotted that gorgeous smile and her bright red sweater, her braids flying out behind her as she flew into his outstretched arms.

He groaned in satisfaction at the rightness of it when he caught her.

She fit so perfectly in his embrace. Her happy sigh was a warm caress on his neck as she wrapped her arms around him, her boots dangling in midair as he held her tight.

"How is it that I missed you?" she murmured against his shoulder. "When I just saw you yesterday? It's crazy."

He pressed a kiss to her temple. "If it's crazy, then we're both nuts, babe."

She giggled. "Two peas in a pod, then, huh?"

"That's right. We can be roomies at the asylum."

She was still laughing as he set her on her feet.

"Come on." She slid her hand into his, her eyes bright

with excitement. "I wanna show you what they've done to the main drawing room. You're not going to believe it."

She led him through the house, and he oohed and aahed at the two newly completed rooms. The drawing room was his favorite. They'd gone all out to make it a cozy place to read and relax. The fireplace, set in stone with its rustic mantelpiece, created the old-world feel, and it only got better from there. The armchairs were plump and comfortable with fall-colored throw rugs draped over the sides, and one entire wall of the room was a floor-to-ceiling bookcase with a sliding ladder. April climbed it, and he pushed her along so she could point out the books they'd been collecting. Some of them belonged to the Kings' great-great-grandparents. The leather-bound editions were no doubt expensive.

After rabbiting on about how she couldn't wait to see the entire wall bursting with books, April turned to him with wide eyes. "Oh man, I've gotten carried away, haven't I? You made plans for us, and I totally forgot—"

He held up a hand to stop her. "You know, I've learned a thing or two about you this past month..." He snagged her hand in his and gently tugged her back toward his truck. "And one thing I figured out, even in that coffee shop back in Portland, is that when you're excited about your work, there's no dragging you away from it."

She chuckled beside him and gave his arm a little squeeze that he felt all the way to his heart. "I'm obsessive, is that what you're trying to say?"

"You're passionate," he corrected. "And I love that about you."

Her eyes were wide with surprise, and he had no doubt she'd heard the gruffness in his tone, the overwhelming emotions he couldn't hide any longer.

So why try?

He reached into the back seat and pulled out the dinner he'd picked up. "I already asked Willow, and she said we could have full use of the kitchen to heat this up."

She took the bag from him with a grin, and when she opened it, she gasped. "The lasagna from Mystic Creek? My favorite! How did you know?"

"I did a little digging…"

She arched a brow.

"Okay, fine. Your grandmother told me when I called for a list of your favorites."

She laughed. "I haven't eaten there in ages."

Her gaze grew a little distant and cloudy.

He knew that look well by now. "I know. I figured there were memories there for you and, uh…" He cleared his throat.

Was this a mistake?

Maybe. He hoped not.

Mostly, he hoped she knew what he meant by this.

"I thought maybe getting the lasagna as takeout could be a first step, of sorts. I know you have a lot of memories in Aspire. Good and bad and everything in between. But I thought, maybe…maybe we could start forming new memories of our own, you know? Like take the good, leave the bad, and maybe this time next year—"

She cut him off with a kiss that made his whole body ignite. He wrapped his arms around her and tugged her close just as she pulled back to whisper, "I love it, Boone."

And I love you.

He didn't have a chance to say it because their lips found each other again, and he was almost certain he was telling her how he felt with his hungry kiss.

And he was just as certain that she was telling him that she felt the same.

"Okay, you two." They were interrupted by Willow, and they broke apart with a guilty laugh.

Which only grew louder when Willow covered her eyes, only peeking to make sure she didn't fall down the steps as she headed out of the inn toward the smaller cabins hidden in the woods where the family was staying.

"Don't mind me," Willow said as April giggled.

"You can open your eyes now."

"Nope. No way am I interrupting your time with lover boy—"

"Lover boy, huh?" Boone teased.

April nudged him with her elbow. "Don't let it go to your head."

Willow called back to them as she rounded the main house. "Help yourself to the kitchen and dining room! Oh, and, April, if you need to stay, you know there's a room waiting for you."

Boone wanted to tell her it wouldn't be necessary. He had every intention of taking April back home tonight.

Back to the ranch and her family, by his side…

Right where she belonged.

But April beat him to it. "Thanks, Willow. Have a good night!"

Then Willow was out of sight, and Boone's heart soared as his gorgeous girlfriend turned to him with love shining bright in her eyes. "You hungry, lover boy?"

CHAPTER 36

Apl had been noticing lately that something in her was broken.

And she was pretty sure it would never be fixed.

Boone leaned over and swiped his thumb over her lower lip. A shiver raced down her spine as his mouth quirked up on one side in a sexy grin. "You had a little icing…"

She laughed and wiped her mouth on the back of her hand.

"You really are a miracle worker," he said. "That was definitely the best lemon meringue I've ever had."

April laughed. "And you are by far the best taste tester I've ever had."

He patted his rock-hard abs. "It's a tough job, but somebody's gotta do it."

They were sitting side by side on one of the stainless-steel counters in the kitchen, dinner long since devoured, and a good portion of the testing dessert menu polished off as well.

"Come on, let's walk it off," she said.

He hopped down and slung an arm around her shoulders, pressing her to his side in a way that never failed to make her feel safe and grounded.

When they walked side by side like this, and he was so close she could smell his soap and feel his muscles...

She could almost forget that she was broken.

But she felt the reminder of it every time he gave her a satisfied grin, or sighed with contentment.

Boone was so very...solid.

She supposed he always had been. That was one of the traits she'd admired about him—the way he seemed to know himself so thoroughly. Even as a middle schooler he had this confidence. This certainty.

He was a guy who knew who he was and made no excuses for it.

He knew where he belonged, and he had no doubts about that.

Boone had it all figured out and was so very sure of himself that there were times—brief moments, really—where being with him made her infinitely more aware of the gaping holes in her own certainty.

Which was all the more annoying, because his confidence was one of the things she loved most about him. But, she supposed, it made her even more aware of the areas where she was lacking.

Truly, she wasn't sure she'd ever had his assuredness. Not even as a kid. Even back then, she hadn't totally felt like she'd fit in at school or within her own family.

And now, with the way her whole history had been blown to smithereens, and all the chaos with her family, not to mention the secret that was eating her alive...

"Let's get some fresh air," she said a little too loudly, slipping out from under his arm to lead the way.

He chuckled behind her, and the sound made her belly quiver with awareness. "Yes, ma'am."

He caught up to her quickly, and her heart gave a desperate little hiccup when he wrapped his coat around her shoulders as she stepped out into the snowy forest.

Her laugh was breathless as a shiver raced through her. The snow was coming down in big, chunky flakes that caught in Boone's shaggy hair. She reached up to brush some aside. "Maybe fresh air wasn't the best idea. I didn't realize it'd started snowing."

He leaned down to kiss the tip of her nose. "It's an excellent idea. But maybe we can have the best of both worlds, hmm?"

She laughed as he grabbed her hand and tugged so she was trotting alongside his long gait until he'd reached the converted barn.

He swung open the doors and kept them open. He'd come to visit her often enough here at the inn that he made quick work of turning on the Christmas lights and the sound system.

He hooked up his phone and turned the volume down low, and soon the barn was her own personal dream world…with the most handsome man she'd ever known standing in the center of it, his hand held out to her.

"May I have this dance?"

Her smile felt wobbly as she crossed to him, letting him sweep her into his arms. "It's perfect," she whispered as he led her slowly, in time with the music.

He leaned down until his nose grazed hers. "You're perfect."

"I'm definitely not."

Her laugh sounded watery. She couldn't help it. Every time she started to think Boone couldn't be any more amazing, that he couldn't do anything more romantic, be any sweeter…

He went and did this.

"Makes me almost glad you weren't in school with us our senior year," he murmured.

"Oh yeah?" She tipped her head back.

He nodded. "I was too stupid by far back then."

She started to laugh. "How so?"

"I was so caught up in my friends and what everyone else was doing…" He shook his head, his gaze fixed and fierce. "I'd like to think I would have realized that the perfect woman was right in front of my face, but I'm not sure I would have. I might've asked some other girl to the prom, and then I would've had to watch you dance with someone else like this."

He leaned down and pressed a kiss to the corner of her mouth. "I don't think I could have borne it."

She smiled against his lips. "Bold of you to assume that I would've gone to the prom at all. I didn't go to the one in Bozeman, you know."

He pulled back a bit. "No?"

She shook her head, her heart aching, but more of a tender ache than the harsh gaping wound it had been back then, just after her mom died. "It wasn't long after my mom…" She lifted a shoulder. "I didn't have much interest in dances at the time."

"Well then, let's call this our prom. What do you say?"

She narrowed her eyes. "Why? Who'd you go with?"

His sigh made her laugh. "Julie Burman."

"I remember her. Cheerleading captain, right?"

"Head cheerleader…and massive lightweight." He tugged her closer. "She and some of her friends decided to have a pre-prom party, and…let's just say, my prom night was spent holding back hair and cleaning puke off my shoes."

April burst out laughing and found herself resting her weight against him as Boone held her close, his chest rumbling with laughter of his own.

"So that's why you want a prom do-over," she teased.

"Mmm." He pressed his lips to the top of her head, and she reveled in the feel of his strong, steady heartbeat beneath her cheek. "If I could go back and do it all over again, knowing then what I know now…I'd drive to Bozeman and throw you over my shoulder and force you to be my prom date."

She giggled. "So romantic."

He let out a huff of laughter. "It sounded better in my head."

They swayed in time to the music for a while longer. His words stuck in a loop in her mind. *"Knowing then what I know now…"*

She supposed everyone had regrets. Everyone had times they wish they could redo.

She swallowed hard. *But his mistakes had led to puke on his shoes, not a tragedy.*

"Fresh air was an excellent idea." Boone spun her in his arms, making her laugh and dragging her away from the painful past.

She tipped her head back to see his smile beaming down at her. That smile and the way it warmed his eyes and made her feel so seen…

She'd never get used to it. She wasn't even sure what the word was for this feeling.

It anchored her into the present moment. It made her feel like she was at the center of her world…and his. Like the planets were spinning madly around them, but she was safe and centered here with Boone.

"You look so beautiful," he whispered.

She grinned. "It's the lighting in here. I love everything the Kings have done with this property, but I swear the way they've done up this barn...it makes everything feel magical."

"It definitely feels enchanted," Boone agreed. "And it suits you perfectly."

"It suits *us* perfectly," she amended. "I kinda wish I could stop time and just stay here. With you. Forever."

Forever.

Her heart lurched.

What was she doing talking about forever? She didn't know how long she was staying, and she'd been doing her best to avoid any talk of the future. And yet here she was talking about...forever?

She took a deep breath, intending to brush aside the silly comment, but she found Boone's gaze fixed on her, more serious than ever.

"Maybe this is the place where we'll get married, then," he murmured.

Just like that. Like it was obvious, and simple, and—

April stopped moving in time to the music. "What?"

His smile was slow and shy. "Sorry, I know it's too early for that kind of talk."

She shook her head, ready to brush it off, even though her heart was doing a tap dance.

He reached for her. "But I do love you, April."

Her heart stopped. Her lungs stopped. Everything just...stopped.

"I love you, and one day, when you're ready...yeah, I want to talk about marriage and kids and the whole deal."

When her heart started up again, it stumbled and tripped. It clip-clopped and clattered like a gangly new pony trying to get to its feet. She couldn't quite catch her breath, and when he gazed at her expectantly…

She had no idea what to say.

The floor felt like it was being pulled out from under her. She wasn't ready for forever.

She didn't even know who she was or where she belonged.

How could he be so certain when *she* didn't even know?

But as she watched the joy fade from his eyes, replaced by a kind understanding she didn't deserve, her brain lurched to find a way to make this right. "We're here now, Boone. Isn't that enough?"

"Of course it is." He pulled her back into his arms, but despite his reassuring tone, she couldn't help but feel like she'd ruined the moment.

"Kiss me," she whispered. Desperation tinged her voice and flooded her veins. She didn't want to lose this.

She might not know where it was going or how it would end, but she wasn't ready to lose the way he made her feel.

His lips curved up in a smile that didn't feel quite as natural as before, but his tone was teasing. "Yes, ma'am."

And then his lips met hers, and she let herself drown in it.

The future faded; the past dissolved. When he was kissing her, at least…

Life was perfect.

CHAPTER 37

Boone hesitated by the driver's side door of his truck later that night.

"You sure?" he asked for the fifth time.

"I'm sure."

He knew better than to pressure her.

But then again…he'd known better than to talk of love and marriage, but he'd done just that, hadn't he?

Stupid, Boone. So stupid.

He could've kicked himself for the way he'd pushed too hard too quickly. And now here he was, doing it again.

"I can just bring you back in the morning," he started.

"Boone, it's already getting late, and the pass might be closed for snow in the morning." Her tone was patient, but April shifted from foot to foot.

She wanted him to leave.

Without her.

He took a deep breath, wishing it would ease this tight knot in his gut.

He'd messed up. He'd moved too quickly, and now she was spooked.

He scrubbed a hand over the back of his head. Everything in him wanted to talk it out. To make this right. But the more he pushed, the more she'd pull away.

With a sigh, he reached for the door handle.

For tonight, at least, he had to give her the space she needed.

But he didn't have to like it.

He leaned over and kissed her cheek.

"Let me know when you get home safe, 'kay?" She looked so hopeful, so eager and regretful and sad and guilty all at the same time.

It was exhausting just to look into her eyes and try to decipher it all. He gave her a small smile. "Will you answer if I call?"

A guilty blush stained her cheeks as she shrugged. "I'll get a message if you send it."

He rolled his lips together to keep from saying anything more.

This was what she did. She retreated. Her phone would go off, and she'd be next to impossible to talk to…until she felt like coming out of her shell.

Crap.

He looked away as he opened his door and then slid inside.

He'd thought they were past this. He thought that since they'd agreed to be a real couple, she wouldn't shut him out any longer.

Looks like you're wrong.

"Drive safe," she said.

He nodded. "G'night, sunshine." Her pet name didn't sound too sunny coming off his lips, and her awkward, closed-mouth smile told him so.

He shut the door, returning her wave as he backed the

truck up. He saw her still standing there in his rearview mirror until he turned onto the road that would take him back down the mountain.

He caught one last glimpse of her before she disappeared from sight, and the vision of her standing alone in the cold, her arms wrapped around herself...

He couldn't shake the lonely, aching way it made him feel.

Music off and his gaze fixed on the road for wildlife and ice patches, the drive back to the ranch felt like an eternity.

He couldn't quite bring himself to head to the ranch just yet, though.

JJ and Dahlia would still be up, and he was in no mood for company. They'd tease him about his date tonight, and he wasn't sure he was up for talking.

He turned onto the road leading to his parents' place instead. They had a key under the doormat and a room always ready for him.

Best part was, they'd be fast asleep by the time he rolled in.

He'd only just turned onto their street when his phone rang from a local number...but one he didn't recognize. "Hello?"

"Boone? Hi, um, this is Ellie? The librarian?" After a beat, she added, "I don't know why I phrased that as a question. This is Ellie."

She said it with more determination the second time, and Boone's lips twitched. "Ellie, hey. Nice to hear from you."

The question was implicit, he supposed. She'd never once called him before. And while they'd spent a fair amount of time chatting recently thanks to her being

April's friend…

They weren't exactly on a phone-chat level with their newfound friendship.

Unease stirred in his gut as he pulled the truck over. "Is everything all right?"

"Oh. Yes. Fine. Everything's fine. It's just…April…"

Every muscle in his body tensed, adrenaline shooting through his veins. "What about her?"

"I can't get a hold of her," Ellie finished. "I tried calling, but it goes right to voice mail. And I texted her asking her to call, but…"

Boone sighed, sinking back in his seat as panic receded. "Yeah, she most likely shut off her phone for the night."

Because of me.

"Oh. That's too bad." Ellie sounded so genuinely disappointed that Boone's brows came down and he shifted in his seat.

"Are you sure everything's okay?" He didn't know much about her personal life, but the little April had let slip, he knew she had a heartbreaking divorce lingering over her. "If you're in any trouble or—"

"Oh no, no. It's nothing like that," she said quickly. "It's actually good news."

Boone stayed quiet. He could practically feel the librarian weighing her options and deciding whether or not to confide in him.

"I'm guessing you'll be talking to April before I do," Ellie finally said in a rush. "And I'm guessing… I mean, you're the one who named it 'the great David hunt,' right?"

He tensed all over again. This was about David Taylor? He straightened, this time reaching for the door handle so he could get out of the truck, which suddenly felt way too small. "Yeah, I know about her father. Is there any news?"

A brief silence, and then… "I found him."

Boone froze, resting his weight against the hood of his truck as air escaped his lungs in a rush.

"I found him, and I wanted to tell April, but—"

"I'll tell her." Boone found his voice coming out easily…even though his lips felt frozen.

"Oh great. Thanks, Boone. Tell her to call me when she wants to get the details. He's in Florida, and I'm guessing she's gonna want to visit him straight away."

He barely paid attention to the rest of the conversation, though he was pretty sure he said all the right things because eventually the call ended.

And Boone just stood there.

He stared up at the stars in the sky as question after question filled his mind.

What would happen now? Would she leave?

Yeah, she would. But for how long?

And then fears crept in—not just for himself but for her. What did they know about this man?

If he was a good man, if he'd had any interest in being a dad…wouldn't her mother or her grandparents have told her?

Would she get hurt? Again?

He rubbed a hand over his own heart. He wasn't sure she'd be able to handle being hurt again by another parent.

She kept saying she had no expectations whenever he asked her what she hoped to gain by finding her father.

But that was a lie, whether she knew it or not.

She'd set all her hopes on this mystery man. And if he let her down…

If he didn't love her the way she deserved…

His gut twisted with concern for the woman he loved. Out of instinct, he went to call her. But he, too, got sent straight to voice mail.

He stared at his phone long after he hit End Call without leaving a message.

He had to tell her. And he would.

But he had to make sure she wasn't walking into another disappointment.

With that much decided, Boone finally shoved the phone back into his pocket. He'd tell her...when the time was right.

CHAPTER 38

One night turned into two, thanks to another unexpected snowstorm.

By the time Brandon gave her a ride into Aspire on Saturday morning, she was itching to see her friends and sisters again.

And Boone.

Her heart twisted with longing. They'd spoken briefly yesterday, but they'd both been busy with work. It'd been enough, though, for her to get some relief.

He didn't seem to be holding her weirdness against her.

And thank goodness for that.

She'd overreacted. And she hated the fact that she didn't know how to deal with overwhelming emotions anymore.

Running away seemed to be her default setting. And when she couldn't run, she hid.

"You sure you're good from here?" Brandon watched her with concern as she stepped out onto Main Street.

She smiled at the handsome older man. Willow liked

to tease her big brother about being stuck in a big-city mentality, and right now, April could see what she meant.

It was morning on a bright, sunny winter day. She knew, or knew of, just about every store owner on this block.

If this were a big city, she could see how he might feel strange dropping her off by herself, but she gave him a reassuring smile. "I've got it from here. Thanks again for the ride, Brandon."

"No problem. If you decide you want to head back to the inn tonight…" He trailed off with an uncertain wince.

Willow knew about a lot of what was going on in her life—as much as anyone, she supposed. And it was clear she'd told Brandon enough for him to know that maybe she might have her reasons for not wanting to be back at the ranch or in Aspire.

Guilt flickered through her. She wasn't the one who'd been wronged, and she had no reason to be angry with Boone or her sisters.

They'd been nothing but wonderful and welcoming. *She* was the one who owed *them* an apology.

Well, Boone, at least. She hated how she'd left things the other night. Hated even more the awkwardness on the phone when he'd called to check on her yesterday.

But that was why she was meeting him and the others for brunch.

"I'll be good for tonight," she assured Brandon. "But thanks."

He nodded, and she shut the door behind her before threading her way through Main Street's busy downtown.

Aspire always got busier once the snow came. They were close enough to some ski towns that they got their share of winter tourism. So it was no surprise that the library was open, or that Ellie was the one working it.

She'd promised Boone and Emma that she'd join them for a big family brunch at Mama's Kitchen this morning, but she had enough time to pop in and say hello to her favorite librarian.

Ellie was talking to a patron but gave her a big smile and a wave when she entered. She held a finger up to say *"One second."*

April browsed the rotating rack of paperbacks near the front of the checkout area while she waited.

"Hey! Sorry about that," Ellie said, all breathless and wide-eyed as she raced over and gave April a hug.

April laughed, pleasantly surprised. "Wow, this is quite the reception."

Ellie pulled back and blinked at her, some of her excitement fading. "Oh, sorry. I guess you've got a lot of emotions going on, huh? I just thought…" Her cheeks turned a pretty pink. "Sorry, I thought you'd be excited."

Now it was April's turn to blink in surprise. "Excited? For what exactly?"

Ellie's head tipped to the side. "I mean, we've been looking for David Taylor for a while, so I guess I thought the fact that we've actually found him might have been—"

"Wait. What?" April shook her head. "Back up."

Ellie frowned. "Didn't you get my message the other night?"

Embarrassment skittered through her belly. "I, um… Sorry. I saw that you called, but you didn't leave a message, so I figured I'd just catch up when I saw you."

"Yeah, I didn't want to leave such big news in a voice mail, so I told Boone, and he said he'd tell you, but—"

"Boone?"

They stared at each other in silence as April's scattered mind caught up. "So you...you found my father?"

Ellie nodded, looking inexplicably sheepish. "I did. He lives in Miami. I called and confirmed it's the right David Taylor, and...it is." She reached for a piece of paper on her desk and handed it over. "He's expecting to hear from you."

April stared at the sheet of paper in her hand. It was a printout without a lot of info. Just his name, phone number, and address.

Her lips parted, but nothing came out.

After all this time...

After all that searching...

He was here, his info in her hands.

And he was waiting for her to reach out.

"I..." Tears filled her eyes suddenly, and she blinked them away as she cleared her throat. This time she threw her arms around Ellie and hugged her tight. "Thank you, Ellie. Thank you so much."

"I'm glad I could help." Ellie squeezed her before patting her on the back.

April swiped at her eyes as she pulled away, staring at the piece of paper again, now that the reality of it all was sinking in.

Ellie had done it.

She'd found April's father...

And Boone knew.

Anger rose swiftly as her fingers tightened, crinkling the paper at its edges.

He knew, and he hadn't told her.

Betrayal swept through her, along with suspicion. His words from the other night. The way he talked of their future and marriage like it was a done deal...

She'd thought he'd gotten carried away, but she should have seen it all along.

He'd never denied the fact that he wanted to stay in Aspire forever…and that he wanted her to be by his side.

But would he really deny her this just to keep her here?

She didn't want to think it. Didn't want to believe it.

But as she stormed out of the library to seek out Boone, she felt it all the way to her bones.

Boone hadn't told her about her father…

And that was all she needed to know.

CHAPTER 39

The booth in the back of Mama's Kitchen was full to bursting when Boone joined his friends.

Rose attempted to squish closer to Dex, who was holding a sleeping Kiara. JJ and Dahlia did the same scooting movement, and Emma did her best to move to "make a space" for him, but her rapidly growing belly had her stuck where she was.

"Don't worry about it," Boone said with a laugh as Dahlia tried to maneuver Emma and her belly.

"But we need to make room for you and April." Emma wiggled a little further into the semicircle.

JJ frowned, stuck smack in the middle of the others. "If I could find a way out, I'd give you my seat, man."

Boone shook his head, still laughing. "Don't worry about it. Seriously. When April gets here, I'm actually hoping to have some alone time with her."

"Right," Dahlia said. "Because you don't get enough of that."

Emma dug an elbow into her older sister's side at the

wry comment, but she ruined the effect by giggling. Rose looked like she was trying not to laugh as well.

Dex grinned. "No one's judging, man."

JJ lifted his coffee cup. "We've all been there."

"Yeah, well…" He shook his head with a rueful chuckle. Let them think he just wanted some alone time with his girl. That was the case most of the time. But today…

Well, he wasn't sure how she'd react when she found out that David Taylor had been found, but he was pretty sure she wouldn't want an audience.

"In all seriousness," Dahlia said, "we're happy for you. For both of you."

Emma and Rose nodded eagerly.

"It's so great to see April settling in." Emma smiled.

"And to see her so happy," Rose added. "After all she's been through, she deserves to be happy."

Boone dipped his head, his chest swelling with too many painfully sweet emotions to name.

"I'm a lucky guy," he muttered.

JJ nodded toward the front of the restaurant. "And here comes the lucky lady now."

Boone turned, his smile growing in anticipation—and then falling flat once he caught sight of her.

"Uh-oh," Rose murmured.

Uh-oh was right. April's expression was filled with rage as she scanned the crowded restaurant. And when her gaze landed on him—

His chin jerked back at the fury that hit him like a tidal wave.

Then she was stalking toward him, weaving her way past busy servers and busboys with a grim determination that was…

Well, it was a little terrifying.

"What did you do, man?" Dex asked.

"Brother, I think you're in trouble," JJ muttered.

Dahlia tried to intervene when April drew close. "Hey, April, we were hoping you'd make it."

April ignored her, her glare locked on Boone as she planted her hands on her hips. "How dare you?" she hissed.

Boone reached for her, his stomach sinking when she pulled back. "Sunshine, what's goin' on?"

Emma wiggled toward the end of the booth. "Um, April? Sweetie? Is everything okay?"

April whipped her head around to face the others as if she'd just now realized they weren't alone. "Did you know?" she demanded.

The sisters all shared a look, and Boone's stomach took another deep dive, because his confusion started to give way to realization and...crap. Maybe April went to the library on her way here, and...double crap, maybe Ellie told her before he could.

"April, I can explain—"

"Can you, Boone? Because I'd love to hear this." She crossed her arms over her chest, her eyes sparking with fire.

Yep. Ellie definitely told her.

In spite of her lethal gaze, Boone still found himself drawn to April. Some masochistic part of him didn't care that he was in trouble because he was too busy admiring her passion. She was like an avenging angel, so beautiful and furious. She was a sight to behold.

"Well?" she snapped.

His jaw clamped shut. Right. Now was so not the time to be admiring her looks.

He cleared his throat. "April, I was going to tell you—"

"When?" April shot back. "When it was convenient for you? Or maybe...after I'd gotten so comfortable here that maybe I'd forget that I have a real family out there? Is that it?"

Boone frowned. *"A real family..."*

He could practically feel Rose, Dahlia, and Emma flinch beside him.

"Um, Boone?" Emma said softly. "What are we missing here?"

April whipped around to face her sisters and their families. "Ellie found my father. My *real* father."

"Oh. Wow." Rose blinked in astonishment. "That's great news."

"Yeah, that is good news." Dahlia sounded less delighted. "But why are you so angry at Boone?"

April shot him a look, her brows arched expectantly.

Boone cleared his throat. "Because I knew."

"You knew and you didn't tell me," she seethed through gritted teeth.

"Oh dear," Emma murmured beside them.

"I was going to tell you," he quickly argued. His chest ached at the look in her eyes. It was betrayal, clear as day.

Betrayal and...something worse. She was looking at him like he was a stranger.

"April, I swear, I was going to tell you today—"

"I don't believe you," she snapped.

"Why would he lie?" Rose asked quietly.

April's brows lowered. "Because he wants me to stay here. With him and with you." She turned to look at the table full of family. Her family. But she still couldn't see them that way.

Maybe she'd never see Boone that way either.

The thought was enough to take him out at the knees.

"That's what you all want, right? You want me to be a part of this happy family of yours," April accused.

"You *are* a part of our family." Dahlia's tone was surprisingly calm and gentle. "Whether you want to be or not—"

"I'm not!" April's cheeks were flushed, and she didn't seem to notice the looks she was getting from the other patrons. "Frank wasn't my real father. He lied to me. They both did." She turned to face Boone, and he knew what she was thinking.

He knew it, but the words still cut like a knife.

"Just like you lied to me."

"I didn't lie, April—"

"I talked to you yesterday," she spat. "And you didn't tell me—"

"Because I didn't think you'd want to hear about it over the phone. You went radio silent on me and Ellie." He was sure his expression was as desperate as his tone. "You closed yourself off, and I knew you'd do it again, so—"

"So that's it, then." She threw her hand up. "You didn't want to see me walk away, so you kept it a secret."

Her words hurt. They sliced into him a little deeper each time she spoke.

Because she wasn't wrong.

He drew in a deep breath and looked away.

"You didn't tell me because you want me to stay here with you." Her voice was quiet but quivering with emotion.

He didn't argue. There was some truth there, and he couldn't deny it. It wasn't the whole truth. But did that matter to a girl who'd been kept in the dark her whole life?

The silence that followed her accusation felt deafening.

Boone was well aware of the stares—from the strangers and from the friends he considered to be his own family. He lifted his head to meet April's fiery gaze.

"I don't want to see you walk away, it's true," he admitted. "But mostly, I don't want to see you get hurt. This man was no father to you, April. He left you—"

"Everyone left me." The raw pain in her voice was a dagger to his heart.

He could see her backing away, closing him out before she'd even taken a step in the other direction.

He heard Rose sniffle, and Emma looked close to tears as well. She reached out to April. "Sweetie, please, let's talk about this."

April jerked away from Emma's hand. "There's nothing to talk about. I've been telling you all from the beginning that this was a mistake. I don't belong here with you." She turned to Boone, her gaze growing so dark and shuttered, he barely recognized her. "I don't belong here with you."

She turned and swept out.

"April—"

He started to go after her, but Dahlia called out, "Boone, don't."

He stopped and saw everyone at the table shaking their heads.

JJ fixed him with a grim look. "Give her space, brother. That's all you can do right now."

"I…" He didn't want to give her space. But as he watched the door shut behind her, he knew JJ was right.

She didn't want him.

There was nothing he could say right now that would fix this. And so he stood there, staring. April's words still ringing in his skull.

"I don't belong here with you."

A second later, Daisy swept in, all smiles and laughter as she reached their table. "Hey, guys. How…?" Her bubbly tone faded as she took in everyone's faces. "Okay, what'd I miss?"

Boone couldn't answer. He was too busy staring at the place where April had been.

But she was gone…and she'd taken his heart with her.

CHAPTER 40

April leapt out of Ellie's car the moment it came to a stop in front of the ranch. "Thanks for the ride."

"You want me to stick around?" Ellie asked through her open window.

April shook her head. "You've already done too much for me. And this next part…" She forced a smile. "I've got to do this on my own."

"Good luck."

"Thanks." April backed away, giving her friend another wave. "You too."

She watched Ellie drive off before heading into the house. She didn't stop to think. Because if she did…

Her mind instantly called up the hurt look in Boone's eyes. The way Rose and Emma had looked so stricken by her words…

Ellie had helped her book a flight to Miami, and the first flight left from Bozeman in three hours. That gave her just enough time to pack and call an Uber. Assuming an Uber would even pick her up way out here.

One problem at a time…

That was the only way she was going to survive this day. Her insides were still in an uproar—her heart battling her gut, which was at odds with her mind.

She was simultaneously angry and guilt-ridden, betrayed and ashamed.

Ugh. She zipped up her bag with a grunt of frustration. She didn't know what she was. But she didn't have time to stop and figure it out.

There was a father out there waiting to meet her. Actual flesh and blood.

Her family.

The only family she had left, aside from her grandparents.

She flinched as she eyed her phone. Even when she'd been so angry with them for keeping Frank's secrets, she'd always been respectful of the fact that they worried about her, and she'd done her best to check in. She'd never told them exactly where she was, for fear they'd come knocking, but she'd always let them know she was safe.

She stuck her phone in her back pocket. She'd tell them where she was heading later. Once she was at the airport.

April hurried down the steps and stopped short at the sight of Nash in the kitchen. They regarded each other in silence for a long moment.

Placing his coffee mug quietly on the counter, Nash finally broke their standoff with a nod toward her bag. "Going somewhere?"

She stiffened. "I have to go, Nash. Don't try and talk me out of it."

He held up his phone. "Yeah, I heard."

She let out a humorless huff of laughter. "Word travels fast."

He gave her a crooked smile. "Want a ride to the airport?"

She swallowed hard. Boone would know any minute now what she was up to. The gossip in this town was no joke, and Nash would feel obligated to tell Emma and the others her plan.

But he'd know either way, and she really did have no idea if Uber made it out this far.

"Come on." Nash reached for her bag. "We'd better get a move on."

She hurried after him, climbing into the passenger seat of his truck. It wasn't until they were on the road that she asked, "You're not going to try and talk me out of it?"

He cast her a surprised look. "No, ma'am."

When she continued to stare in disbelief, he chuckled. "Even if I wanted to talk you into staying for Emma's sake, it's not my place. You're a grown woman, and you can make your own choices."

She nodded. "Thanks."

"Besides," he continued, "no one understands the need to connect with family more than Emma and the rest of your sisters. That's how they all came to be here, you know."

"Yeah." She nodded, her heart aching in a way she couldn't explain as they drove away from the ranch house. "Yeah, I guess you're right."

"They'll understand." At her look of disbelief, he added, "Even if they don't like it."

She felt a smile tug at her lips, but it faded quickly. Maybe her sisters would understand that she had to do this. But would Boone?

Her heart tripped and fell. Her lungs struggled to draw

in air. She'd been so angry that she hadn't even given him a chance to explain.

And now…now she desperately wished she had.

But would it have made any difference? She'd still be on her way to Miami.

"Do you…?" She stopped and started, not realizing how long they'd been driving in silence until her voice cut it like a knife. She cleared her throat, her gaze still fixed on the landscape outside her window. "Do you think I'm making a mistake?"

"No." He said it so quickly and so easily, she believed him. "I don't think it's a mistake to go looking for your father. I think…" He paused to choose his words. "I think with the death of your father—and, for you, your mother as well—I think you O'Sullivans have been left with a lot of questions. A lot of loose ends that can't be resolved because the one man who could put things right died too soon."

April held her breath. The guilt was expected but still as painful as ever.

He died too soon.

She shut her eyes, focusing on Nash's words like they were a lifeline. "It makes sense that you'd want to see this through. Your biological father might not be able to answer all your questions, but I think everyone who knows you and your situation can understand why you need to see him and talk to him."

April drew in a deep, shaky breath. "Not Boone."

He was quiet for a long moment, and April felt petty for having said it. But she was curious too. And since Boone wasn't here to ask, his cousin was the next best thing.

"I think Boone understands, all right," Nash said simply.

She blinked, her eyes welling with tears. "He didn't tell me."

Nash didn't respond. Maybe he was just giving her space to work it out. Or…maybe he had no idea what she was talking about.

She really had no idea what Emma had told him on the phone.

Clearing her throat, she fingered the edge of her jacket and fixed her gaze on the trees out her window. "He thinks… I mean, Boone thinks this is my home."

No, that wasn't quite right. He thought *he* was her home.

Her heart kicked and fought like it was under attack. But she swallowed down the swell of emotions and turned to face Nash.

His expression was serious and placid. She had this feeling that nothing she said would rattle Nash.

This cowboy would make an excellent therapist if he ever got tired of cattle.

She started to smile at the idea. But then she instantly thought of how she'd say that to Boone, and how Boone would laugh, and…

Her smile fell flat.

"Only you can say where your home is, April. And I guess that's why you have to meet your father, right?"

He glanced at her, and she nodded. But her insides fell with disappointment. She couldn't ignore the way her heart was aching, and she couldn't pretend she didn't know why.

She missed Boone. Terribly. She missed the guy, and she hadn't even left town yet.

She rubbed a hand over her eyes. Regret was kicking in the more her anger had a chance to recede.

She wished she hadn't ended things like that. If those were the last words she ever said to him…

No. She squeezed her eyes shut and forced her thoughts into submission. She would not go there. Not right now. Not with Boone.

Her phone dinged, and she turned it off.

"Not talking to him, huh?"

April frowned. It wasn't like that. "I don't know what to say."

When it came to Boone, she was all messed up. How could she think straight when her heart was so intent on toppling her world upside down whenever she thought of him?

They drove in silence for a while, and when Nash finally spoke, he wore a small smile. "Look, I don't know what happened between you two, and I have no desire to get involved."

Hope rose swift and fierce. "But…?"

Tell me he loves me. Tell me he'll forgive me.

Tell me he had a good reason to keep me in the dark.

"One thing being in a relationship with Emma has taught me is that…we all speak our own language…" Nash gave her a sidelong glance as if to check she was keeping up.

"Like…love languages?" She couldn't help a wince. It sounded so corny.

He laughed. "No, more like… Part of being in love with someone is learning to see the world through their point of view. To figure out where they're coming from…"

She nodded slowly, but really, all she kept thinking was *What does this have to do with me and Boone?*

Nash seemed to change tacks. "Believe it or not, Emma and I had a whole lot of misunderstandings when she first arrived at the ranch."

"Oh, I believe it," she said quickly.

He arched his brows in surprise.

"Sorry, it's just…" She cleared her throat. "Lizzy and Daisy love to gossip."

Nash chuckled. "Then I'm guessing you're well aware that every one of your sisters had to figure out what 'home' means to her."

April blinked at the change in topic. "I don't follow."

Nash shrugged. "Kit was a single dad who'd been burned by love. Lizzy was a bridezilla who'd been cheated on by her fiancé." He shot her a wry look. "Trust me when I say that finding a common ground did not come easily for them."

April let out a snort of amusement. This was not answering her questions about Boone, but she had to admit that the distraction was welcome.

"Then there's JJ and Dahlia. They're both lone wolves, used to taking care of everyone but themselves."

"Okay." April drew the word out, a not-so-subtle "What's your point?"

"Rose will be the first to tell you that she had to learn how to stand on her own two feet before she could be a good partner to Dex. And Dex…well, he had to learn how to let her make her own mistakes."

"Yeah, I get that," she said.

"And Daisy had to learn how to take responsibility for herself and her actions, while Levi really had to learn how to move forward and—"

"Okay, if you're trying to teach me something here, I'm a little lost."

"I'm not trying to teach you anything." Nash shook his head. "I guess I just want you to know that whatever you and Boone are going through...it's all just part of learning how to see the world through the other person's eyes."

"So you think he's right," she clipped, irritation creeping up before she could stop it. "That I should just settle down in Aspire and—"

"Nobody's saying that." He said it so quietly that she instantly felt guilty for getting riled.

"Then what *are* you saying?"

"You've had dinner at Boone's house, right?"

The question caught her off guard, but then she nodded.

"You ever notice that embroidery over the kitchen table?" He shot her a quick look. "It's a circle, and it says—"

"Home is where the heart is," April filled in.

Nash grinned. "Now, you and your sisters know how complicated that can be. But for Boone..."

April found herself holding her breath.

"For Boone, that's always just been a simple truth."

April felt her lips twitching again, even as her heart ached. Because...yeah. That was Boone for you. Things may have come easily for him his whole life, but because of that, he had this purity and goodness in him that made her feel like...like...

What? What was this feeling?

"For Boone," Nash continued in a low voice, "it's that simple. The sky is blue, the grass is green, and home is where the heart is."

She let out a soft laugh as she nodded. "He should've told me, though."

Nash nodded. "I'd guess he thought he was protecting you."

Before she could get annoyed again, Nash quickly added, "But you're right. He should've told you."

She nodded. They fell silent again, each lost in thought until the airport came into view.

"Thanks for the ride, Nash," she said. "Tell Emma and...everyone..." She cleared her throat. "Tell Boone... I'm okay. And I'll be in touch, okay?"

He nodded. When she went to reach for the handle, he stopped her. "April..."

She glanced back.

"I'm gonna be praying for you. Praying that your birth father is the man you need him to be. You're gonna find your home." He smiled. "Just remember that if it's not in Florida...it could be here."

She stared at him in surprise.

He smiled. "One thing I've learned from Emma? You don't have to share the same blood to be part of the same family."

April blinked away tears as she nodded. "Thanks, Nash. Thanks for everything."

CHAPTER 41

Boone's heart was going wild in his chest. Adrenaline was coursing through him, and his limbs shook as he took the steps up to the ranch house two at a time. "April?"

He called her name again when he reached the kitchen.

Emma's and Dahlia's voices came as soft murmurs as they followed him in. Boone's heart rate was skyrocketing as he took in the silence of this house.

She wasn't here.

"Boone, honey," Emma said. "Why don't you have a seat and try to relax?"

"Relax?" His tone was incredulous. "My girlfriend is God knows where—"

"She's at the airport." Kit's lazy drawl came from the back door, and Boone whirled around to face him.

"What?"

Kit toed off his muddy boots. "Or she's on the way." He squinted at the clock on the microwave. "Should be getting there soon, though."

"But…the airport?" He didn't ask where she was going. Any fool could figure that out.

But he was the fool who hadn't actually thought she'd do it. At least, not like this. Not without saying goodbye first.

JJ had driven the ladies home, and he came up to Boone now, settling a hand on his shoulder and nudging him into a nearby chair. "Sit down, brother."

Boone sat.

Kit was regarding him with a sympathetic wince. "Sorry, man. I didn't realize it would be a surprise. I got a text from Nash that he was driving her and… You didn't know?"

Emma turned to Kit, lowering her voice like she didn't want to upset Boone any further with the recap of that epically awful scene at the diner. "April sort of stormed out," she finished.

Kit grimaced, scrubbing a hand over the back of his neck. "Lizzy's gonna be upset she didn't get to say goodbye."

"None of us did," Daisy murmured, an uncharacteristic frown marring her brow.

Boone hadn't even heard her come in, but he supposed Rose wouldn't be far behind. This was what they did when one of their own was in trouble.

Even if she didn't want to belong to this family…

He dropped his head into his hands. "This is all my fault."

"No, don't say that." Dahlia patted his shoulder.

"We all knew she'd take off to find her father as soon as she got a lead," Rose said. Her voice came from the hallway leading to the front door, and Boone heard Kiara's coo.

"I should've told her right away. I just…I was hoping she'd look into him first. Maybe schedule a phone call."

"You didn't want her to go," Daisy said simply.

He lifted his head. "I didn't want her to go." He looked around to each of the sisters. "But I wasn't trying to stop her. I wasn't going to keep it a secret forever. I'm just…I'm worried about her."

"We all are," Emma said.

"Nash shouldn't have taken her." Boone sounded like a petulant child, but he couldn't bring himself to care.

"No, he was right to take her." Daisy caught his glare and gave him an apologetic shrug. "She needed to go. She needs to get answers to at least one of the questions that are haunting her…"

"And she can't do that from here," Rose finished.

Boone winced. "I screwed up. I pushed her away."

"It wasn't you." Dahlia sighed. "She's always had one foot out the door."

He wished he could argue, but he couldn't deny it. He'd known from the start that she didn't really want to be back here. That she didn't consider this her home.

But he'd thought she was coming around.

He'd thought she was starting to feel at home here. With him. He'd thought…he'd thought…

He shut his eyes with a weary sigh. "I thought I'd be enough."

"This isn't about you." JJ's voice was gentle. "You can't make someone love you or trust you. They have to figure that out for themselves."

Boone shot to his feet, pacing into the middle of April's family. They were watching him with concern, but to Boone's mind, they all seemed way too okay with this.

Didn't they understand how fragile she still was after

her parents' passing? "What if he isn't what she's hoping for?"

Rose flinched. Dahlia sighed. Emma nibbled on her fingernails, and even Daisy started to pace.

"He didn't want her when she was a baby," he continued. "And we don't know anything about this guy."

"He's right," Emma murmured.

Dahlia crossed her arms with a scowl. "Now I wish we *had* hired an investigator. I guess we'd thought…we'd hoped…"

Boone nodded. He'd thought it too. That if enough time passed, and April grew comfortable here with them…

She'd drop the idea of needing her biological father to be her family.

But if he didn't want that? If he rejected her?

Boone's heart couldn't take it. With a shake of his head, he declared, "I'm going after her."

"No, Boone," JJ said. "That's not the answer this time."

"How are you so sure?"

"Because this is something she has to do on her own." Rose gave him a firm, steady look, bobbing Kiara in her arms. The baby's little fingers curled into her mama's sweater as she rubbed her nose against Rose's shoulder.

"If she'd wanted you along for the ride, she would have asked you to come," Daisy added.

But she hadn't wanted him here for this. Not for the first time since he'd watched her walk away, Boone found himself wondering if he'd gotten it all wrong.

If she'd ever cared for him the way he cared for her.

"Even if she doesn't…" He didn't realize he'd been talking out loud until Dahlia arched her brows in question.

He cleared his throat. "She might not love me like I

love her," he rasped, the words shredding his chest and throat as they came out.

The sisters exchanged looks that could only be called pitying.

"But," he continued, "even if she doesn't...I can't just sit by and let her get hurt."

"Boone..." Daisy sidled up next to him and slid an arm around his waist, pressing her head to his chest. "We love you. And one of the things that makes you so great is that you always want to be the hero."

Rose nodded. "You'd make an excellent knight in shining armor."

Dahlia let out a huff of amusement as she listened to her sisters.

Boone frowned down at Daisy, who was still clutching him like a stuffy. "Where are you going with this?"

Kit, who was watching the scene unfold with a lopsided grin, gave Boone a wink. "I think what they're trying to say is this is one of those times when the real test isn't if you can run to her rescue, but...can you let her go?"

"No," he said. "I can't."

"I think maybe you have to," Emma whispered.

"You know what they say." JJ's shoulder hitched. "If you love them, let them go. If they're meant to be yours... they'll come back."

"So you just want me to wait around in the hopes that she *might* return?" His voice was strained with disbelief. "Surely that's not the only way I can show my girlfriend how much I care. Because quite frankly, it stinks."

"We all know April has been feeling lost and alone for a long time," Dahlia said. "You can't force her to find closure, Boone, and you can't make her choose you. Or us. Or...any of this."

He looked away. He knew she was right. But it still made him feel like he was being sliced down the middle to think of April out on her own.

He eyed the door. His truck was there, key still in the ignition. He could hop on the next flight.

But Dahlia's words clung to him, and he knew she had a valid point.

Even if he could convince her to come back here with him, to stay by his side…

How long until she resented him? How long before those demons she'd been battling got the better of her and she ran again?

He scrubbed a hand over his face, his thoughts a mess as he tried to figure out what April needed.

"What if her father's a jerk?" he said, his voice a little too loud and aggressive. "Or what if…?"

Some of his anger faded as he caught Emma's gaze. She looked so sympathetic. So understanding.

Like she knew what his biggest fear was.

"What if he's wonderful and gives her the home she's always wanted?" he muttered. "What if she's gone and she's never coming back?"

A long silence followed his question, and he saw his own fears reflected back to him on every other face in this room.

Everyone wanted her to come back. They all wanted her to choose this ranch and this town…to choose this family.

He fell into his seat with a groan as he realized they were right. They'd been right all along.

JJ clapped a hand on his shoulder in sympathy.

"I have to set her free," he croaked.

Everybody he turned to wore the same expression of

sympathy and resignation. It was the only thing any of them could do.

"All selfishness aside," he said when the silence had grown too thick, "I really don't feel comfortable about her meeting with some stranger in a strange city where she doesn't know a soul."

"Agreed." Kit nodded.

"Miami, right?" JJ scratched his beard, and his gaze met Dahlia's. "When are Sierra and Cody flying back for Thanksgiving?"

Dahlia's lips curved into a grin as understanding dawned.

Daisy straightened. "Miami is where they have a layover, right?"

Hope swelled in Boone's chest as he looked to Kit, who was already pulling out his phone. "On it! I'm calling Cody right now…"

CHAPTER 42

I t was the longest travel day of April's life.

Which was saying something considering April had recently done a big ol' road trip with Boone.

But it turned out that trying to get from Montana to Miami last minute at budget prices meant layovers. Lots of layovers.

By the time she got into the Miami airport, she was exhausted, dirty, and more than ready for a bed.

But she had a father to meet first.

She'd called him on her last layover, and while her heart had been pounding something fierce, she'd managed to introduce herself. The good news was, thanks to Ellie, he'd been expecting her call.

The bad news was he hadn't exactly sounded thrilled to hear from her. She put it down to the fact that some people aren't great on the phone and hoped he'd be better in person. Maybe he was just one of those quiet, reserved guys. Frank had been that way when meeting new people.

Her stomach did a flip as she joined the others on her plane as they shuffled down the aisle, carry-on luggage awkwardly held in front of them, and eventually deboarded the plane.

She paused at the gate, taking a moment to stretch after being cooped up for so many hours. A glance at the clock overhead had her walking quickly toward the exit.

She had one hour to get to the spot her father had chosen for lunch.

Her father.

She was actually going to meet her father!

She took a deep breath and readjusted the bag on her shoulder. She'd never been to Miami before, but hopefully an hour would be enough time to get wherever it was she was going.

"I'll see you there." That was all he'd said after he'd given her the address and a time.

"I'll see you there." Click. He'd ended the call so abruptly, April was still a little unsettled.

But then again, how was a guy supposed to react when talking to his daughter for the first time in more than twenty years?

It wasn't like there was a playbook for this sort of thing. And for all she knew, with her heart pounding the way it had and her palms all clammy…

She could have sounded like a robot.

What mattered was she was finally going to meet the man who was her father by blood.

And she wished Boone was here by her side.

She pushed away the thought just like she'd been pushing away this longing. No, an aching. It felt like a limb was missing, and she alternated between wanting to call him to make things right and not wanting to talk to him at all until she had some clue of what she was going to say.

Her brow furrowed as she fell into step behind a large family that was walking at an irritatingly slow pace.

She was still angry with Boone, truth be told. Maybe he would've told her eventually—okay, yes, he definitely would have. And maybe he had his reasons for holding off.

Actually, she was sure he had his reasons. Maybe even good ones.

She nibbled on her lower lip as she glared at the teenager who was walking at a snail's pace in front of her.

But one other thing that April knew? Boone wanted her to stay. And the guilt she'd seen in his eyes when she'd confronted him only confirmed her suspicions that while he might have had some very good reasons for staying quiet about the news of her father…

He'd had some selfish reasons too.

So yeah, she was still a little annoyed. But…not nearly as much as she'd been before all these long flights in which she'd had way too much time to think and ask herself some difficult questions. Like…

Didn't he have some right to be worried about her?

She'd let him in. He was her boyfriend, after all. Maybe he should have been quicker to tell her the news, but also…

Maybe she shouldn't have gone radio silent on him after he'd told her he wanted to marry her.

She groaned aloud, which earned her a curious glance from the teen boy in front of her.

The kid was lanky and had an awkward gait, and he turned back around quickly when she flashed him a smile.

The question she'd really been grappling with was what would she have done if the tables were turned?

She still didn't know, no matter how many ways she

tried to twist the situation. If she thought his feelings might get crushed by some stranger he'd never met... would she willingly send him off?

And if she was the one who was perfectly content to live in Aspire for the rest of her days, would she just...let him go?

Her heart twisted so violently that she stopped walking, causing the person behind her to bump into her, muttering a curse as he walked around her.

She shuffled slowly the rest of the way into the arrival terminal, her heart still hurting as she realized she'd just answered that question.

No. She wouldn't have been able to watch him walk away. Not without fighting for their relationship, at least. Entering this crowded terminal with families hugging and reuniting...

The loneliness she felt nearly knocked her off her feet. She missed Boone. She'd only left him twenty-four hours ago, but she missed him. The ache spread from her heart and all the way out to her fingers and toes.

She missed his arms around her, and the warmth in his eyes. She missed the way he made her feel loved and cherished, without even trying.

She missed the way he always knew how to drag her out of her thoughts and into the sunshine.

Sunshine. That's what Boone called her, and that's how he made her feel. Like she really was made of light, and that joy was her birthright. Like she deserved to be happy and free. Like when he was around, at least, she was filled with warmth and love and...

Tears stung the back of her eyes.

Dang it. Now was not the time to get overwhelmed

with emotions. She still had an epic meeting to endure…or no, not endure.

This was not some torturous moment. It was the moment she'd been waiting for ever since she'd seen the adoption certificate in that file.

She blinked rapidly, but her sight was still blurred by unshed tears when she heard it. "April!"

She jolted, her head turning to scan the crowd. Surely she was hearing things. But then…

"April!"

A second later, she was rushed and pulled into a hug before she even knew what was happening.

Like any sane person, she froze at the unexpected hug. And for half a second, she thought that maybe this tall woman squeezing her around the shoulders had been sent by her father.

But then her gaze fell on the equally tall and stupidly handsome man standing behind the stranger. "Cody?"

Her voice came out as a squeak, and the woman embracing her finally let her go, grabbing her by the shoulders and looking her over from head to toe the same way Daisy had the first time they'd met.

Between that memory and seeing Cody, she really should've made the connection. Later, she'd blame it on exhaustion that she still just stood there gaping at the woman with the bright red streaks in her dark hair.

"I'm Sierra." She grinned.

And then, finally…it clicked.

"Sierra," she echoed.

"Your big sister." As she said it, she turned and slung an arm around her shoulders, holding her close to her side. "And I guess you remember Cody here."

Cody gave her a shy smile. "It's been a while, April. I wouldn't be surprised if you didn't remember."

Her stupid brain called up Boone in that moment. She had this memory of telling him how every girl in their grade had a crush on Cody Swanson.

"Yeah, I...I remember you."

They stood there grinning at her. Cody's smile was easygoing, and maybe even a little sympathetic. Like he knew just how weird it was that she'd met the sixth and last O'Sullivan sister here in the Miami airport.

Sierra, on the other hand, was beaming at her like this was the best thing that'd ever happened. "Okay, look, I know this is unexpected," she said when she caught sight of April's expression. "But I've been dying to meet you. We both have."

Before April could respond, Sierra kept talking, all the while guiding April toward the airport exit while Cody took her bag from her and slung it over his shoulder.

"Trust me when I say, I get it. It's super weird to meet random women who claim to be your sisters."

"Yeah, I'm getting used to it," April murmured.

This made both of them laugh.

"But what I don't get is...what are you doing here? How...I mean...when...?"

"Your boyfriend sent us." Sierra winked down at her.

Boyfriend. The mere mention of Boone made her heart hurt all over again. It took a second for her brain to catch up, and when it did...she had no idea what to think.

They walked out into the sunshine, but April was too caught up in her spiraling thoughts to care. Why had Boone sent them?

On one hand, she was touched that despite how they'd left things, he still cared.

On the other hand…

Her brows drew down. "He thinks I can't handle this on my own?"

Cody fell into step on her other side. "Nah, it's not you he's worried about."

Her frown deepened.

"Look, it's our fault," Sierra said. "Dahlia and I were talking about how we should just hire that same investigator and have him look into David Taylor, and…" With a huff, she dropped her arm and turned to face April.

It was only then that April realized they'd led her to the shuttle stop for a rental car.

"I think all of us…all us sisters, I mean…" Sierra pursed her lips. "I think we all kinda hoped that once you got to know us, and once you came back to the ranch and made peace with the past…"

April shifted from foot to foot, keenly aware that Cody still had that sympathetic look in his eyes…and she hated it.

She didn't deserve any of their sympathy.

"You thought I'd give up on finding my biological father and just…decide to stay?" April guessed.

Sierra wrinkled her nose. "Wishful thinking, huh?"

April didn't respond.

"Anyway, in hindsight, I think we all realize we should've been helping you more."

"Boone too," Cody murmured, so softly that April almost missed it.

She whipped her head to the side to face him. He really did have Kit's good looks. All the girls in her class must've wept into their pillows when they found out he'd been taken off the market by one of the O'Sullivan sisters.

"He said that?" April asked.

Cody and Sierra exchanged a look. "I think Boone's the one you want to talk to about this," he finally murmured.

"But Boone and all of us sisters are in agreement about the fact that we dropped the ball. We were so hoping you'd want us to be your family that we didn't help you look into this David Taylor guy, and…" She reached out, clasping April by the shoulders, her expression serious. "We just want to make sure someone's got your back, okay? He may be your father, but he's still a stranger, you know?"

Pride warred with good sense, and April fought between telling them she didn't need anyone's help and weeping with gratitude because…

They had her back.

When was the last time someone had her back?

And just like that, he returned. Boone was filling every space in her mind's eye as memory after memory flooded her. A sort of mental highlights reel of every time Boone was there for her.

There were a lot of memories. So many she found herself nodding to Sierra and Cody, emotions making her throat tight as she whispered, "Thanks."

CHAPTER 43

B y the time they got the rental car and arrived at the agreed restaurant, April had come to the realization that she genuinely liked these two.

They were easy company, for a start. Cody, in particular, had this calm, cool, laid-back vibe about him that was a relief to be around considering the ever-intensifying state of her nerves.

With each minute that ticked down toward her meeting with David Taylor, her pulse seemed to ratchet up another beat.

And Sierra, April discovered, was a nice combo of Daisy and Dahlia. She had Dahlia's take-charge mannerisms, which was actually really useful when dealing with the car rental and directions. But she had an easy smile and a ready laugh like Daisy, which helped to lighten the mood as they drove her to the meeting spot.

The comparison made her wonder about the rest of her sisters, and guilt nagged at her. Rose would be worrying about her right about now and had probably brought

Kiara to camp out at the ranch so she'd be there if April called. And Emma would be fretting like a mother hen, baking and cooking like a fiend because that was what she did when she was worried.

Lizzy, she knew without a doubt, was right there with them, but she'd be making threats to come after April and drag her back home.

The image of Lizzy on one of her mama-bear tirades had her lips quirking into a smile as they parked across the street from the upscale bistro.

"This is it," Sierra announced, as if they all hadn't been staring at the restaurant for five minutes in tense silence.

April unclicked her seat belt. What was she waiting for?

Cody turned in the driver's seat to look at her. "We'll get a table on the far side of the restaurant, okay? Far enough that we won't hear anything, but..."

"But we'll be ready and waiting if you need us," Sierra finished.

April nodded. She was almost positive her biological father wasn't an axe murderer and all this stakeout talk was overkill, but the knot in her belly eased somewhat as she nodded and opened the car door.

She led the way across the street, though she heard Sierra and Cody following a few feet behind her.

My very own security detail.

Her lips hitched up in a smile that was almost immediately followed by the urge to sob.

Boone had done this. For her. He was looking out for her even now...even after she'd left, and after all the things she'd said.

The things she'd said...

Her steps faltered as she entered the restaurant, but it

wasn't nerves over meeting David Taylor that had her stomach twisting.

It was the things she'd said.

Bile rose in her throat at the memory of her fight with Frank. Of the last words she'd said. And how she'd never had a chance to make things right.

Suddenly, the thought that she'd left Boone with those harsh words between them, that she'd never told him how much he meant to her…

It was unbearable.

Panic made her heart pound, and she reached for her phone as she stepped into the cold air-conditioning of the dark restaurant's entrance.

"April?"

Her head snapped up, and she found herself staring at a middle-aged man who'd risen from his seat at a table for two nearby.

"Yes." Her smile was polite and automatic as she walked over to her father. She found herself taking in his appearance in an oddly clinical manner. He was shorter than Frank with paler skin. Frank always had a sun-kissed olive hint to his skin, whereas David looked like he'd burn in a heartbeat.

His smile seemed strained. It was in sharp contrast to Frank's grin that would split his face from ear to ear whenever he saw her or her mother.

It'd always been that way. They could've just been gone for an afternoon or just coming home from school, but he'd always smile like it'd been too long. Like her coming into his life made everything better.

"David," her father said by way of greeting as he stuck a hand out.

She shook it, noting how clammy and weak his hand-shake was compared to…

She gave her head a little shake. *Focus.*

Why was she comparing him to Frank?

And why did she feel like she was watching this inter-action as a spectator and not a participant?

"Please, have a seat." He indicated to the chair oppo-site him.

She pulled it out, the chair scraping along the floor as she sat and scooted it toward the table. Threading her fingers together, she rested them between the neatly set cutlery and looked at her…well, her father, she supposed.

He gave her an awkward smile.

And then he grew quiet. So quiet that April felt compelled to fill the silence. Words started tumbling out of her mouth, and it was with a vague sense of horror that she found herself prattling on and on about how her mother had passed and how she'd only then discovered that she'd been adopted and…

All the while, it felt wrong.

It felt like she was telling her innermost secrets to a stranger.

"He may be your father, but he's still a stranger, you know?" Sierra's words from earlier came back to her, and with a start, she glanced around, eyeing the crowded restaurant until she spotted Sierra and Cody.

They were sitting side by side in a booth and keeping a not-so-subtle eye on her.

When they caught her looking in their direction, she got a little wave from Sierra and a wink from Cody.

"So, anyway," she said, out of breath as she turned back to the still too-quiet man across from her. "That's, um…that's why I was looking for you."

Silence.

He nodded, but his expression was…wary, if anything.

She blinked in horror as she realized what he might be thinking. "I'm not looking for anything. I mean…I wasn't looking for you because I need money or anything."

Was it her imagination, or did his shoulders slump in relief?

"I just thought…" She cleared her throat.

Why wasn't he saying anything?

Why did she feel like she'd dragged this man here unwillingly?

Maybe you did.

She forced a smile. "I just thought it would be nice if we could get to know each other, that's all."

She'd thought it a fairly benign comment, so his wince of discomfort caught her off guard.

Her smile faltered. "Was I…wrong?"

He eyed her for a long moment, then leaned forward, resting on his elbows with a sigh. "Look, April…I can see that you're a great kid…"

Her heart sank, and the meager contents of her stomach churned.

His tone, that look of reluctance in his eyes.

She knew what he was going to say before he even opened his mouth.

"Look, I knew Loretta was pregnant." He sighed. By the way he spoke, April was certain he'd rehearsed this. "We were never serious, your mother and me. And I told her up front that I wasn't ready to be a father."

April blinked, and for a moment, his words came to her all garbled as she realized what was happening here.

He didn't want her.

He'd never wanted her.

"It took a long time for me to get to a place where I'd be ready for fatherhood." He gave her a smile that was at once condescending and pitying.

April smiled back out of habit, but everything in her wanted to run. Wanted to turn back time.

Everything in her wanted one more minute with Frank. Just one minute to tell him how sorry she was for the things she'd said.

One minute to tell him she loved him.

To tell him that he was her father, no matter what the paper said.

But she couldn't have one more minute, and it was all her fault.

Her stomach heaved, and April barely heard David's next words.

"April, I…I have a family of my own now. Two kids. A beautiful wife."

"Oh, I…I'd love to meet them." She didn't even know why she said it. Maybe just to get to the point. To end this miserable meeting.

And sure enough…

He looked pained as he shuffled in his seat. April took an odd sort of satisfaction in watching him squirm.

"That's not going to happen, April," he finally murmured. "My wife has no idea I fathered a child when I was in my early twenties. How do you think it's going to look if I confess that now?"

She stared at him. At this man. This…*stranger*.

"I don't want to upset her." He winced.

April wanted to bolt. But this was the only parent she had left. And she had so many questions. And stupidly enough, the least important one was the one that came out first. "Then why did you agree to meet with me?"

He smiled in a way that felt staged, so fake it made her stomach turn. "I wanted to see how much like Loretta you looked. And I figured this kind of news would have been a little cold over the phone."

"It's cold now." April's voice hardened. "I'm your daughter, your own flesh and blood, and you don't even want me."

"I wish I could. I wish things had been different, but when I agreed to let Frank adopt you, I...I let you go."

Frank.

The mention of her father—her real father. It was too much.

Her eyes filled with tears, and before she even knew what was happening, Sierra and Cody were at her side.

She barely recognized Cody. She'd never seen him angry, and right now, he looked ready to punch David.

Her father leaned away from his angry scowl.

"Is everything okay here?" Cody's voice was hard and clipped.

April nodded but then shook her head. This was not okay. She'd shouted at Frank, she'd left Boone behind...for this.

For this man to reject her.

"Who are these guys?" David asked, his voice hushed like he didn't want to cause a scene.

Sierra didn't have that issue. Her voice was loud, cold, and filled with fury. "We're her *family*." She pulled April out of her chair and wrapped an arm around her shoulders. "Let's get you out of here."

As soon as they left the restaurant, April felt the dam break. That wall she'd been so desperately trying to keep in place suddenly crumbled as every pain she'd been denying herself rose like a tidal wave.

Before she could stop it, her body started to shudder as sobs punched out of her mouth.

Sierra pulled her into a tight hug. "Come on, sweetie. Let's take you home."

CHAPTER 44

Boone scraped his hands through his hair as he paced. His footsteps formed a steady beat on the kitchen floor as Cody's voice came from the speaker of Kit's phone, which was sitting on the table as Emma, Nash, and Lizzy crowded around it.

Kit stood frowning, leaning against the doorframe as he listened to Cody speak.

"And then he told her he had a family of his own…"

Boone flinched as if he'd actually been struck. Kit noticed and gave him a sympathetic grimace.

Cody's recounting of what had gone down during April's meetup with her father wasn't easy for anyone to hear. But for Boone, it was sheer torture.

He should've been there.

He could've protected her.

How?

He filled his cheeks with air and blew out a slow exhale.

He had no idea how he could've shielded her from this

blow, but at the very least, he could've been there to hold her afterward.

"And then he said he didn't want her," Cody said.

Boone stopped short, the air rushing from his lungs with an "Oof" that had Nash glancing over with a frown of concern.

"You should've seen her face, man," Cody continued with a sigh. "I wanted to punch the guy in the throat."

Emma leaned forward, her face pale and her fingers clenching the mug of tea in her hands. "Where is she now? Is she okay?"

Lizzy leaned over and wrapped an arm around Emma. "Is she with someone?"

"Yeah, Sierra's with her. But…" Cody sounded hesitant. "She hasn't stopped crying, and I'm kind of worried."

Boone's heart slammed against his rib cage. His girl. His sunshine.

"Where is she now?" Boone stalked toward the table. "I know y'all want me to stay put, but she needs me."

"Boone…," Emma started gently.

"No, he's right," Cody said so quickly it caught Boone by surprise.

"What?"

"She keeps mentioning you, man. I think maybe she's more upset with the way she left things with you than anything."

The blood seemed to rush from his head all at once, and he couldn't think, let alone speak.

Lizzy's voice held a hint of amusement. "You can go ahead and tell her she's good on that front. If Boone's dumbfounded look is anything to go by, he's still just as head over heels for our little sister as ever."

Kit snickered, and even Emma looked like she was fighting a smile as she shushed Lizzy.

"I can be in Miami by tomorrow morning," Boone rushed out. Heck, he didn't care how pathetic he sounded. If April needed him, he'd go anywhere on earth to be by her side.

The world seemed to shift around him as he realized what that meant.

He scrubbed a hand over his face. He'd been so set on keeping April here. With him. But he loved her enough to leave everything behind.

He found everyone gaping at him, and Cody had stopped talking.

"What?" he demanded. "There's gotta be a flight to the East Coast I can make, and—"

"Easy, tiger," Lizzy murmured, her smile small and sweet. "Let's see what April wants to do first before you go flying off, okay?"

He sighed with frustration. "Cody? If she needs me…"

"She does, man, but let us bring her to you. I think she needs to be back home, you know?"

Nash had been frowning down at his phone, but he spoke up now. "If I book 'em now, I think I can get all three of you back to Bozeman by morning." He looked to Boone. "Then Boone can meet you there."

"Yeah, that's a good call," Cody said.

Boone pressed his lips together, his jaw clenched with frustration.

Kit clapped a hand on his shoulder. "Brother, we all know what you're feeling."

Nash, Emma, and Lizzy nodded.

"It's the worst, not being able to help the one you love." Emma gave him an understanding smile.

Lizzy's glossy lips pulled into a sad pout. "That poor girl. I wish we could take this from her somehow."

Boone's tension eased slightly at the sight of his own impotent frustration reflected back at him. Maybe they did know how he felt to some extent.

Still.

Staying put until the morning was gonna be torture.

Nash was typing on his phone. "I'm gonna book these flights. I'll send you the info as soon as they're bought."

"Thanks, man," Cody said. The guy sounded tired. "I'm gonna go get us back to the airport and return the car. I'll see y'all tomorrow…I hope. Kit, tell Mom and Dad the new plan, will ya?"

"You bet, bro. Drive safe…and take care of our girl."

Cody hung up, and a silence fell in the kitchen.

Boone had to get out of this room and into fresh air before he lost his mind. To Nash, he said, "Give me the flight numbers when you have them. I'll pick 'em up."

He nodded, still concentrating on his task.

"Poor April." Emma sniffed as Lizzy rested her head on Emma's shoulder. "How could someone do that to their own child?"

"Frank did it to us," Lizzy said softly.

"But he regretted it." Emma seemed to hear how lame that excuse sounded, and she sighed. "I don't know, it's different somehow. I may not have known Frank well, but after reading his journal and hearing April's stories, I don't think it was us, you know?"

Lizzy nodded. "Yeah. Rose and I were talking about it the other night, and we're both starting to think that Frank didn't know how to love or be loved until Loretta and April came into his life. And by then…"

"It was too late," Kit finished.

Boone listened intently. He wished April were here to hear them talk. Maybe it would help ease her guilt if she knew they didn't resent her for her role in Frank's life.

That they were grateful for her part in helping him understand what it meant to be a father.

Even if it was too little, too late.

"I think he wanted to fix things. To do right by us," Emma said slowly.

"But he didn't know how," Lizzy finished.

Emma nodded. "The more time that went by, the harder it must've seemed."

Lizzy sighed. "And then he ran out of time."

Boone, Nash, and Kit exchanged looks of understanding.

Emma and Lizzy might not have even realized it, but they'd just taken a big step toward forgiveness and closure.

And he just hoped April could find the same.

Emma broke the silence with a shuddering sigh that had Nash coming over to settle a hand on her shoulder. "If we'd seen him…if we'd reached out to him and tried to connect…" She ran a protective hand over her belly as she looked at Lizzy. "I don't think he would have pushed us away."

Lizzy sighed sadly as her gaze fell on the phone still sitting in the middle of the table. "No, I don't think so either."

CHAPTER 45

April was a wreck.

She'd been exhausted from crying by the time they'd boarded that first flight but unable to sleep for all the thoughts swirling through her head. And even though she'd been hungry, she couldn't eat during their layover, despite Sierra's attempts to force food in her mouth.

By the time they rolled off the last airplane and into the Bozeman airport the next day, April was a disaster. But it wasn't food or sleep that she needed most.

She needed Boone, and the closer they got to Bozeman, the more desperate she felt. When she caught sight of him waiting at the bottom of the escalator, she burst into tears of relief.

He'd come.

Cody had said he would, but she'd been too afraid to hope. After the way she'd run off and the things she'd said…

She flew down the last few steps of the escalator and straight into his waiting arms.

Boone scooped her up and held her to him. And there,

crushed against his hard chest by ridiculously strong arms, his embrace so tight her feet dangled off the ground as she buried her face in his neck...only then could she fully breathe.

The crush of his embrace gave her the relief she'd so desperately needed, and she drew in air with a horrible sob.

"Shh, baby. It's all right." He spoke in a low croon as he carried her away from the other passengers and into a quiet corner. He stroked her hair and back, shushing her, soothing her, telling her she was safe and loved and...

And home.

Her arms tightened around his neck. This feeling, the one she'd been unable to name before...

She had the name for it now. The way Boone made her feel cherished and protected, the way he made her feel grounded and free, the way he looked at her and made her feel like she was whole and perfect and utterly lovable despite all her mistakes and flaws...

Or maybe even because of them...

This was home.

He was home.

And she'd been so very stupid.

He shushed her again when she tried to say as much. But then again, with all her blubbering, he probably hadn't understood.

She pulled her head back so she could look him in the eyes. "I love you."

His gaze grew so tender so fast, she would've lost the ability to stand on her own two feet—if she'd been standing on her own two feet.

As it was, her feet still dangled as he gave her a crushing kiss.

"I love you, too, sunshine," he whispered against her lips.

"I'm so sorry—" she began, but he stopped her with another kiss, which made her laugh. "I'm serious, Boone."

"So am I. You have nothing to apologize for."

"The way I left things, what I said…"

"Babe, listen to me." He rested his forehead against hers. "Love is messy. Love is complicated. But when it's real, it's worth it. And you…you are worth fighting for."

Tears filled her eyes again, but this time they were happy. "I don't deserve you."

His gaze grew so sad that she felt sorry she'd said it aloud. "I hate to hear those words from you, sunshine. You sell yourself short. And if it's that David Taylor guy who put that idea in your head—"

"No." She said it quickly, because quite frankly, his anger on her behalf was a little frightening. Endearing, but frightening. "I mean…" She wet her lips, wishing like heck they were somewhere more private than an airport.

She heard Sierra clear her throat behind them, and April turned her head with a sheepish expression that made Cody chuckle.

"So, we're gonna rent a car." Sierra pointed over her shoulder toward the rental desk. "We kind of want the freedom of our own transport, and, well…it's probably a good idea to give you two lovebirds some privacy." She wiggled her eyebrows, making April's cheeks burn red. "We'll meet you at the ranch."

Boone nodded. "Thanks for getting her home safe."

"Our pleasure." Cody gave her a wink, and April giggled when Boone tightened his hold on her with a playful growl.

"See you at home," Sierra said as they turned away.

"Home," she echoed.

Boone was watching her closely. "Hey, just because this meeting with your dad didn't go the way you wanted doesn't mean that you suddenly have to call the ranch home. Or make a commitment to me, for that matter. I was rushing you. We all were—"

"No." She gave a decisive shake of her head. "That's one thing that I realized during this whole disaster of a trip. I've been looking for a home out there, but all this time…it was here. With you."

He kissed her long and hard. "I realized the same thing, sunshine."

She smiled against his lips. "You always knew where home was for you. It's Aspire."

"No." He shook his head, his gaze as serious as she'd ever seen it. "I mean, yeah, it is. But ever since I've met you, I've known it. *You* are my home. It doesn't matter if you want us to stay in Montana, or move to Miami, or live life on the road in endless motels…"

She laughed as tears filled her eyes again. "What are you trying to say, Boone?"

"What my parents have been telling me and my sisters all along. Home is where the heart is. And, sunshine…you are my heart."

Her eyes flooded with a fresh wave of tears as she held him tight.

"Oh, babe, please don't cry."

"I can't help it. I'm so lucky I found you."

"Actually…" He stroked her back and hair, his tone teasing. "If you'll recall, I'm the one who found you, remember?"

Her laugh was watery but light. "Yeah. I remember."

He kissed the side of her head. "What do you say? You

ready to head home? I happen to know there are six women there just dying to see their little sister. Not to mention a whole lot of husbands, fiancés, and a handful of nieces and nephews."

She laughed. "Can't wait. But, Boone…" She pulled back to look into his eyes. "There's one stop I'd like to make first, if you don't mind. I want to have a future with you. With them. And I want that future at the ranch. But… if I want to have a future, I have to make peace with the past."

Boone nodded and then kissed her nose. "Lead the way, sunshine. I'll be by your side for every step."

CHAPTER 46

April's grandmother fussed over them so much, Boone teasingly told April they should unexpectedly drop in on her grandparents more often, just for the homemade goodies.

April laughed, and for that, Boone was grateful. On the way over here, she'd told him everything.

All about her father's death, and her guilt. All about the anger she held toward two parents who she adored. Even about how angry she'd been with her grandparents. "I shut them out," she'd said with a frown in the truck. "I tried to do right by them as a granddaughter, but I shut them out. I need to fix that."

So here they were, her grandmother fussing and her grandfather watching April with a gaze so warm and bittersweet, there was no doubt in Boone's mind that the older man was looking at April but remembering her mother.

"I'm sorry," April said when her grandmother finally sat. "I'm sorry for the way I ran off…"

What followed was a tearful exchange, and there wasn't a dry eye in the house. Not even Boone's.

Hearing his girl talk about the guilt she'd been suffering was the hardest part.

And he nearly wept with relief when her grandmother pulled April into her arms. "That accident was not your fault, baby."

He watched April go pale. These were the words she needed to hear, but he also could see her fighting them, not certain she could forgive herself.

But she had to. Boone clasped his hands together in prayer. *Please show April the light. Let her find forgiveness... for herself and for them.*

"I shouldn't have taken off like that." April slashed a tear off her cheek.

"Oh, honey, that car shouldn't have run through that red light either. That's not on you."

"But he was rushing to get to me. He called out my name, and I..." April's eyes filled with even more tears. "I ran away from him. I wanted to hurt him for hurting me, but I didn't want him to die."

"Oh, baby girl." Her grandmother pulled her into a hug. "He loved you so much. He would have moved heaven and earth to make you happy. He didn't tell you about your sisters because he didn't want to admit his shame. And your mama made him promise not to speak of the adoption. She never wanted you to know what a selfish person David Taylor was. She so desperately wanted Frank to be your daddy."

April sniffed and nodded.

Boone watched her, drinking her in. He held his breath as he waited for her to speak.

And then his heart swelled with gratitude when she

lifted her head with an expression of peace and resolve as she finally whispered, "He was my dad. And I loved him so very much."

Her grandfather reached for her hand and met her gaze. "He knew that, April. There was never a doubt in his mind, no matter what was said or left unresolved. He knew you loved him because he knew you."

April nodded. "Thanks, Grandpa."

After mopping up their tears and eating a few more goodies, it was time to go. It turned into a tearful goodbye, with her grandparents promising to come out to the ranch to visit soon.

They were largely quiet on the way back to the ranch, but with April's fingers intertwined with his and her beautiful eyes meeting his gaze whenever he glanced over, Boone's heart was full to bursting.

She'd been through so much, and it wasn't over yet. Maybe in some ways it never would be. She'd always have grief to contend with, and memories that were both bitter and sweet. But first there were her sisters.

Her arrival was akin to the prodigal son's. They hadn't so much as parked in the drive when the porch was overflowing with O'Sullivan sisters and kids and cowboys and even some excited dogs.

"It's chaos," Boone said with a laugh as he reached for his door handle. He turned back to see April grinning at the scene before her.

"It's perfect."

He'd no sooner lifted her down from the passenger seat than she was surrounded. Tears flowed, and poor April looked like she might be drowning in hugs and kisses at one point.

"Should we save her?" JJ teased.

Boone, Cody, Kit, and Nash followed his gaze to the circle of crying, laughing, loving women.

"Nah," Boone said. "She's exactly where she needs to be."

Nash nodded. "She's home."

Boone couldn't stop watching her with what Daisy and Lizzy would not stop referring to as his dopey grin.

"I love this smile," April said as she went up on tiptoe to kiss him. Then she whispered, "And I love *you*."

And with that, he decided he didn't care who thought he was dopey. Not so long as April loved him.

The hubbub moved into the kitchen, and talk turned to April's trip.

"It's in the past," she said. "David Taylor is back where he belongs. A stranger who might have helped give me life, but he was no father to me." She wet her lips, her gaze traveling over her six sisters. "That term only applies to my real father. My dad...to Frank."

Boone watched her swallow hard, and he reached for her hand.

She gave his fingers a squeeze of thanks before starting in on the tale he'd heard twice now. "Frank was looking for me. The day of his accident. He saw me on the street and called out to me. He wanted me to come back home and resolve it, but...I was still too angry at him, and I... I..." She huffed out a sigh. "I ran, so he chased me, and—"

"April," Emma interrupted quietly. She glanced at Sierra, who looked to Dahlia, who gave the other three a quick questioning look.

It was Dahlia who spoke. "We know, sweetheart."

April blinked in shock. "What?"

Sierra winced. "Your grandmother told me the whole story when I went there looking for you."

April turned to Boone, but he could only shrug. He hadn't known about the specifics of the accident. But apparently her sisters had.

"You knew," April echoed.

Lizzy took a step forward and reached for her hand. "Hon, we knew, but, you see…we didn't know if *you* knew."

"We didn't know the part about him seeing you and you running, but the truth is…that doesn't make any difference." Daisy's forehead wrinkled.

"Because we all know it's not your fault," Rose finished for her.

April's lips parted as all six of them nodded eagerly, each seeming to talk at once, and all trying to convince her that she wasn't to blame.

April turned, burying her face in Boone's chest. His arms came around her, and he held her tight. "You okay, babe?" he murmured into her hair.

"No. Yes. I mean…" She pulled back with a shake of her head. "All this time, I've been so worried that if you found out, you'd hate me for taking him from you."

Every single O'Sullivan sister burst into tears as they rushed April for another effusive group hug that left the men in the room chuckling when it ended in every sister toppling over.

Soon they were laughing and crying as they tried to right themselves.

"This family," Kit said with a tender look at his wife, who was wiping away tears of laughter as she tried to help Emma up off the floor. "You're huge!"

"You're mean," Emma shot back.

That had everyone laughing again, and April tore

herself away from the sisters to snuggle back into Boone's arms. "Thank you," she whispered.

"For what?"

"For everything. For this." She nodded toward her loud, chaotic family. "For bringing me here and being my friend and helping me understand what it means to be loved."

He kissed her, and they both ignored the childish teasing that came from her sisters.

CHAPTER 47

A few days later, Boone turned to April in the stables, eyeing her pretty black dress that was nearly hidden beneath a down jacket. "You sure you don't want to drive with the others? There's a lot of snow on the ground."

April grinned up at him, hitching her dress to reveal knee-high cowboy boots. "Bring it on."

Boone's head tipped back with a laugh. "Man, I love this girl."

She giggled and took his hand when he offered to help her up on the mare.

"Your grandparents are driving up in the four-by-four with Emma and Nash," he told her. "They've got the ashes, and the minister will be meeting us up there. JJ's gonna drive him there."

April nodded. This plan had come together quickly, but at this time of year, if they were going to have an outdoor memorial service for her parents, it had to be done sooner rather than later.

Her grandparents had loved the idea of giving both her parents closure at the place they loved most.

She'd chosen a spot high on a hillside overlooking the property and the pond where Frank used to take her fishing when she was little.

"It's perfect," Boone said when he helped her down a little while later, cold but invigorated by the fresh air.

The others arrived in small groups. All of her sisters and their families were there, along with her grandparents and Ellie, who gave her a shy hug.

April broke away from the others to thank her for all she'd done to help her these past weeks. "Now it's my turn to help you," April promised.

Ellie gave her a sad smile. "I don't know how, but I appreciate the sentiment."

"April, hon," Emma called. "The minister's ready."

Ellie smiled. "Go. Be with your family. I'll catch up with you later."

April hugged her grandparents, then took Boone's hand and went to stand in the middle of her sisters, who were already gathered around the marker JJ had carved out of stone.

The minister's words were kind and heartfelt, and April bowed her head in prayer along with the others as they laid her parents to rest in the land they loved so dearly.

"Amen," she whispered when the prayer came to a close.

The minister made the rounds, speaking quietly to her grandparents and the children. Boone and the other men gathered in a cluster by the horses and vehicles, leaving April and her sisters to themselves for a moment.

"That was beautiful." Lizzy grinned. "It may not be my

place to say, but I think they would have appreciated this ceremony."

"Me too," Rose said.

April nodded. "This is where they belong. Here with me..." She looked to her sisters with a smile. "With us."

"So, it's official, then." Dahlia surveyed the land. "We're really going to keep this place."

"It's settled." April smiled. For the first time in a long time, she felt totally at peace here at the ranch. She tipped her head up to the sunshine that was peeking out from behind a cloud. She had a feeling that this peace came from her mom and dad. A parting gift.

Thank you. Thank you for the life you gave me, and the love I still carry in my heart.

Rose rested her head against April's shoulder. "We're going to have a lot to give thanks for on Thursday."

Daisy came up behind them and rested her chin on April's other shoulder. "Our first Thanksgiving here at the ranch as a whole family. It's perfect."

"It definitely feels like a dream come true." Emma sighed, wrapping her arms around her belly, tears in her eyes as Lizzy linked her arm through Emma's and Dahlia rested an arm around Lizzy's shoulders.

"Maybe it is." Sierra was still gazing out at the landscape, but she turned and grinned at the sight of the six of them. She came to stand between the two clusters of three sisters and bound them all together by linking arms with Emma and Rose. "Maybe it was his dream."

Sierra nodded toward the marker and the land beyond.

April's throat grew tight, but she smiled as she nodded. "I think you're right."

Emma sniffed, but she kept her chin held high as she spoke to the plaque that covered her father's ashes.

"Frank...Dad...thank you for this place. You somehow knew we all needed it, and whether it's by the grace of God or some other magic, we've all found a home here. I just wanted you to know that we're gonna look after this place, and...if it's okay..." She looked around the group. "I think we should rename it the O'Sullivan Sisters Ranch."

Rose made a squeaking noise as she tried to contain a sob, which made Daisy burst out in a watery laugh. "I love that!"

Dahlia nodded, her lips quivering as she smiled. "It's the perfect name for this place."

Lizzy grinned. "It's the dawn of a new day at the O'Sullivan Sisters Ranch!"

Everyone cheered, and no one louder than April.

If it seemed odd to the others that the sisters were laughing and cheering after a funeral, no one seemed to mind. The men were watching them with indulgent smiles, and the children were more than happy to join in on the celebrating.

The kids quickly turned it into an impromptu snowball fight, and April found herself crying tears of laughter as she watched the oh-so-serious sheriff knocked onto his butt by a flurry of snowballs from his kids.

He wiped snow off his face as a laughing Daisy pulled him to his feet.

"I taught them baseball too well," he grumbled. But he was grinning from ear to ear, just like his kids were.

Not to be outdone, Kit and Lizzy's twins turned on their parents, and all of the sisters howled with laughter as they watched Lizzy try to run away in her boots, which were far more fashionable than functional.

JJ came up behind Dahlia. "What do you say, babe? Should we show 'em how it's done?"

Dr. Dex made everyone laugh when he handed Kiara over to April and rolled up his sleeves. "Step aside, JJ. This job calls for a doctor."

Nash joined in the mix, and it soon became evident that he and Dahlia were a formidable team. They were declared the victors, and that was when Emma finally cut in. "Who's ready for lunch?"

"Me, me, me!" the twins shouted in unison.

"Me, me, me!" JJ echoed as he scooped Dahlia up in his arms.

Dr. Dex wrapped an arm around Rose. "We should probably get Kiki out of the cold too."

And so the families headed back to the house, and the other guests went with them, leaving April and Boone alone in the peaceful silence.

"So, what do you think of your new home?" Boone asked as he wrapped his arms around her.

She sighed dreamily. "I'd say he's perfect. But then that might go to his head."

Boone chuckled and nuzzled her neck. "You know what I mean."

"I love it," she whispered. "This was the right decision. Staying at the ranch. With you. All of it."

"Glad to hear it, sunshine."

She pressed a kiss to his lips.

"So you're not going anywhere anytime soon?"

She shook her head. "So long as you and my family are here, I'm here. Because a wise man once told me—" She laughed as he lifted her into his arms. "—home is where the heart is."

"Ain't that the truth." He cut off her giggle with a kiss that stole her breath.

The first of many kisses on this ranch, she decided. The start of a new life and a bright future.

Lizzy's words came back to her, and she smiled up at her boyfriend.

The dawn of a new day, indeed.

EPILOGUE

I t was the double wedding of the century!

At least, that was what every O'Sullivan sister declared during the reception in the magical barn at The King's Inn.

A light December snow whirled around the barn, but inside, the soft orange glow of twinkling lights gave the wedding a magical radiance.

But it was the laughter and the smiles that truly made this night one to remember.

April paused to survey the crowd as Daisy's hand-picked band started up a fast-paced number that had everyone whooping and hollering.

Willow stopped bustling about long enough to bump April with her hip. "Ya done good, O'Sullivan."

April laughed. "Thanks, King."

Willow turned to face her. "Seriously, thank you. Did you see how happy Bailey and Brandon were after the speeches? This wedding is such a hit, and you were a big part of that."

April blushed and ducked her head. "I was just a small part. The rest was you and your family. And if this wedding is anything to go by, I'd say your new business is off to an excellent start."

Willow beamed. "It is, isn't it?"

April straightened when she saw one of the waiters with an empty tray.

"Uh-uh." Willow stopped April with a hand on her shoulder. "You are officially off duty. It's your sisters who just got married, and besides…" She cast a teasing glance behind April.

April turned and…

Swoon.

Her insides melted at the sight of Boone Donahue in a tux, his shaggy hair slicked back into submission and the most gorgeous smile in the world aimed right at her.

In fact, his gaze was so fixed, she might as well have been the only woman in this room.

Nay, in the world.

"I think I might get in trouble if I don't let you off duty for the rest of the night." Willow laughed as she pushed April in Boone's direction.

Smoothing her hands over the red silk skirt of the dress Lizzy had made for her, she felt almost…nervous as she approached Boone.

Which was ridiculous. Because he was her boyfriend.

But right now he was also Boone Donahue.

The Boone Donahue—the hot young quarterback who'd always been out of her league.

He moved toward her, and his hot smile turned into a crooked, cocky grin.

Note to self: never ever tell him you thought that.

She bit back a smile. She knew better now, obviously. He wasn't nearly as egotistical as she'd always believed.

But in moments like this one, she still felt like she had to pinch herself.

He was hers.

And she was his.

He moved toward her but stopped short when they reached each other. He held a hand out as the music changed.

She started to laugh as one of the slow songs they'd both loved on the road trip started to play. "Did you ask them to play this?"

His smile was now a full-blown smirk. "May I have this dance?"

She laughed as she slid her hand into his. "Is this your way of giving us the prom date we never had?"

He arched a brow as he pulled her into his arms. "Maybe it's my way of giving you a preview of our first dance at our wedding."

Her eyes widened as her heart swooped and soared. But he mistook her silence. Kissing the tip of her nose, he murmured, "Relax, sunshine. I'm only teasing."

She melted into his arms, a smile on her lips. "I love you. You know that, right?"

"I do." He kissed her gently. "And have I told you how proud I am of you lately? Because…dang, girl." He turned his head to take in the lights and the cakes and the decorations. "You are incredible."

"We did do a pretty great job, huh?" She followed his gaze, her smile growing as it landed on the two happy couples at the center of it all. "You know, it got me thinking…maybe we *should* get married here."

He stopped dancing, and she laughed when she looked up to see his mouth hanging open. "You're messing with me, aren't you?"

She shook her head, not even trying to hide all the love in her eyes. "I do want to marry you, Boone." She went up on tiptoe to kiss him lightly before she added, "One day."

She winked, and he started to chuckle.

"That's good enough for me, babe." His arms tightened around her. "When it comes to you, I'm in no rush. Just knowing you'll be mine someday in the future is enough."

She tipped her head to the side, her heart swelling in her chest until all this love felt like it couldn't be contained. "I'm already yours, Boone Donahue."

He clutched her hand in his as they swayed to the music, and he pressed that hand to his heart. "Your home is right here, sunshine. And if I have my way, it will be until the end of time."

Thank you so much for reading Boone & April's story. I love the way this series wraps up and how the sisters rename the ranch and really cement this special place as their own.

But April will still be working at The King's Inn and I can't wait for you to get to know this new family. Long held secrets and a rivalry that spans decades will come to light as we head to Paradise Springs and watch Bailey, Willow, and their brothers, fall in love in small-town Montana.

If you want to be the first to hear about this new series, then make sure you sign up for my newsletter here:

www.subscribepage.com/
sophiaquinn_newsletter_exclusive

You'll also receive a bonus prologue to Kit and Lizzy's romance and a free Mama's Kitchen recipe book.

ACKNOWLEDGMENTS

Dear reader,

Wow. I can't believe this series has wrapped up. It feels very bitter-sweet. I've loved hanging out in Aspire and watching Frank O'Sullivan's family grow into something he would have been so proud of. For all his mistakes, he did one thing so right… he created six beautiful women and adopted a seventh who was meant to be. It's so satis-fying watching these ladies fall in love and get the home they all longed for.

Because this world has burrowed so deeply into my heart, I'm not quite ready to let it go, which is why The King's Inn has been born and why you'll still get to see glimpses of the O'Sullivans in future novels. I'm very excited to unravel the history of Paradise Springs and introduce to a whole new set of characters all centered around The King's. Two sisters and three brothers will each get their own romance and I can't wait! Planning is already under-way. And I'll keep you posted on progress.

If you enjoyed the final O'Sullivan novel, I'd like to encourage you to leave a review on Amazon and/or Goodreads. Reviews and ratings help to validate the book. They also assist other readers in making a choice over whether to purchase or not. Your honest review is a huge help to everyone.

And speaking of help, I'd like to acknowledge and thank my lovely team. Deb—another gorgeous cover. Thank you for your talent. Thank you, Kristin, for your eagle eyes, and to my other proofreaders who helped me polish off this book and get it as shiny and mistake free as possible.

Thank you to my amazing review team and all my readers. Writing these books for you has been nothing but a pleasure and it warms my heart to know how much you've enjoyed them. Thank you for the lovely emails and comments. It's truly such an honor and privilege to write these books for you.

And, as always, I'd like to thank my heavenly father—my life force, my love and my true inspiration. Thank you that love presents itself in so many different ways. Thank you that redemption and forgiveness go far beyond anything we can truly fathom. Your mercies are new every morning and you love never fails.

ABOUT THE AUTHOR

Sophia Quinn is the pen-name of writing buddies Maggie Dallen and Melissa Pearl Guyan (Forever Love Publishing Ltd). Between them, they have been writing romance for 10 years and have published over 200 novels. They are having so much fun writing sweet small-town romance together and have a large collection of stories they are looking forward to producing. Get ready for idyllic small towns, characters you can fall in love with and romance that will capture your heart.

www.foreverlovepublishing/sophiaquinn

Made in the USA
Middletown, DE
21 April 2024